**Kincaid said, "I love a woman with long hair."**

"You love all women, long hair or no." Fiona remov
hairpin from one place and tackled a particularly un
curl near her temple.

He sent her a roguish wink. "I especially love w
with long brown hair and green eyes."

"Kincaid! Stop that."

"Stop what?" he asked, all innocence and amaz

"Stop flirting with me."

"Was I flirting?"

"Aye. As easily as you breathe. With you, ev
tence is an offer."

He leaned back, crossing his arms over l
chest. As he settled, his thigh slid over to pre
hers once more. "And with you, my love, ever
is a challenge."

## *Acclaim for Karen Hawkins's be*
## *romantic novels . . .*

"Luscious, romantic, witty, sexy, and emo/

—

"Fast paced, lively, sexy and laugh-out-l
—R

"Delightful . . . sparkling."

# How to Abduct a Highland Lord

# KAREN HAWKINS

POCKET BOOKS

New York London Toronto Sydney

An *Original* Publication of POCKET BOOKS

POCKET BOOKS, a division of Simon & Schuster, Inc.
1230 Avenue of the Americas, New York, NY 10020

This book is a work of fiction. Names, characters, places and incidents are products of the author's imagination or are used fictitiously. Any resemblance to actual events or locales or persons, living or dead, is entirely coincidental.

Copyright © 2007 by Karen Hawkins

All rights reserved, including the right to reproduce this book or portions thereof in any form whatsoever. For information address Pocket Books, 1230 Avenue of the Americas, New York, NY 10020

ISBN-13: 978-0-7394-7891-2

POCKET and colophon are registered trademarks of Simon & Schuster, Inc.

Front cover and stepback illustration by Alan Ayers, handlettering by Ron Zinn
Interior design by Andrea C. Uva

Printed in the United States of America

*To Nate V. N.*
*Thank you for never getting tired of my endless quest*
*for "just the right word" and for keeping your*
*snickering to a minimum when I sing in the shower.*
*Nate, you make my heart smile.*

*T. A. I.*

# Acknowledgments

I would like to acknowledge my agent, Karen Solem, who never says, "You want to write WHAT?"

And a huge hug to my new editor, Micki Nuding, who was also my old editor from a long time ago. Micki, you were right! We're working together again! WOOHOO!

# How to Abduct a Highland Lord

# Prologue

Och, lassies! Such doubters ye are! I've met men who were cursed. And women, too ...

OLD WOMAN NORA OF LOCH LOMOND<br>TO HER THREE WEE GRANDDAUGHTERS ONE COLD NIGHT

*Stirling, Scotland*
*April 9, 1807*

Jack Kincaid died as he had lived: awash in a haze of fine bourbon, his perfectly tailored coat pockets stuffed with his winnings from a night of wild gaming, and reeking faintly of the perfume of another man's wife.

Jack had whiled away this particular evening at a grand house outside Stirling, lured from London by the charms of the lovely Lady Lucinda Featherington. Lord Featherington, ambassador to a distant foreign clime, was due home any day. Jack had overcome the lady's qualms at his presence with a heated kiss and a murmured suggestion that had sent a delighted flush through that not-easily-shocked woman. "Black Jack" lived lustily, and many were the hearts tossed his way only to be smashed upon the hard rocks of his heart. Women were always guaranteed a good time in his bed, though.

Hours later, the sound of a carriage rumbling up the drive had caused the lady to gasp, throw back the covers and scramble from Jack's arms. Jack just laughed. He didn't fear Lord Featherington; the man was a pitiful shot and had never hit his man. Jack never missed.

But Lucinda had no wish for a scandal. Concern for her reputation outweighed her feelings for Jack, and she begged him to leave.

Amused and a mite tipsy from sampling her husband's excellent cellars, Jack allowed himself to be coaxed into climbing out the window. Just as the doorknob of the master bedchamber turned, Jack leapt from the trellis to the garden below.

Whistling to himself, he sauntered through the gardens to the stable, where he gathered his horse from a surprised groom. Then he was off, flying back to the amusements to be had in London. If he changed horses along the way, he would arrive in two days, in plenty of time for Lord Mooreland's private card party. Mooreland was a fool, but he entertained with a lushness that was unparalleled.

A more prudent gentleman would have taken the York Road, with its wide avenue and frequent inns. Jack took the stage road to Ayr, a dark and lonely road notorious for its highwaymen. The Ayr Road was doubly dangerous for a lone man on horse, especially one dressed in London finery, a ruby flashing on one hand, his head muddled by Lord Featherington's best bourbon.

Jack urged his spirited horse to a gallop, heedless of the darkness and highwaymen alike.

As he turned a corner, the calm, balmy weather changed with an abruptness that stunned him. The skies suddenly opened with a clap of thunder, and a heavy, drenching rain slashed down. Cold and sharp, it soaked him in a second, and the thunder caused his horse to rear. Jack's hands slipped from the wet reins, and he fell. As the ground rushed up to greet him, the faint scent of lilacs tickled his nose, then the fall stole both his breath and his consciousness.

Sometime later, he awoke to the stinging slap of rain on his face. He lay in a deep puddle of mud, its thick ooze gluing him in place. His hair stuck to his forehead and clung to his neck, rain running over him in rivulets. The warm mud that held him to the ground was in striking contrast to the cold rain sluicing down upon him. Rain that smelled like lilacs . . .

*Fiona MacLean.*

But surely not. He hadn't spoken to her in fifteen years, though he could still picture her exactly as he'd seen her last: rich brown hair falling about her face, her tears hidden by the rain—

His heart tightened. There was no sense in remembering that. And to think that this accident involved

Fiona merely because of the scent of lilacs was ridiculous. He must have hit his head harder than he thought. Indeed, it was difficult to think at all, his temples ached so much.

Bloody hell, he didn't have time for this. There were women to be bedded, wagers to be won, bourbon to be tasted.

But as with all things in Jack Kincaid's badly lived life, it was too late.

Far too late.

Groaning, he rolled to his elbow, the mud sucking at him, his head protesting with a burst of colors and pain as he moved. Suddenly, he knew this was the end. He wasn't going to make it. *This is death. And here I am; cold, sodden, and alone.* He'd never meant to die like this. He'd never meant to die at all. His eyes slid closed as a wave of blackness descended upon him, and he fell backward into the mud.

And there he lay, the rain slowing to a faint splatter on his upturned face.

# Chapter One

*The MacLeans are an ancient family, long of grace and fair of face. 'Tis a pity they know their own worth, fer it makes 'em difficult to bargain with. Shrewd they are; 'tis rare they come out on the bottom side of any bargain. Yer own pa says he'd rather be bit by a sheep than dicker with a MacLean.*

OLD WOMAN NORA OF LOCH LOMOND

TO HER THREE WEE GRANDDAUGHTERS ONE COLD NIGHT

*Gretna Green, Scotland*
*April 9, 1807*

Fiona MacLean forced herself to smile. "Father MacCanney, we've come to be married."

The heavyset priest looked uncertainly from Fiona to the groom and then back. "B-but—he's not—I canna—"

"Yes you can, Father," Fiona said in her calmest voice, her hands fiercely fisted in the strings of her reticule.

Come hell or high water, she was about to end the

longest, most drawn-out, and most foolish feud in all
Scotland. And thereby lose her freedom, her carefully
planned future, and perhaps even a bit of her heart.

The thought made her stomach sink lower. But
this marriage was necessary if she wished to keep her
brothers safe from their own foolish tempers. *It's the
only way. I cannot waver.*

"Fiona, lass," Father MacCanney said in an exas-
perated voice, "he's not fit to be a groom!"

"All the more reason for me to marry the fool." At
the priest's blink of surprise, she quickly added, " 'Tis
a known fact that a good woman can turn even the
most contrary, rotten, stubborn ne'er-do-well into a
responsible man."

The priest glanced uneasily at her prospective
groom. "Aye, but—"

"Have no fear for me, Father. I know he's no prize,
but he's the one I want."

"Fiona, I know the lad might benefit from the
match. 'Tis just—"

"I know," she said, sighing bravely. "He's a philan-
derer who's been with every woman from the North
Sea to the fleshpots of London."

The priest flushed at the mention of fleshpots. "Yes,
yes. So everyone knows, but—"

"He is also a complete wastrel who has made no
effort to embrace a useful life. I know he's not the best
choice of groom, but—"

"He's not even conscious!" the priest burst out. "He
canna even say his own name!"

Fiona glanced down to where her man, Hamish, had dropped her groom on the cold flagstone at her feet. Muddy rivulets dripped onto the church floor from Kincaid's clothing. "I was afraid that was your problem." Even unconscious, Jack was a royal pain. Some things never changed.

"Lassie, ye canna drag an unconscious man to the altar."

"Why not?"

"Because—because 'tis just not done, that's why!"

The priest eyed Hamish with suspicion. Fiona's massive guard stood silently behind her as he'd done since she was a child. A large sword hung at his side, three primed pistols were stuck into his wide leather belt, his bushy red beard bristled, and his fierce gaze pinned them all in place.

"How did the lad come to be unconscious and muddy?" Father MacCanney asked pointedly.

Fiona hated to lie. She really did. But the less the priest knew, the safer he'd be from retribution from her brothers. Torn in pain at the loss of their youngest brother, they raged through Castle MacLean, fists lifted to the sky, fury pouring from them.

The curse of the MacLeans had flowed then. Rain and thunder had flooded from the skies for days, threatening those who lived in the village below Castle MacLean. The river had already been swollen from early spring rains, and the danger of flooding was imminent.

Fiona could not let that happen. And she knew

how to stop the feud. First, she'd had to find Jack Kincaid. Thank goodness Hamish had heard rumors of his dalliance with some woman in nearby Stirling; it was simple to find the wastrel then.

She could only hope that the rest of her plan would follow so easily. Somehow, she greatly doubted she'd be so blessed. She shrugged and said with as much cheerful indifference as she could muster, "We found him."

"Unconscious?"

"Yes."

"Where?"

"In the road. His horse must have bolted."

The priest did not look convinced. "How did the lad get so wet?" He eyed her with deep suspicion. "There's not been any rain in this part of Scotland in over three weeks."

Fiona had to distract him. "Hamish, can you awaken the lout? Father MacCanney will not marry us unless he's conscious."

Hamish grunted, then bent over, grabbed the unconscious Jack Kincaid by the hair, and lifted his head.

Fiona's gaze fell on his face, and her heart leapt. Even splashed with mud, his dark red hair plastered flat from the rain, Jack Kincaid was painfully handsome. Fine, firmly cut features with a strong jaw and masculine nose, deep auburn hair, and, had they been open, the blue, blue eyes of an angel.

But angel he was not.

In the distance, a faint rumble of thunder caused

the priest to look toward the open windows. Outside, bright sunshine warmed the stone walls, nary a cloud in the blue sky.

Fiona's gaze remained on Kincaid. It took all of her moral strength not to kick him—just a little—while he was so conveniently at her feet.

Since that dark day fifteen years ago when she'd discovered Jack Kincaid's true nature, she'd kept her emotions and thoughts about him locked away. She'd thought they'd died, but apparently some anger and resentment remained.

Still grasping Jack's hair, Hamish shook his head, then looked at Fiona. "The jackass is not awakening."

"I can see that." Fiona sighed. "Let him be."

Hamish dropped his burden, ignoring the thud that made the priest wince.

Relief filled Father MacCanney's face. "Ye can't marry him, then."

"Yes, I can," Fiona said firmly. "He will awaken soon."

The priest sighed. "Ye are the most stubborn lass I ever met."

"Only when I must be. You cannot deny that 'twill be good for the lout to be in the care of a strong woman."

"No," Father MacCanney said in a constricted voice. "I canna deny that."

"I'll put up with neither drinking nor carousing. He will also be made to attend church regularly. Whether he knows it or not, Jack's wild days are over."

Something like pity flickered over the priest's face.

"You canna make a person change, lassie. They have to *want* to change."

"Then I shall *make* him want to change."

The priest took her gloved hand in his. "Why do you wish to embark on this madness, lassie?"

" 'Tis the only way to stop the feud. Callum's death must be the last," she said in a hard voice.

The priest's eyes had filled with tears. "I mourn your brother, too, lass."

"You cannot mourn Callum more than I. And as if his death is not enough to bear, my older brothers are calling out for vengeance. If someone does not stop this nonsense now—" Her voice broke.

Callum, beautiful Callum. Her youngest brother, with his quicksilver grin and equally fast flashes of temper, was now lying six feet under, a stone marker the only reminder of his life. And all because of an idiotic feud that began hundreds of years ago.

The MacLeans and the Kincaids had been fighting for so long that no one remembered the true cause of their hatred. Now, because of Callum's stupid refusal to let a silly insult from a Kincaid slide, things had come to a head. Callum had pushed the argument, pushed the fight. And paid the price with his life.

One blow, the edge of the stone hearth . . . and that was it. Callum was dead, and the banked fires of the age-old feud had erupted into flames.

The priest pressed her hand. "I've heard that the Kincaids feel Callum's death was not their fault. That perhaps someone else—"

"Please, Father. Do not."

The priest looked at her face. She knew what he was seeing: the circles under her eyes, the paleness of her skin, the tremor of her lips as she fought desperately to keep her tears at bay.

"Father," she said softly, "my brothers blame Eric Kincaid for Callum's death. Nothing I say can cool their thirst for vengeance. But if I marry Jack, he and his kin will be a part of our family. My brothers will be forced to let go of their plans." Her determined gaze locked with the priest's. "I will not lose another brother." Anger surged through her, raw and furious.

Outside, the ominous rumble of thunder darkened the otherwise clear day. Hamish nodded, as if agreeing with an unspoken thought. Father MacCanney, meanwhile, paled.

The priest was silent a long moment, and Fiona could see he was on the verge of agreeing. He just needed a little push.

"Besides, Father, if I make this sacrifice and marry to end the feud, it might break the curse."

Father MacCanney swallowed noisily and pulled his hand from her grasp. "Hsst, lass! I'll have none of that curse talk in this holy place."

That was because he believed it. According to the old tales, a white witch, disgusted with Fiona's great-grandfather's temper and self-serving ways, had declared that from then on, every member of the MacLean family would be given tenuous control over something as tempestuous as they were—the weather.

Whenever a MacLean lost his or her temper, lightning caused thatched houses to catch afire and made the ground tremble. Hail tore away the leaves of every tree and greenery within sight. Floods roared through the valley, ruining harvests, washing away homes and, sometimes, people.

When the people of the village saw clouds gathering at Castle MacLean on the hill, they huddled in their houses in fear.

Fiona closed her eyes. They were her people. *Hers.* Just as Callum had been her brother. She could not fail in this. If she did not defuse the situation, her brothers' fury would unthinkingly destroy everything.

The only way to break the curse was for every member of a generation to perform a "deed of great good." So far, no generation had succeeded. Perhaps this would count as Fiona's deed.

Fiona looked at the priest from beneath her lashes. "The curse has been proven time and again, Father."

The priest shook his head. "I feel fer yer family, lass. But this mad idea—"

Desperate, Fiona pressed her hands over her stomach. *My last hope.* "Father, I have no choice. Kincaid *has* to marry me."

Father MacCanney's eyes widened. "Blessed saints above, ye can't mean—ye haven't—ye didn't—"

"Aye. I am with child."

The priest whipped out a handkerchief and mopped his brow. "Dear me! Dear me! That changes everything, it does. I'll not have a bastard born in my parish."

Fiona threw her arms about the priest's neck. "Oh, thank you, Father! I knew I could count on you."

He returned the hug, sighing. "Ye'd just find another if I didna assist ye, anyway."

"I wouldn't wish anyone else to marry me, Father." Of course, she'd never thought to marry this way at all. She'd thought that someday, she'd meet a bonny man who would fall deeply in love with her, and they'd have a lovely wedding here in the church, surrounded by flowers and her family. None of that would happen now.

Sadness for what she'd never have pressed on her heart, but she resolutely pushed the feeling aside. "Father MacCanney, this is the right thing. It will be a new beginning for us all."

The priest sighed again, then turned to Hamish. "At least bring the lad to his feet. No man should marry from the dirt on the floor."

"Thank you, Father," Fiona said again. "You won't be sorry."

" 'Tis not *me* who might be sorry for this day's work, lassie."

Fiona hoped he was wrong.

Hamish prodded the fallen man with his huge boot. "Perhaps I should dunk his head in some water." He turned to gaze at the cistern.

Father MacCanney gasped. "That is *holy* water!"

"I dinna think God would mind. Besides, 'tis his wedding day and—"

"No," Father MacCanney said firmly. He pursed his lips. "Perhaps a wee dram would stir the man."

Hamish stiffened.

"Hamish," Fiona reproved. "We must all sacrifice."

"Ye ask a lot," Hamish growled. He reached into his coat and pulled out a flask. Reluctantly, he opened it, tilted back Kincaid's head, and poured a bit into the man's mouth.

Kincaid sputtered, but he didn't push the flask away. Still half-conscious, he reached up and grabbed at it, then poured it into his mouth.

"Damn ye!" Hamish yanked away the flask. "Ye drank half me whiskey!" The Scotsman grabbed Kincaid's jacket collar and hauled him up, looking ready to punch him.

"Thank you, Hamish," Fiona said swiftly, moving to stand beside Kincaid.

Kincaid blinked, then looked around woozily. "This is . . . church? I've never before dreamed I was in a church."

Fiona slipped an arm through his, trying to steady him. He slumped against her, his masculine scent of sandalwood and musk enveloping her. She immediately had a memory of another time, long ago, of hot hands and hot desires, the desperate ache of wanting—

Outside, thunder rumbled again over the sun-drenched garden.

Father MacCanney seemed to have trouble swallowing. Hamish sent Fiona a hard look.

She blushed, then cleared her throat. "Kincaid, you are indeed in a church. You are here to marry me."

"Marry?" He looked down at her, and she was struck by the vividness of his gaze, the brilliant blue of Loch Lomond.

She felt herself drawn into that gaze, pulled in, sinking as if into a pool of heated water.

A faint smile curved his lips. "Fiona MacLean." The words tickled her ear, smoky and seductive.

To her utter dismay, a low heat simmered at his nearness, building with a rapidity that made her gasp. The thunder rumbled louder, and a stir of heated wind sent the flowers bobbing, the grass rippling.

Fiona clenched her hands into fists, forcing her heart to resume a steady beat. She could not let herself lose control. She'd known the dangers of this errand. Jack Kincaid had this effect on every woman. *Every woman. None is special,* she reminded herself.

Her passions cooled at the thought. "Kincaid, stand alert," she said in a brisk tone. "We've important things to do this day."

His gaze flickered over her face, lingering on her eyes, her lips. He lowered his face until his whiskey-scented breath warmed her ear and cheek. "Tell me, love, if I marry you in this dream, will I win my way back into your bed?"

Her breath caught, and she whispered back, "Yes, you will be welcome into my bed. This is a real marriage, though we do not care for each other."

"Speak for yourself."

She raised her eyes to his, her heart strangely still. "What . . . what do you mean?"

"I mean I do care for you. I lust at the thought of touching you, of—"

"That is not caring." Why had she thought he'd meant anything else? If her time with Jack had taught her anything, it was that he was not capable of caring. Not really. "We can discuss all of this later. Right now, we must marry."

His gaze drifted over her face again, resting on her lips. A slow, seductive smile curved his mouth. "I will marry you, Fiona MacLean, and bed you well, as is meant to be. That is indeed the stuff of dreams."

She whispered furiously, "Jack, this is serious. If we marry, we can end the feud."

"Feud?"

She blinked. "The one between our families."

"Oh. *That* feud. I'd worry about that myself, if I weren't already dead and dreaming." He slung his arm over her shoulder. "What the hell! Do your worst, Father," he said grandly. "It's just a dream."

Father MacCanney met Fiona's gaze. "Are ye sure, lass?" he asked again.

Outside, the wind was dying a bit, though the heavy taste of rain and the unmistakable scent of lilac filled the air.

Fiona took a deep breath. In a few moments, she would be married. Married to a man who would shortly be sober and furious at the events she'd forced upon him. Married to the man who had long ago betrayed her. A man who would betray her again, if she were foolish enough to give him a chance.

She straightened her shoulders. There would be no more chances.

"Yes, Father," she said in a steady voice. "I am ready."

# Chapter Two

❧❧❧

*Long, long ago, before there was an England or even a Scotland, seven clans lived in this valley. Times were peaceful, and everyone strove to get along. Everyone, that is, but the MacLeans. Och, a proud clan they are, and fiery of temper. Even back then, before kings drew their lines on the land and called them countries . . .*

OLD WOMAN NORA OF LOCH LOMOND
TO HER THREE WEE GRANDDAUGHTERS ONE COLD NIGHT

*J*ack awoke slowly, drifting to awareness as if he floated on a feather pillow. He turned his head slowly, then frowned. He *was* on a feather pillow, covered with fresh-smelling white linen. Cautiously, he spread his hands and discovered that he was resting on an equally soft feather mattress.

This wasn't death. This was an overstuffed featherbed.

Jack slitted open his eyes, struggling to focus against the painfully bright light. His head throbbed at even that small effort. By Zeus, what had happened?

He remembered riding in the woods. A sound in the brush. Thunder, then the feel of icy cold rain—

Rain. And the smell of lilacs. Fiona.

Good God, it couldn't have been. And yet . . . rain and lilacs? It had to be.

Jack frowned, struggling to remember more. He had a distinct image of Fiona and her giant of a servant, Hamish, standing over him in the rain.

Other images followed. Fiona and Hamish and . . . Father MacCanney? In a church? Jack had a vivid impression of the taste of whiskey, bright and burning, and the deep green of Fiona's eyes. Eyes he'd thought he'd managed to forget.

Apparently not.

He rolled to one side and sat upright, wincing at the shrill sunlight coming through a crack in the curtains. What a strange, oddly disturbing dream. Perhaps it would teach him not to drink more whiskey than God intended a man to have in a single sitting.

Jack swung his legs over the edge of the bed, his stockinged feet finding the cold floor. Bloody hell, it looked as if they'd built this tavern on a ship, the way the room was rocking back and forth. He carefully stood, gripping the bedpost tightly.

Where the hell was he? The chamber was appointed in the finest of two-decades-old fashion, carefully preserved but well worn. There was a large oak wardrobe and a marble-topped table holding a bowl and pitcher and a neatly folded towel, flanked by a sturdy but threadbare upholstered chair. The scent of lemon and wax tickled his nose; the floor and woodwork were scrubbed and shiny, even in the dim light.

No tavern sported such cleanliness. Where was he, then? He leaned against the bedpost, his forehead resting on the thick, worn blue velvet draperies, his gaze dropping to his knee. The breeches he wore weren't his. He looked at his shirt and found that it, too, belonged to someone else. He'd never possessed a shirt with such silly lacings on the sleeves. The only familiar things in the room were his boots, which sat in one corner, cleaned and neatly shined. But why? Why was he here, and wearing someone else's clothes?

A rustle sounded in the passageway outside the door, then the brass handle turned and the door swung open. The bright light from the hallway outlined the figure of a woman. Small and curvy, she presented an intriguingly vague picture.

Jack knew her instantly. Knew her from the scent of lilacs that permeated the room. Knew her from the curve of her cheek where the light caressed it. Knew her from the graceful way she held the door. Knew her from the way his loins leapt at the sight of her.

It hadn't been a dream, after all. "Fiona MacLean," he said, his voice rusty and deep. "What is all this?"

She closed the door and walked forward, the beam of sunlight from the window sparkling on her hair.

Jack's jaw tightened. It had been fifteen years since he'd last seen her. Her eyes were greener than he remembered, her lashes casting mysterious shadows over them. The sunlight burnished her rich chestnut hair gold, and framed her delicately shaped face. He'd thought he'd forgotten her, but this moment proved otherwise: he remembered everything.

Her lips were plump and lush. Her nose was short and sprinkled with freckles. She was also more rounded than when he knew her before—no longer a young maid but a woman grown.

He could tell her breasts and hips were luxuriously full, though she was dressed in the height of propriety, her sedate morning gown an innocuous dove gray, her pelisse tightly buttoned to her throat.

Jack had avoided such women in London. Prim, proper misses you dared not talk to for fear of ending up leg-shackled. He'd learned to avoid such obviously dangerous women from this very one.

Fiona wet her lips nervously, drawing an instant response from his loins again. "Kincaid, I am sorry about this."

Low and husky, her voice sent a shocking quiver of heat through him. "Where the hell am I?"

"My brothers' hunting lodge. I dared not take you to Castle MacLean. Especially now."

Damn it all, his head was splitting, and she was speaking in riddles. Jack took a step forward, but the world immediately swayed to one side, then the other, his stomach roiling right along with it. Tight-lipped, he gripped the bedpost again.

Her green gaze flickered from him to the door, then back, her eyes shadowed by long, sable lashes. She'd always had the most intriguing eyes—large and lushly lashed and slanted ever so slightly at the corners, accented by fly-away brows. They were exotic, those quick slashes of impudent brows and seductive eyes, on a face that was otherwise angelic.

Of course, he knew otherwise. "Fiona, why am I here?"

A flicker of uncertainty touched her face. "You . . . you don't remember?"

"Remember what? I was riding home and—" Bits of memory returned in a painful rush. He'd left Lucinda's house because her husband had returned. The ride in the woods. The sudden rain. The lilac scent. Darkness, followed by the church, and Father MacCanney telling Jack to— He gripped the bedpost tighter. "We're *married*?"

She paled slightly but did not deny it.

Bloody hell, it hadn't been a dream at all! The room tilted, and he swayed unsteadily.

Fiona started forward, but he waved her off as he sank onto the edge of the bed. "Do not touch me, witch."

The last word quivered in the room. Her eyes flashed, her lips compressing dangerously. "I am not a witch."

"I know otherwise," he growled.

"If you are speaking of the MacLean curse, then yes, I am capable of some"—she gestured vaguely— "activities."

"You can make it rain." He snorted. "You just can't make it stop."

She colored a bit, the cream of her cheeks bright pink.

What a coil. He'd been captured and forced to wed a woman cursed with the ability to make clouds gather and rain fall, cursed like all in her family.

She made a dismissive gesture with her hand. "None of that has anything to do with why you are here. Why we are married."

*Married.* He couldn't wrap his pained head around the thought. "It cannot be binding."

"Yes, it is. I—I made certain it would be." Some of his fury must have been evident, for she put out a placating hand. "Please, Jack. I only did what I had to do. I had no choice."

He stood and took a step toward her, every fiber of his body pulsing with anger. "*You* had no choice? *You* were not the one who was dragged to the altar unconscious!" She had stolen his freedom from him. She, of all people.

She stepped away, her back near the wall. "Jack, I am truly sorry. I only did what I had to."

"*Had* to? What was so urgent that you felt such a thing was necessary?"

"I had to stop the feud. Our families are at risk."

"Are you crazed? That argument is as old as the mountains."

"Not anymore." Her eyes flickered with a flash of emotion deep within. "Jack, surely you know about Callum?"

He paused. "Your brother?"

"Yes. He was my youngest." Her voice caught on the last word, her lip quivering.

Jack blinked. "Was? Fiona, what happened?"

"There was a fight in a tavern a week ago. Your half-brother Eric fought Callum. Callum died. Surely you knew—" She broke off, her expression uncertain.

"The last time I saw anyone in my family was five years ago, at my grandfather's funeral." They'd been none too happy to see him, either, especially after they'd discovered that his grandfather had left his entire fortune to Jack. "I have not seen Eric or anyone since."

"Eric and Callum met in a tavern. They had an argument. Blows were exchanged. Callum died."

He frowned, unable to look away from her tear-bright gaze. "I didn't know."

"Your family says it was a simple brawl, that Callum's death was an accident. But my brothers do not believe him."

The sharpness of her voice told him it wasn't only her brothers who believed Eric's guilt.

Jack had been born almost a decade before either of his half-brothers. By the time he'd been fifteen, he and his stepfather had already reached the nadir of their relationship, a fistfight that had left them bloodied, bruised, and too angry ever to live under the same roof again.

So at the tender age of fifteen, Jack had packed his portmanteau, strapped it to the back of his favorite horse, and left for England. He rarely came home to visit. His family were all strangers to him now, and Jack was used to being alone. In fact, he treasured it.

"None of this has anything to do with me," he said.

She paled, her lips tight. "Callum is dead. Do you understand that?"

"Talk to Eric," he said harshly. "This has nothing to do with me."

She grabbed his arm, her fingers pressing through his linen shirt. "Someone killed my brother."

He looked down at her for a long time, noting the tension around her mouth, the tiredness around her eyes. She was exhausted. The realization sent a quiver of something through him, a faint sense of . . . worry? Regret?

He pulled his arm free. "You have the wrong Kincaid. You should have captured Eric or Angus, someone other than me."

Her eyes blazed. "How can you say that?"

"I do not concern myself with my family, nor they with me. I never have. Why would I begin now?" He could still remember the day he'd left his house. Stiff with anger and pride, he'd hoped one of them—his mother or stepfather or even one of his little brothers—would ask him to stay, beg him not to leave. Instead, there was an air of palpable relief. In the months following, the lack of further communication had cemented the fact all the more—they didn't care and never had.

Jack had decided that he didn't care, either. He had a decent income, provided by his mother's brother, and he'd rented rooms in the fashionable part of town. He fell all too easily into a life of ease as he gambled, gamed, chased women, drank to excess, and learned to treasure the one and only thing that was truly his own: his freedom.

By the time he was nineteen, he had a reputation as a hardened libertine and an inveterate gambler. He was also known for his outrageous good luck. Fortune, it seemed, really did smile upon those less lucky in areas of the heart. Until, at the age of twenty-two, on one of his sporadic jaunts to his homeland to run his hunters through the moors, he'd met Fiona MacLean. He would not become entangled again. "I will not be involved in this, MacLean. Find yourself another."

She lifted her chin, her eyes blazing up at him. "It's too late, Jack."

"I refuse to believe that."

Her brows rose. "Do you think me a fool? That I would go to this much trouble for something that could be undone so easily? Our marriage will stand, Kincaid. It will stand forever."

Jack stared at Fiona, a sinking sensation in his stomach. Was she right? Was there no setting this union aside?

Damn it all, how had this happened? And why with the one woman he hadn't been able to resist?

Only once in his life had he allowed himself to be swayed by his heart. He'd gambled it all—and lost. He'd been mad for Fiona from their first meeting. Within a week, he'd decided that she was the one, and with all the passion of youth, he'd pleaded with her to run away with him.

She'd reluctantly agreed. He'd made arrangements, bought a carriage and six, and waited for her at the assigned location. Night had drawn, but she had not come. In her place had arrived a thunderstorm like none he'd ever witnessed, along with two of her brothers. Gregor and Alexander had brutally informed him that their sister had changed her mind.

Jack had thought they were lying, until they'd given him the letter she'd written.

*Dear Jack, I cannot do this. Please leave and do not look for me again. My feelings for you are not what they should be. I am sorry if you believed otherwise. Sincerely, Fiona.*

His jaw tightened at the memory. He'd been left with nothing to do but turn the carriage and ride away, humiliated and furious.

Damn it all, he'd known better than to put his faith in something as fickle as emotion, yet he'd been unable to resist.

It was a mistake he never made again. Emotion was to be sipped and savored briefly, like champagne, before it went flat.

"I refuse to believe this marriage will stand."

Her jaw firmed, her eyes narrowing. "I made certain it would. With you as a member of the family, my brothers will halt their quest for blood."

"I know your brothers. It would take more than a mere marriage to keep them at bay."

She dropped her gaze. "Perhaps."

Jack tensed, his gaze narrowing. "Perhaps?"

She shrugged and began to turn away.

He grabbed her arm and yanked her back around. "Explain yourself."

"No! Not while you're holding me so!"

"You bloody witch," he snapped. In two short steps, he had her trapped between his body and the wall, the warmth of her skin seeping through her pelisse. For some reason, that only angered him more. "Whatever it is that you've done, you will undo. I will *not* be married. Not now, not ever!" He lowered his face until their eyes were even. "I will not give up my freedom, and I don't give a damn about Callum or my brothers or anyone else."

There was a moment of shocked silence. Fiona might pretend to be brave, but he could see from the way her lips trembled and her chest rose and fell with her short breaths that she was frightened.

"I will not undo anything," she said in a low, breathy voice. "We are married. We will stay that way. I am sorry, but there is nothing you can do about it."

He had the sudden impression of being held underwater, unable to breathe. His fingers tightened on her shoulders cruelly.

She did not look away, though her lips whitened. "Let me go, Kincaid."

"No."

She struggled, kicking back against the wall. "Let me go, now!"

"No. Not until you—"

The door to the room slammed open and Hamish

stalked in. Red-haired and red-eyed, he looked like a fiery angel seeking vengeance.

"Bloody hell," Jack muttered. He released Fiona and turned to stand before her. "Hamish. What a pleasant surprise."

Hamish's red brows lowered as he glanced from Jack to Fiona, then back. "What's goin' on here?"

"Nothing that concerns you," Jack said.

"I am pledged to watch the mistress. If ye lift a hand to her again, I'll end yer miserable life."

"Did you have anything to do with this damned marriage?" Jack felt his head, wincing when his fingers brushed a sore knot. "I've a feeling you assisted her far more than was necessary."

"I wish I'd given ye that knob, but I didn't. Ye fell from yer horse and smacked yer head." Hamish flexed his hand, the size of a large rock. "Had it been me, ye wouldn't be awake now."

"Hamish." Fiona stepped around Jack. "There was no need for you to intrude."

"I heard ye call out."

"I fell against the wall."

"Baldercock," Jack said rudely. "I pushed you."

Hamish's huge hands balled into fists. He started forward, but Jack was ready. He lifted a foot and sent the lone chair flying directly in the path of the big Scotsman.

Hamish grabbed the chair and threw it to one side, where it smashed against the wall and splintered into a dozen pieces.

Jack raised his fists and—

Fiona shoved him back, the edge of the bed catching him behind the knees and sending him thudding to the mattress. The distant rumble of thunder echoed.

"That is enough!" Fiona snapped, her eyes sparkling with anger. "Hamish, leave us! Kincaid and I must speak."

"I'm not leavin' ye with the likes of Black Jack Kincaid!"

"If I need you, I will call," Fiona said firmly.

The Scotsman didn't look convinced. "I don't—"

"Hamish," she said in a quiet tone. "Go."

Jack raised his brows, distracted from his own irritation by the strength of the rebuke in her voice.

Hamish must have heard it as well, for he flushed a deep red, then turned to the door. "I will be in the hallway." He paused to lock gazes with Jack. "I can be back in here in a trice."

Fiona nodded. "That won't be necessary."

The Scotsman grunted his disbelief but obediently left, closing the door behind him.

Fiona had changed, after all. There was some steel to her now, a determination he'd never seen before. For some reason, that made him more uneasy than facing Hamish.

Still, Fiona MacLean was responsible for this mess. Jack did not deserve to be punished for the sins of his less-than-loving family. Hell, he didn't deserve any of this. Jaw tight, he turned to his enemy. "Fiona, I will never accept this marriage."

Fiona fought to hold on to her tenuous control. She'd known Jack would be angry, but nothing had prepared her for the rage burning in his gaze. Her shoulders still ached where he'd gripped them, and she shivered from the cold fury in his face. "Jack, please. You must accept this."

"Why?"

Slowly, she placed her hand upon her stomach. "Because I have told everyone I am carrying your child."

He stepped back. "You did *what*?"

"I sent word to both of our families that I was with child and that was why we'd married."

He blinked.

"That's the only reason Father MacCanney agreed to wed us. He thought I was carrying your child."

"You bloody *bitch.*"

She winced. She deserved that, she supposed. "Kincaid, I would not have involved you if I'd had any other choice. The feud—"

"The feud is nothing more than squabbles over boundary lines and livestock."

"No, now it's different. Callum died. If something is not done, and quickly, neither of us will have a moment's peace for the rest of our lives. We'll be too busy tending graves to enjoy anything."

Jack's expression darkened. He spun on his heel, took a quick step toward the wall, then halted. He turned back to fix a cold blue stare upon her. "You really believe your brothers would do something rash."

She thought of her brothers' expressions when she'd last seen them—the hatred and anger. "Yes," she said, her voice barely audible. "They will seek vengeance. And they will succeed. Then their actions will be answered. If not by your father, then a cousin or an ally. You know how it is done."

He nodded abruptly. "Aye. I do know." Jack raked a hand through his hair, wincing when he touched a tender spot over one ear. "And so it will begin." He crossed to the window. "Does my father know of all this? Of your brothers' vow for vengeance?"

"I wrote to him and told him everything."

He turned, his face in the shadows. "You told him that you planned to capture me? To force me to marry?"

She bit her lip. "Not that part, no."

"Of course not."

She sighed, her knees a little weak. It had been such a long week, filled with sadness and emotion. "I told my brothers the same thing: that I was with child and you were the father."

Jack leaned a shoulder against the bedpost and crossed his arms over his broad chest. "Who is the father, Fiona? I should know, in case the bastard arrives to take retribution."

Her cheeks burned. "There is no child. I mean, not yet. I haven't been with anyone since you and I—" She bit her lip. Blast it, she hadn't meant to tell him that.

His expression shuttered. "I don't believe you."

"It doesn't matter what you believe. What matters

is that—" She crossed the few steps that separated them. "Jack, you were right in what you said before: just getting married won't stop the feud."

He scowled, his clear blue eyes locking with hers. "Then what will?"

Lord, he was going to force her to say it. "To end this feud once and for all, we must also have a child. And soon."

# Chapter Three

❧

*The worst part of a MacLean is that when they think they're right, they usually are. 'Tis a most annoyin' habit, and I feel a bit of pity for the lads and lassies who marry into such a prideful clan.*

OLD WOMAN NORA OF LOCH LOMOND
TO HER THREE WEE GRANDDAUGHTERS ONE COLD NIGHT

Disbelief warred with shock on Jack's face. "You are crazed if you think I will agree to that!"

She took a hasty step forward, so close that her skirts brushed against his knees. "We have no choice."

Jack's hard blue gaze glinted down at her, deep white lines beside his mouth. "Speak for yourself. I have many choices."

"No, you don't. Our families are on the brink of disaster." Suddenly, the urgent words locked in her throat as a lost thought quivered in her brain: *I am going to fail.*

It was all too much. Callum's death, her brothers' anger and their determined plans, abducting Jack, Father MacCanney's reluctance, the hurried marriage,

Jack's own fury . . . Every strained moment of the last week dropped upon her shoulders in a silent *whoosh.*

Tears filled her eyes. She clenched her fists, swallowed a sob, and pressed her fingernails to the tender flesh of her palms, hoping the tears would fade.

But the sob grew. She gulped hard in an effort to control it, but with a hiccup, her hold on her emotions cracked, slipped, then shattered. An entire week's worth of pent-up emotions and deep grief broke free, swamping her in pounding waves.

She dropped her face into her hands and let the sobs flow, unable to stop the torrent. She cried and cried. She missed Callum so much. He'd been her friend and confidant, understanding her better than anyone else in her family. And now he was gone.

*Gone.*

Sobs racked her body, draining her strength as tears fell from between her fingers. Grief, anger, pain, all of it rolled through her, wave after wave.

A warm hand closed over her wrists, and she was unceremoniously hauled against a broad chest. "Stop it," Jack whispered, his cheek against her hair, his voice soft. "I hate it when women cry."

Fiona cried harder. She didn't want to do this in front of him, but now that the tears had begun, she couldn't stop them. In trying to keep her brothers' fury from exploding and destroying them all, she hadn't allowed herself to grieve for Callum. Now the future stretched before her, bleak and cold and lonely without him.

The sobs came harder and harder still, until she thought her heart might break.

"*Fiona*," Jack said, his voice deeper. "You cannot— Oh, blast it all!" He sank his hand into her hair and pressed her face to his chest, holding her tight. "Easy, lass."

She buried her face against him and let the tears fall. She was no gilded miss who'd been sheltered from reality; she'd had her share of loss. But this time, life seemed brutal beyond acceptance. *Callum, I miss you.*

"Lassie, that's enough," Jack said, his voice resonating against Fiona's ear. "We will deal with this."

*We?* Fiona's heart clutched at the word, a faint ray of hope warming her. The thought that she might not be alone, that maybe Jack might find a way out of this mess, slowed the flow of her tears bit by bit.

Yet, though her crying lessened, Fiona didn't move. She drank in the strength of Jack's embrace, the warmth of his body. Her pain began to ease. Finally, her tears ceased, her body racked now by a deep hiccup.

Jack rubbed his chin against her hair and said gruffly, "I mean it. I really hate it when women cry."

"So—so—do I." She gulped.

He sighed, his breath stirring the tendrils at her temples. "I am sorry about Callum."

The tenderness in Jack's voice brought more tears to her eyes. She was a mess; red eyes, wet cheeks, and embarrassing hiccups. Suddenly self-conscious, she attempted to step out of Jack's arms. "I need a hand-kerchief."

Jack's embrace tightened, his hand rubbing up and down her back with comforting strokes. "I would give you my handkerchief, but someone has taken mine."

Fiona gave a watery chuckle. "I had Hamish change your clothes. You were wet, and I did not wish you to catch the ague."

"How thoughtful of you. Not many men who've been abducted and stripped can say they were so well tended."

She smiled against his damp shirt, her head resting on his muscled chest. Her ragged breaths gradually evened out, and a soft, intimate silence enveloped them.

The steady beating of his heart, mixed with the scent of starch from his shirt, calmed her somehow. The rise and fall of his chest beneath her cheek warmed her from head to toe, and she gave a contented sigh.

Jack bent and pressed a kiss to her forehead.

Fiona's breath hung in her throat. The kiss was chaste, almost innocent, and incredibly intimate.

"You've been through hell, haven't you, love?"

He'd called her "love." Not "my love," but just "love." She wondered how many women he'd called that, and how many had felt their hearts flutter the way hers had.

Though she'd wept against his shirt and basked in the comfort of his arms, the truth was that Jack Kincaid would have treated any other woman who'd melted into a weeping mass the same way. As he said, he couldn't stand to see a woman cry.

Fiona stepped out of Jack's protective arms into the cold of the room, reaching for a towel from the washstand.

She mopped her eyes, then blushed. "I didn't mean to soak your shirt."

He glanced down at the large wet spot on his chest, a wry smile softening the hard line of his mouth. "I don't know whose shirt this is, but you can take it up with them."

"It's Dougal's."

"Dougal's? There's *lace* on the cuffs. Your brother would never wear *lace*."

She gave a watery chuckle. "Dougal is a dandy now. You wouldn't believe how all the-crack he has become."

Jack looked down at her for a moment, his eyes dark and unfathomable. He reached out and twined a tendril of her hair about his finger. "This is a pretty mess."

"I know," she said, wishing she could just disappear. Her hair was falling about her, and her nose was pink from crying. "This entire week has been a nightmare."

"I am sure it has." He pursed his lips as he considered her. "Only desperation would have made you think of this harebrained plan."

She stiffened. "My plan may have its faults, but I thought this through. I have thought of nothing else for a week, night and day."

"There must be another way," he insisted. "Why didn't you tell someone of your brothers' plans? Someone who could stop them?"

"Who? Jack, my brothers can turn someone into a cinder merely by losing their tempers. Who would dare face them?"

"One of my brothers didn't seem to have any problem doing just that," he retorted grimly.

She stiffened, her eyes flashing dangerously.

Jack winced at her expression. "I didn't mean to be coarse. It's just that, though some believe your family can make it rain—"

"And lightning. And hail. Don't pretend you don't believe in the curse. I know you do."

He shrugged, careful not to meet her gaze. "It doesn't matter what I think. What matters is how to calm tempers so we can return to a normal life. When you discovered your brothers were planning ill, you should have told someone."

"Oh? And who would have been able to turn their plans to good? Your father, perhaps? The man who said he'd kill any MacLean who came within sight of the property gate?"

Jack frowned. "He said that?"

"Your stepfather is not a temperate man. Besides, if I had exposed my brothers' plan, they would have merely thought up another and made certain I didn't know of it."

He rubbed his neck. "You tried to talk them out of it?"

"Of course!"

"You pointed out the consequences and—"

"Kincaid, I thought of all of this. There is no other way but this one."

He regarded her for a while, his gaze never moving. Her shoulders slumped a bit. Perhaps he *would* find a way out of this, a way she hadn't yet found. Perhaps he would see some path she'd missed, some—

"Damn it to hell." He turned and walked to the end of the bed, leaning against the bedpost. "What a muddle." He raked a hand through his hair, wincing when his fingers brushed his bruise again. "Your brothers are as hotheaded as my own, if not worse."

She stiffened. "My brothers have reason for their anger."

"Not enough to justify planning a murder."

"Jack, I do not condone their plan, but you do not know what we've been through."

"Fiona, don't—"

"No! Don't *you!*" Her hands fisted at her sides, rage giving her the energy she'd lost. Outside, a shadow passed over the sun and a sudden wind blasted across the window, rattling the shutters. "Callum is gone, rotting under six feet of dirt. We are angry, we are *all* angry!" She pointed a finger and stabbed it into his chest. "Do you know how much I hate all of this? I hate having to see you again in such circumstances. I hate having to lie to my family and Father MacCanney. And I hate that I am forced to marry the worst possible man on earth!"

The words rang in the room, clear and stark.

Jack stared at her, his blue gaze so dark it appeared black. "You already regret marrying me."

"Just as much as you regret being married to me."

"We are agreed in one thing, then: we are not suited."

"We never were," she returned hotly.

"Then you will also agree that bringing an unwanted child into the world will not solve anything."

"Our child would not be unwanted! I will take good care of him, and gladly."

His gaze narrowed. "It is not as easy as that. Having a child is a serious proposition." His lips twisted. "Even I am aware of that."

"I didn't mean to suggest otherwise," she said stiffly.

"But a man you have deemed unworthy of marriage could not possibly be a good father."

Her cheeks heated. "Jack, don't—"

"No, we will speak the truth. How is this child going to feel, knowing he was conceived only to stop a stupid feud?"

"He doesn't need to know that."

"Those things have a way of making themselves known."

He was right. She clenched and unclenched her hands. Finally, unable to think of a retort, she said in a sour voice, "I cannot believe you even care about such a thing."

His expression grew grimmer. "Your opinion of me

could not be lower, could it? To you, I am just Black
Jack Kincaid, the man with no heart."

"No, no," she said, regretting her words. "I didn't
mean—"

He threw up a hand. "Forget it. I shouldn't be surprised. There is really no reason for you to believe otherwise." He turned from her and stalked to the window. The pale afternoon sun lit the planes of his face,
his auburn hair a slash of color against the deep blue
curtains, his body rigid with anger. "What a damnable
mess."

Fiona shivered a bit in the chill of the bedchamber.
She thought longingly of the warmth she'd felt tucked
against Jack, of the way his hard chest muscles had
pillowed her cheek, of the way his scent had tickled
her nose. A slow heat began to warm her, beginning
down low and moving higher, a deep tug of attraction, rich and sweet.

Heaven help her, she was *lusting.* The realization
sent a flood of heat to her cheeks. "If our families
think I am already with child, they will have to halt
their animosity, which will give us some time to—"
She closed her mouth. Heavens, how would she finish
*that* sentence?

His gaze narrowed. "Time to what?"

"Time to—to—to—" *Dear Lord, please open the
earth and swallow me whole!* How had she let her
tongue get her into such a fix? "You know what I
mean."

"No," he said slowly. "Explain yourself."

"You know what I meant!" Fiona snapped, crossing her arms over her chest. "While it will not be pleasant for us—"

"Speak for yourself." An unexpected smile twisted his lips. "Making the child is the only good part of this plan. If you remember anything, you should remember that."

Oh, God, she did remember. She remembered every sweet, delicious, breath-gasping moment. Slowly, she nodded.

His gaze traveled over her, hot and possessive, leaving a sizzling trail. "I'd take you here and now, if it suited you and we had the time."

Fiona's gaze flickered to the bed, then back, a delicious shiver feathering over her skin. She imagined them there, legs twined, hearts pounding as he—

No. She had to stay focused. She could not become distracted by such things.

"Fiona?" His gaze rested on her mouth.

"Y-yes?" Her lips tingled as if he'd touched them.

"You said you'd notified your brothers that we are married?"

"Yes. I sent a note to both my family and yours."

Jack sighed. "I was afraid of that. Your brothers will arrive soon."

She shrugged. "I suppose so."

"Wonderful," Jack muttered. He stalked to the window, then back, pausing before her. "How did we get here?"

"In my carriage."

He turned on his heel and went back to the window, pushing aside the curtain to peer outside. "It's getting cloudy and the wind is picking up."

Fiona sighed. "That was me, I fear. You have sorely tried my patience."

"As you have mine." He released the curtain. "I am not going to wait for your brothers to get close enough to open the skies."

Fiona wished she could ask Jack for reassurance that everything would be fine, but such luxuries were for real marriages. The thought made her shoulders sag.

"The carriage is away from the front door, which is good." Jack yanked the latch up and pushed the window wide. Fresh air blew into the room, lifting the curtain and shaking the tassled ties.

"Jack?" she asked, bemused. "Why does it matter if the carriage is near the door or not?"

Securing the curtains to either side, he turned and walked back to her, then bent and swept her into his arms as easily as if she were a feather pillow.

Fiona grabbed him around the neck and held on tightly. "Wh-what are you doing?"

He grinned, all dark auburn hair and deep blue eyes, and her heart skipped a beat.

"Kincaid, this is not funny! Put me down now."

"No, love. You've planned things this far; now it's my turn."

"Your turn?"

He shook his head. "You always were a bit on the

bossy side. Probably because of all those brothers of yours."

She gasped. "Bossy? I am *not* bossy."

"Hmph. Your brothers certainly used to think so." He turned toward the window. "It's time you stopped orchestrating the lives of everyone you know."

"I don't do any such thing!"

He glinted down at her. "No? Look at you now, getting married to save your brothers from a mess of their own making."

"This is an emergency."

"I know, I know. Lives are at stake. I understand. But you are not allowing your brothers to find their own answers; instead you're attempting to manipulate them to *your* outcome." He sat on the windowsill. "I call that bossy."

"I call it necessity."

"Whatever you call it, it's time someone else was in charge."

She squirmed, but his arms merely tightened. "Kincaid, put me down this instant! Hamish is not going to like this!"

"Good." Jack swung one foot across the windowsill, then the other, then he was standing in the shrubbery. He grinned at her. "Hamish is not invited."

She stilled a moment, as caught by his smile as by his words. "Invited where?"

"On our honeymoon." Jack walked across the lawn to the carriage, his muscles rippling as Fiona clung to him. "We're going to London."

"But I thought we'd live at my house!"

"With your brothers?" Jack scoffed. "The ones who've sworn to kill every Kincaid they find? I think not."

"But—"

"My lady?"

It was Simon, the footman.

"Oh, ah, Simon," Fiona said, wondering desperately what she should say

"Simon, good man," Jack said smoothly. "Good news! Your mistress and I were married this morning."

"Wh—you—the mistress—" Simon looked from Jack to Fiona, then back.

Jack nuzzled Fiona's cheek. "Tell him, love."

Fiona barely managed a smile through the shivers from his cheek against hers. "It is true. We are married."

Jack quirked a brow at the footman. "So open the carriage door; we've no time to waste."

"B-b-b—"

"And hurry, before I drop your mistress," Jack continued, walking briskly past the astounded footman. "She may not have much height to her, but she's an armful."

"Jack!" Fiona protested.

Simon scurried to the coach and threw open the door.

"Thank you," Jack said, tucking Fiona inside, then settling close beside her on the leather seat. "To London."

"London?" Simon squeaked. "But that's a long way—"

"London," Jack repeated in a voice that brooked no argument. "We'll stop along the way to change the horses. I have some boarded on the London Road."

"Aye, my lord, but—"

"Now." The word dripped with rebuke.

Simon flushed, then bowed and closed the door.

Almost immediately, the carriage began rocking over the uneven road. Fiona sent a sidelong glance at Jack, noting the hard set to his jaw.

This was it. She'd married Jack Kincaid and won his reluctant agreement to support her plan. Now she'd have to pay the price for that agreement.

*London,* her bemused mind thought. Her family was left behind. Her friends and the servants she knew and trusted.

In London, there would be no one. No one but her . . . and Jack.

*Good God. What have I done?*

# Chapter Four

Of course, pride and strength are not always bad. If ye're ever in a fight, ye want a couple of MacLeans with ye in case things go from bad to worse. If there's one word they dinna know, 'tis the word "cease."

OLD WOMAN NORA OF LOCH LOMOND
TO HER THREE WEE GRANDDAUGHTERS ONE COLD NIGHT

The trip to London was long and tortuous. Though the carriage was of good quality—Alexander would have nothing less for his sister—it still swayed and bumped over the roads because of the speed Jack insisted upon.

Fiona, heart weary, fell into a deep sleep after the first few hours. The next two days passed in a blur. Every time the carriage stopped to change the horses, Jack would rouse her and escort her inside. There, she'd blearily partake of the inn's fare, then they'd be off, the carriage careening madly toward London.

Finally, late on the third day, Fiona awoke with a start. She'd been deeply and dreamlessly asleep. She lifted her head, blinking into the dark as she surfaced to awareness.

Slowly, she realized she was in her carriage, snuggled in a corner, her cheek resting against . . . a waistcoat.

Fiona bolted upright.

*Jack. The marriage. London.*

Oh, God. She swallowed, painfully aware that her thigh was intimately pressed against his.

She had been sleeping against him. She scooted to one side, pressing her hands to her face.

"What's wrong, love?" Jack's voice rumbled through her. "Am I not soft enough?"

Fiona closed her eyes a moment. *Oh, please, don't let me have drooled.*

There was a spark and a flash, followed by a faint hiss, as Jack lit one of the lanterns that hung in the far corner.

A warm golden glow suffused the coach and lit Jack's auburn hair to a deep, rich brown as he settled back in his seat, his leg once more against hers.

Fiona's gaze flickered over his clothing. Thank goodness no splotch of drool marred his waistcoat. Relieved, she smoothed her hair, pins scattering here and there, wisps of curls tickling her hands. "Look at my hair!" She caught Jack's amused gaze and flushed. "I must look a mess."

His eyes, almost black in the lantern light, raked over her, and a faint smile touched his lips. "You look like a woman just roused from a very well-used bed."

Fiona had an instant image of herself and Jack, unclothed, their bodies entwined, memories she'd thought long dead.

She bit her lip, hoping the pain might drive out the thoughts.

"Don't attempt to seduce me with that look."

Her look was seductive? She lifted the edge of the curtain and regarded her face reflected in the window. "I don't look seductive at all. I just look— Oh, blast! My hair!" Two large curls poked up in the back, giving her a faintly devilish look. "Why didn't you tell me I had horns?"

"Perhaps I like women with horns." He crossed his arms over his chest, looking handsome and wolfish.

She tried to smooth her curls. "So you like horns? It's *so* tempting to make a comment about you and livestock."

He burst into reluctant laughter. "B'god, you are a fresh one."

"I always was." She gave her hair a final pat. "How is my hair?"

His dark gaze flickered over her hair, then lower. *Much* lower.

"I meant the hair on my head!"

Jack's lips quirked in a smile, and he shrugged. "I won't apologize for being a man."

"You should apologize for being a *rude* man." She folded her hands in her lap. "What did you mean when you said I was giving you 'that look'?"

"I find it very erotic when a woman bites her bottom lip."

"You must be teasing," she exclaimed.

The blue of his eyes deepened. "You *are* an innocent, aren't you?"

Her cheeks heated. "You, of all men, know that is not true."

"There are many kinds of innocents, Fiona."

She shrugged. "I have no regrets about our previous relationship, except that it did not end as it should have."

"That was not my fault."

"Yes, it was. You were not ready to settle down."

"I offered to marry you! I waited for you, but you didn't come. Instead, you sent your brothers with a damn note and—"

"You still had a mistress."

Silence met this. Jack's expression darkened. "I do not see what that has to do with anything. Many men have mistresses. I wished to marry *you*, Fiona. That was what should have mattered."

An odd flicker of hurt burned through her. "Our values are quite different. I would not have countenanced my husband having a mistress."

He shrugged. "Perhaps I would have given her up had you asked. We'll never know, will we?"

"Do you have one now?" The question was out before she could recall it.

His lips tightened. "That is none of your concern."

Fiona realized that her hands were clenched into fists, and she forced her fingers to relax. It *was* her concern. She could not accept a marriage that was othewise. And therein lay the only flaw in her plan: she'd married the one man she could not cajole, control, or persuade.

She regarded him from beneath her lashes. Every line of his body spelled defiance. From the way he planted his feet on the floor of the carriage, to the way his arms were crossed over his chest, to the proud tilt of his head, he was informing her without words that she had not won this battle. That she may, in fact, lose.

Fiona did not like losing. "Everything you do is my concern. We are married."

"Not for long. The second I reach London, I will see what can be done with this mess."

Fiona shot him a look from beneath her lashes. "The marriage cannot be set aside. I have already told you that."

Jack quirked a brow at her. "You aren't always right."

"I know that," she said with some asperity, "but even you must admit that I am right more often than not."

He smiled suddenly, a spontaneous, lopsided grin that stole Fiona's breath. "You haven't changed a bit."

If there was one danger in her current plan, it was that she might succumb to Jack's attractions. Then there would be nothing but heartbreak, and she'd already had enough of that.

"You are biting your lip again." His eyes glinted. "I am going to tell you why that gesture is so erotic, but I warn you, it's quite reprehensible."

"Anything that involves you tends in that direction."

His lips twitched, but he replied easily enough, "When you bite your lip, it makes me think of all the other things you could do with your mouth."

"Oh." Like eat and kiss and— "*Oh.*" Her cheeks burned, yet she was also a bit intrigued. Jack had always had that effect on her. He could embarrass and tantalize all in the same breath.

But perhaps this was useful information. The time might come when she'd need to seduce him—especially if he proved recalcitrant about performing his "husbandly duties" once they reached London. Which he might be, if he had a mistress. Fiona pressed her lips together to keep from scowling. She had never been very good at sharing her things, and she was certain she'd be quite possessive about a husband.

"You have lost some of your pins." Jack picked up two from the folds of her gown and held them out to her. "Your hair is so long. Longer than the last time I saw you."

"It's almost to my waist." She made a face. "I have thought of getting it cut."

"I love a woman with long hair."

"You love all women, long hair or no." She sniffed, tackling an unruly curl near her temple.

He sent her a roguish wink. "At this moment, I especially love women with long brown hair and green eyes."

"Oh, just stop it."

"Stop what?" he asked, all innocence.

"Stop flirting. With you, every sentence is an offer."

He leaned back against the squabs, his thigh sliding over to press against hers. "And with you, every sentence is a challenge."

She didn't know how to answer that. If she replied, it would confirm his comment. If she didn't say a word, she left a wealth of sharp retorts unsaid.

He flipped up one corner of the leather curtain and glanced briefly out into the racing darkness. "We're entering London. It's almost two in the morning." He settled back in his corner, his leg moving against hers once more. "I like traveling fast."

She glanced to her other side. It would be cold to lean all the way into the corner, for the night air was seeping from every seam. She supposed she would have to accept his leg against hers. At least there was a good deal of clothing between them—her chemise, petticoats, gown, and cloak. Jack was wearing breeches and . . . She looked at his legs. What else? Could he be naked beneath his breeches? They seemed molded to him, outlining the powerful lines of his thighs and the swell just above—

Oh, God. She closed her eyes. She'd been looking at his— Not only was it rude, but it had sent an amazing tingle through her, almost as if she'd touched it.

"Fiona, if you ever look at me like that again, I will not be held responsible for what I do." Jack was so close that she could feel his breath on her temple. "Do you understand?"

Fiona managed a jerky nod, relieved when he moved back.

Jack from a distance she could deal with. Jack in the close carriage, his thigh a mere inch from hers . . . the memories were too bright, too raw. She'd been young and impetuous, and fortunate that nothing more had come of their brief liaison than some uncomfortably vivid memories.

She cleared her throat. "I was just remembering *us*."

"I think of us, too."

She blinked at him. "I didn't think you would."

He sent her a darkly amused glance. "No? How could I not? You were my first."

"That's impossible. You already had a mistress! Alexander said she wasn't your first one, either."

"So I have your brother to thank for that slip of the tongue, eh? Remind me to thank him properly when I see him."

"I would have found out anyway."

Jack didn't argue. "Yes, but you were special; my first virgin."

Embarrassment flooded through her, and she fixed her gaze on the tips of her half boots where they peeped out from beneath her skirts. If only she were something as simple as a slipper that did not have feelings or memories or anything else so uncomfortable.

She frowned a bit. Shoes really did lead the perfect life. They were polished and taken care of and not expected to do anything more painful than occasionally step in a bit of mud or a rare puddle. She'd wager her shoes never wished they could just disappear.

Fiona looked at her hands, the hem of her pelisse, the seat opposite, anywhere but at him. "My goodness, it is certainly warmer here than in the countryside, isn't it?"

"Yes." He stretched out his legs so that his thigh pressed even more firmly against hers. "It is much warmer."

She snuck a look at him. When had his eyes grown so hard, so intense? Though he did not scowl, his entire stance still spoke of an undercurrent of bitter anger. Some part of her had hoped that he'd accept the circumstances of their marriage and not struggle against fate. That had been a vain hope.

She sighed. "When will we arrive?"

"Soon. We stopped to change horses in Barnet, so they're fairly fresh."

"Barnet? I don't remember changing horses there."

"We stopped while you were sleeping. I told your man—"

"He has a name," she said shortly. "It would be more polite if you'd use that rather than calling him 'your man.'"

Jack's brows lowered. "You aren't one of those reformer women, are you?"

"The only thing I wish to reform is your poor manners."

Jack looked incredulous. "My what?"

"Your poor manners. I daresay you don't know the names of any of your own staff, do you?"

"I haven't the time for such nonsense. There are dozens of them."

"Dozens? How large is your town house?"

"Large enough." He caught her gaze and held up a hand. "Hold. Before you get more out of sorts, let me try to remember that blasted man's name." He frowned. "Seth?"

"Simon."

"Simon, then. He came to the window when we stopped to change the horses. I explained I did not wish to wake you, so he had the carriage propped up so we could change the horses. Your Simon is quite ingenious."

"I don't remember any of that."

"I explained you were tired from our honeymoon activities."

Fiona gasped. "You did not!"

Jack's eyes glinted in the low light from the lantern. "No, I did not. But I thought about it." He slipped an arm about her waist and slid her across the small space between him. "It's not every groom who would be so understanding of his bride on their wedding night." He cupped her face, his thumb tracing the line of her cheek. "Fortunately for you, I am a patient man."

An odd flutter danced in Fiona's stomach, her skin prickling with goose bumps. He'd always had the ability to make her bones melt with just a simple touch and a soft word. He was so certain of himself—while she was filled with uncertainty, an unwelcome experience. For the first time in her life, she did not know what the future held, and it terrified her.

He feathered his thumb over her lips, his gaze following the movement. "You have the most beautiful mouth, Fiona. So lovely and lush, like a strawberry plucked at just the right time, red and sweet . . ."

He bent forward and raked his lips softly over hers. It wasn't a kiss; it was more of a promise, a whisper of what could be.

Fiona shivered again, her skin hot, her breasts tight. She should fight this attraction. Fight it and keep her own emotions well in control. But the last week had been nothing *but* control, and she was tired of not feeling, not touching. She wanted comfort and acceptance and passion. After a week of death, she wanted to taste *life*. To hold it to her, to savor it and revel in it.

She slid her arms around his neck and kissed him.

Jack saw the exact moment she gave herself over to the passion that hovered between them. While she'd slept in his arms, the scent of her hair and the warmth of her skin beckoning to him, he'd had to fight the desire to touch her, taste her, possess her. It had been a *long* carriage ride. During a rough section of road, her hand had fallen into his lap, and he'd thought he would explode.

It had always been this way between them. Since their first meeting, something hot and primal had drawn them together.

Now, finally released, his passion exploded with

the touch of her lips to his. He pulled her closer and nipped her bottom lip, savoring its plumpness.

But he wanted more than a kiss. Far more. He slid his hand up to her breast, cupped her, and ran his thumb over her nipple, making it harden through the thin material.

Fiona gasped, her mouth parting, and Jack slid his tongue between her lips. She moaned, pressing closer, her arms tightening about his neck.

God, but she was sweet. He deepened the kiss, tasting her ripeness as he slid his hands down her back to her waist, to her hips. She was so lush and full. This was a woman made for love, made for him.

A sudden rocking yanked him back to reality as the carriage stopped.

"Damn it!" he growled. "We've arrived." Jack looked down into her eyes. She sat on his lap, her lips swollen from his kisses, her skin touched with a ripe flush.

His groin tightened, but he ruthlessly ignored it. She was his for the taking. He knew it. But before he made that leap, he had to discover for certain if their marriage could be annulled.

In the meantime, it would cause no harm to remind her who had the upper hand. Let her taste the cost of being married to a man who didn't wish to be. Jaw clenched, he pulled Fiona's pelisse back into place and smoothed her skirts.

A soft rap sounded on the door.

"Oh, no!" Fiona struggled to get off his lap, but Jack held her there.

"Jack!" she hissed. "Simon will see."

"Then let him." He tightened his hold, his expression grim. "You are my wife now. That gives me the right to hold you whenever I wish."

Fiona had the damnedest effect on him, making him possessive and irritated at the same time. It was yet another reason to end this farce, and quickly.

The carriage door opened, and Simon flushed at seeing Fiona in Jack's lap.

"The steps," Jack ordered.

Simon nodded, his gaze directed at the ground. He let down the stairs, then moved aside.

Jack lifted her and stepped out of the carriage, carrying her to the broad steps that rose to the doors of his house.

"Jack!" Fiona hissed. "Put me down. Your servants will see, too."

"Let them."

Fiona wished she dared struggle but feared that would only make their entrance appear more ridiculous.

As Jack began to climb the stairs, Fiona looked up at her new home. Five stories of stately mansion rose above her head. Heavy molding around the large windows and doors bespoke a quality and craftsmanship that was obvious even in the dim night. "Good God! It's massive!"

Jack paused with his foot on the last step. "I do wish you'd keep those comments until we are in bed, love. I would appreciate them all the more there."

Fiona's cheeks heated. "Stop that!"

Jack's wicked grin flashed as he stepped onto the portico. The huge doors opened as if by magic.

Within moments, they were inside, the doors closing. Fiona had a hurried impression of black and red marble flagstone, rich carpets, and the glitter of a huge chandelier presiding over a foyer elaborate in gilt-edged side tables and large, golden framed mirrors.

Jack walked briskly past a stiff individual who could only be the butler and a stern, gray-haired woman whose keys proclaimed her the housekeeper. The shadowy figures of at least a dozen footmen blurred in the background.

"My lord," the butler said as Jack walked past. "We didn't know you were returning. There is no fire lit in your chamber. Shall I—"

"No," Jack said, taking the stairs two at a time. "That is not necessary." He paused at the top, his gaze insolently caressing Fiona. "Please bring a large breakfast in the morning. A *very* large breakfast."

Fiona had thought she couldn't get more embarrassed, but she was wrong. Her entire body flushed. How dare he do such a thing in front of the servants?

*He is angry. I knew he would be.* She just hadn't expected he'd be so bitter.

Jack carried Fiona down a long hallway, his footsteps muffled by thick red carpet.

Fiona put her irritation behind her. Tomorrow,

she'd have Jack introduce her to the servants properly, and all would be set to rights. For now, she wanted to stop thinking. To stop feeling. She yearned for the delight of losing herself in a large featherbed and fresh sheets.

He opened a large door and carried her inside a huge chamber to a bed that towered at the center of one wall. He paused at the edge of the mattress and looked down at her, his expression inscrutable.

Fiona's breath shortened. She was agonizingly aware of the bed beneath her, of Jack's arms around her. This was it; the moment he'd take his rights as her husband. Her body tingled, her breath shortened.

Jack lifted her a bit higher and then, without ceremony, tossed her onto the bed.

Fiona bounced, gasping as she tried to find some purchase in the sea of covers and pillows. "Jack!"

He was already crossing the room to the open door.

She scrambled to her knees, her hair falling about her, her skirts flipped this way and that. "Where are you going?"

"To see my solicitor."

"At this time of the night?"

"For what I pay him, he can drag his lazy arse from bed." His expression was hard. "Meanwhile, you may sleep here. At least for tonight."

Her chest ached as if he'd struck her. "Jack, the feud—"

"Will resolve itself, with our help or without it."
He opened the door. "Sleep well, wife. This will be the
only night you enjoy my bed."

"But you can't just—"

The door slammed, the sound echoing through the
high-ceilinged chamber.

# Chapter Five

*The MacLean curse is an old one, placed upon the family in the times of Robert the Bruce by the infamous White Witch. She resides in the forest outside of Muir da Og. They say she's as lovely as a sunrise, and her only pleasure is in eating the hearts of the human men she's spurned.*

OLD WOMAN NORA OF LOCH LOMOND
TO HER THREE WEE GRANDDAUGHTERS ONE COLD NIGHT

Fiona awoke, aware before she opened her eyes that she was not alone.

Stretching, she turned to her side and saw Jack sitting beside the fireplace, the flames casting shadows over his face. His cravat was untied, his coat thrown across a chair, his shirtsleeves rolled back from powerful forearms. He held a glass of amber liquid as he gazed unseeingly into the flickering flames.

Fiona rolled to one elbow and pushed her hair from her eyes. "Well? What did your solicitor say?"

Jack did not even turn to look at her. "You know damn well what he said. It would take an act of Parliament to get the marriage annulled, unless you agreed to say I'd not touched you." His lips twisted. "You wouldn't, would you?"

"No."

He never looked away from the fire. The flames cracked and popped, a faint warmth reaching the bed.

Fiona was glad for the heat. She'd fumed when he'd left, but the cold of the room had made her seek shelter in the huge bed. She'd taken off her pelisse and attempted to untie her boots, but the laces had knotted and her cold fingers had been unable to loosen them. She'd finally climbed between the sheets fully dressed, buried her head in a pillow, and fallen asleep almost immediately.

From his chair, Jack now regarded her stonily, his glass held tightly in one hand, his gaze hard.

She plucked at the heavily hemmed edge of the sheet. "I daresay you're tired. Perhaps you should sleep—"

He slammed his glass onto the side table, his blazing glare silencing her. "I don't need anyone to take care of me! I am stuck with this marriage, but I do not have to put up with the mewing of a wife I never wanted!"

Fiona gripped the sheet with both hands. "Very well," she said in a reasonably steady voice. "I will never again inquire after your well-being. But do not think I will accept poor behavior. We can at least be pleasant to each other until we have the child. After that, I will move back to Scotland."

"And the child?"

She frowned. "He will stay with me."

"Fine. So long as you leave me in peace."

His words should have had no power to wound her, for they were exactly what she expected.

Jack stood and pulled off his untied cravat, tossing it to one side. He paused long enough to refill his glass and take another drink, wavering a bit as he did so.

He was drunk. Fiona's heart sank a bit lower. He would come to her bed now and do his duty, and she . . . what would she do? Her body and mind seemed strangely divorced, and she dreaded the coming moments. Dreaded what had once been the most amazing event of her life.

Her memories were deeply colored by their passion, but now it would not be the same. Gone was the concern, the caring. All that was left was anger and distrust.

Jack yanked his shirt over his head and tossed it to the floor. Within moments, his breeches followed suit, and he stood before her, naked.

The firelight flickered over his body, tracing the ridges of his chest, caressing the flatness of his stomach, limning the powerful muscles of his arms and shoulders. He was beautiful. She'd forgotten how just the sight of him could warm her with anticipation, even now.

"Why are you still dressed?" he asked harshly.

"I was cold."

His lips twisted into a semblance of a smile. "If we are to make a child, you will have to make sacrifices."

She managed to nod. "Of course." She reached up and untied her gown, her gaze still fixed upon him. There was something intent about him, something coiled. His eyes were dark, his body tense, as if he were about to pounce.

Which wasn't necessarily a bad thing, she decided, looking up into his blue, blue eyes and noting the thick curl of his lashes. He would pounce, and it would feel ever so wonderful. She knew that already. He was a heartbreaker, exquisitely skilled in bed and ready to take his pleasure by giving it.

She bit her lip to fight a shiver. She wanted to throw her arms around Jack and kiss him mindlessly, encourage him to continue with this seduction.

She wanted to put a hand to his cheek and rub her palm over his shadow beard, letting the stubble rasp against her skin.

She wanted to twine her arms around his neck more tightly and pull his mouth to hers and taste once again that hot, smoky passion that simmered between them.

*Oh, God, this is really it.* They were alone in his bedroom, they were married, there was nothing stopping them from consummating their union. Nothing at all.

She gave a nervous glance around. "Ah, this is a lovely room."

His gaze never wavered from her. "Lovely, indeed."

Cheeks hot, Fiona tried to find something to distract her unruly thoughts long enough for her to regain control of herself. "It's an exquisite chamber. Is the rug an Aubusson?"

"Yes." Jack walked across that very rug toward the bed, his movements fluid and deadly. "The rug is Aubusson."

"And the clock is—"

"Ormolu." He paused beside the bed. "The chairs are Hepplewhite. The table is a Pembroke, and the painting over the mantel is by Rubens. Anything else you wish to know?"

"You certainly know your furnishings. I don't believe my brothers even notice ours." Fiona sent Jack a curious look. "Why do you know the names of all this?"

"Because it is mine."

"And yet . . . you didn't bother with the name of my footman?"

"Footmen, like all people, come and go. This house will be here as long as I am."

She forced herself not to look at him, standing so beautiful and naked beside the bed. Ah! The picture above the fireplace. "Th-that is a lovely painting." It depicted a red-haired lady looking into the face of her lover, her expression one of sensual longing. "She's, ah . . . naked."

"As all beautiful women should be." The bed sagged where he sat on the edge, his hip now against her leg.

She tried to move away, but the sheets held her in place.

He placed his hand over her knee. Fiona sat stock—still, her heart pounding so loudly she wondered if he could hear it. "Jack, perhaps . . . perhaps we should wait a bit, until—"

"No. You wanted this marriage, MacLean. You wanted it so badly you took my freedom to get it. And now you've got it."

She glared up at him, anger burning away some of her trepidation. "I didn't want to be tossed onto the bed and—" She tried to calm her quavering voice. "Jack, there is no reason we cannot at least proceed with civility."

"Civility? Was it civil when you had me abducted and dragged to the altar like a sack of potatoes?"

She hated it when he was right. Really, *really* hated it. She took a deep breath and tried again. "Look, Jack—"

"If I am to do this, then it will be on *my* terms."

He gave her no choice. She only wished he would not argue with her while he was naked; it was difficult to make a coherent point with such a distraction. "What are your terms?"

He leaned forward. "When you are in my home, you will stay in my bed."

She couldn't swallow. Or breathe. Or even make a sound. She could only nod.

"Furthermore," he continued, his gaze traveling down to her lips, "you will do so with appropriate enthusiasm."

She found her voice. "You would have me pretend to feel something I do not?"

His hand cupped her breast, and Fiona jerked, her skin aflame, her breathing ragged as pure lust shot through her.

He smiled, a satisfied look on his face. "You won't have to pretend with me, love."

Fiona wished she could leave, run away as fast as she could and never look back. But if she returned home without Jack, her brothers would be furious. She would never make them believe that she'd walked away of her own free will; they'd think Jack had left her, which would be an unforgivable insult.

She took a deep breath. "Very well. You are right that we cannot do this halfway. We—we must do this with 'enthusiasm.'"

The fire crackled and popped. Jack cupped her chin in his large, warm hand and turned her face to his. She almost gasped at the burning expression in his eyes; if she was aflame, he was afire. He wanted her, desired her passionately.

Fiona's body quivered with answered need.

He slowly lowered his lips to hers, and Fiona was lost in a flood of heat and sensation. Without another thought, she gave herself over to the passion that Jack's kiss stirred.

He felt her body soften into his, and he slid his hands up and down her body, cupping her to him, pressing his manhood to her.

He burned with lust and passion, seasoned with

the faintest hint of anger. Distasteful as it was, marriage was now his lot in life. But if he had to be married, he might as well get something from it.

He ran his hand down her back to her hip, then her thigh. She moved restlessly, pressing against him, her mouth seeking his with increasing desperation. "Is this what you want?" he murmured against her lips. He pressed his hand between her thighs. "Or this?"

She moaned, shuddering with need, and Jack's body tightened in response. He wanted her so badly, ached with a lust that burned so hotly and so deeply, he feared it might destroy them both.

She was fumbling with her gown. "Let me," he said, his voice thick even to his own ears.

She nodded, her cheeks flushed, her lips swollen from their kiss. He quickly undid the remaining ties. He wanted to see her naked, her hair spread about her, her arms and legs open for him—him and no one else.

The thought gave him pause. He was not given to possessiveness; his liaisons were entertainments to be taken as they came, enjoyed, and then left. The freedom of the encounters gave spice to it all.

But with Fiona, it was different. Perhaps it was because she was the only woman he'd ever lost before he'd tired of her. Perhaps it was because she was the only woman who'd ever sent him away. Or perhaps it was something as simple as ownership. She was his *wife*. The word sent a possessive thrill through him. His chest expanded at the thought, his body quickening.

The last tie of her gown came free.

With a simple tug at her neckline, Fiona loosened her gown, pushed it wide, and it slid down to her waist, a discarded froth of lace and silk and innocence. She shimmied a bit, kicking away the sheets as she pulled the gown free, and tossed it off the bed.

All she wore was a thin chemise, and the rosebud circles of her breasts pressed wantonly against the material and made his mouth water.

She sat upright and reached down to undo her boot laces, her chemise pulling lushly over her rounded ass.

Jack admired the curve, his fingers curling at the thought of cupping her to him.

"The laces are knotted," she muttered, bending down farther to examine the problem. Her hair fell to one shoulder, pins pinging to the floor as the heavy strands fell loose. She sighed with exasperation, then took out the remaining pins and tucked her hair behind her ears.

Jack watched, his heart pounding a bit harder. Her hair was silken and thick, gleaming rich sable in the firelight. He wanted to slide his hands through her hair, sink into the clinging softness.

God, she was beautiful.

Unaware of his barely held control, she pulled and tugged on the knot. "Blast it!" she fumed. "I can't untie them; the laces are in knots."

He caught her wrist. "Leave them. I cannot wait." He pulled her against him hard and took her mouth once more, kissing her deeply as he slid her chemise from her shoulders, pushing it down her arms, to her waist, and over her boots.

A lace caught on a heel, and he yanked it free, ignoring the tearing sound. Jack slid his arm around Fiona's waist and lifted her to the center of the bed, where she lay clothed only in her pale skin, glossy hair, silk stockings, and dark blue leather half boots.

Jack stepped back to enjoy the sight before him. There was something about the contrast of her wanton body and the prim boots that stirred him even more. Something about the way her stockings rose from those boots to caress her pale skin and travel up her legs to the middle of her bare, rounded thighs.

Her creamy skin contrasted vividly with the long sable hair fanned over his pillows and the tight curls that hid the secrets between her thighs.

Never had Jack seen anything so enticing, so lovely. She lifted her arms and pulled him to her, her naked chest against his. Jack sank into her embrace, soaking in her sweetness. He tasted her lips, her cheeks, pressing kisses to her slender throat and shoulders. Every inch of her fascinated and intrigued him. Every kiss drew a gasp from her lips and urged him on.

He found her lips again and kissed her deeply, caressing her, exploring her, inhaling her.

She moaned against his mouth, and with that one, primal sound, Jack finally lost control.

He pressed against her, her legs parting beneath his, her hands tugging at him, pulling him closer.

She was intensely aroused; he could see it, smell it, taste it. So turgid he ached, he hooked his hand beneath one of her knees and pulled it high to his waist, his manhood pressing against her soft, damp opening.

Fiona gasped, her head thrown back, her eyes closing. "Yes!" she said between panting breaths. "Please!"

Still, he held back. As crazed as he was to be inside her, he wanted her to want him even more.

Slowly, ever so slowly, he pressed himself into her, gritting his teeth as her tight wetness encircled him with the firmness of a gloved hand.

Her lips parted, and she gasped loudly, her eyes flying open to meet his. "*Jack.*"

She pressed against him, encouraging him to move faster, her hands tight on his shoulders.

He increased his movements, captured by the pure pleasure of her expression.

"Yes," she gasped.

Jack moved faster, consumed with the feel of her. She stretched about him, deliciously warm and wet, gasping his name, writhing beneath him, her heels pushing against his ass, pressing him forward. Sensations spiraled through him at the touch of hard leather, at the sounds of her gasps of pleasure, at the scent of her mingled with lilac.

He hovered on the razor-sharp edge of control.

"God, yes," she said, pressing him forward, straining to take even more of him.

One of her leather boots rubbed against his hip,

and he groaned at the shock of sensation, erotic pleasure flooding him. As he took her with renewed passion, she arched against him, clinging tightly.

"Jack!" she gasped.

The sight of her face, the pleasure that suffused her skin with a flush of pink, forced him to grit his teeth and hold back.

She clutched at his shoulders, lifting her hips, pressing against him, gasping for him to go faster.

In all his life, Jack had never had to fight for control the way he fought now. He'd never before flamed with such passion, desired anyone more. It was as if she'd cast a spell on him, making him hers with each touch and gasp.

Sweat beaded on his forehead, and he twined his hands in her hair, clenching his fists about the softness.

Her moans increased, and she moved frantically. He caught her shoulders and pressed deeply into her, holding himself rigidly in place.

Her eyes flew open. Her breath caught. Her lips parted, but no sound came out. Suddenly, she thrust her hips forward, her heels pressing into the backs of his thighs as she came, her waves of tightening pleasure grasping at him, tugging him, making him crazed with lust as she gasped his name over and over.

Yet she did not stop. Her orgasm over, she bucked against him again, pulling him closer with her booted heels, spurring him on.

Jack thrust forward, sinking deeply into her and

sending her over the edge once more. With a cry, she arched against him, clamping her legs around his hips as wave after wave of tightness clenched him.

He fell over the pinnacle with her, falling through a tumult of ecstasy, rasping out her name as he finally allowed himself release.

Gasping, he collapsed over her, keeping his weight on his elbows. She quivered below him, her eyes closed, her mouth parted, her face flushed with passion.

Jack rolled to his side, pulling her with him, and they lay in a tangle of legs and damp skin, hearts thundering, souls reeling.

Fiona thought she'd never be able to catch her breath, so hard was her heart pounding in her chest. But moment by moment, her heartbeat slowed, and she became aware of Jack's broad chest against hers, the tickle of his breath in her hair, the deliciously sensual slide of his damp skin over hers.

She slid her arms around his neck and held him there, unable to move, incapable of thinking. She closed her eyes and savored the feel of him, the scent of their lovemaking, the freshness of the sheets, and the warmth of his skin.

Did Jack feel the same wonder? Had their passion surprised him as much as her? Or was it what he'd expected? Good God, what if sex was *always* like this for him—with every woman he'd been with?

Some of the glow began to subside. Fiona could feel his heart beating more steadily now, feel his even breaths in her hair.

She turned to look at him, at the way his lashes rested on the crests of his cheeks. Perhaps she should ask him, find out what he was thinking and feeling.

But . . . what if he wasn't thinking the same things she was thinking? Of how wonderful, how special it was? Worse, what if it hadn't been that good for him at all?

The uncertainty began to pinch at her. She had to ask him, had to know. She couldn't just lie there and wonder. "Jack?"

He did not answer.

Oh, no, he had guessed what she was about to ask and was afraid to answer.

Fiona gathered her nerve. "Jack?" she said a bit louder.

A soft snore was her answer.

# Chapter Six

The tale is a bit blurred on how MacLean came in contact with the White Witch. All we know for certain is that meet they did, and that neither of them would be the same afterward. Often that's the way love is, sneaky and unrelenting.

OLD WOMAN NORA OF LOCH LOMOND
TO HER THREE WEE GRANDDAUGHTERS ONE COLD NIGHT

"Umhph!" A thump in Jack's side awakened him. He blinked and struggled to focus on the face in front of him.

Full, soft lips folded in a displeased line. A pert, upturned nose was splashed with dusky freckles across the bridge, barely noticeable in the light from the fireplace. Thickly lashed eyes glowed a lovely, mossy green.

All of this surrounded by a cloud of sable hair so thick it dared a man to—

*Fiona.*

*How did— Where had—*

*Oh, yes.*

The scent of their recent lovemaking and the feel of her bared legs twined with his slowly stirred his memory, though his sated body struggled against the lethargic effects.

"You were snoring."

He opened his mouth, then closed it, unsure of the accusing tone of her voice.

"*Loudly.*"

He supposed it was annoying being awakened in such a way, especially if she had been as sound asleep as he had been. "Sorry, love." He yawned. "After a good romp, I always sleep deeply."

Silence. "A good romp?"

Normally, Jack would have recognized the outrage in her quiet voice. Unfortunately, he was deep in the euphoric grip of after-sex stupor.

So he merely turned and spooned Fiona to him. She fit against him perfectly, her head tucked beneath his chin, her rounded ass pressing against him, her legs entwined with his.

Her hair tickled his nose, and he smoothed it back with his cheek, enjoying the feel of her silky skin and the faint beat of her heart. "Let's sleep a bit, shall we?"

He closed his eyes and—

She pushed herself out of his embrace, cold air touching his skin where she and the blankets had once been. He frowned, opening one eye. "Hm?"

She had turned to face him, her expression serious. "Jack, we have things to discuss."

He sighed. "What things?"

"Things like"—her lips tightened with distaste—"our 'little romp.'"

There was no missing the outrage this time. Jack passed a hand over his face, struggling to push his sleepiness aside.

He had a "no talking after" rule which he zealously guarded. Any woman who didn't adhere to the rule was never allowed back in his bed. So far, he'd been able to enjoy his after-tupping stupor luxuriously.

Perhaps he should have explained this to Fiona before they fell into bed. The problem was, he had been too angry and far too intent on getting between her thighs to manage any discussion. Being with her so many hours in the carriage had fed his lust until he could barely keep his hands on the right side of her clothing in front of the servants.

He wasn't capable of speaking right now, either—not about anything of substance—and he had a feeling that was what she wished. He wanted to savor the repleteness of his body, enjoy the worry-freeing effects of passion, and sleep the deep sleep that always came after a particularly satisfying tumble.

He slowly closed his eyes again, his thoughts melting behind images of their tryst, of her skin against his—

"Jack!"

Her insistent voice tugged his eyes back open. She was now leaning on one arm, her hair falling over it and pooling on the sheets in a thick swath of sable.

Damn, but she was beautiful. And lush. And all too tempting. Suddenly, Jack wasn't quite as sleepy. His body was even beginning to stir, much to his delight. Smiling a bit at his own randiness, he rolled up onto his elbow to face her. "Very well, love. What shall we talk about?"

Jack kissed her heated cheek, trailing his lips to hers.

"Jack," she said, a bit breathlessly, "we may have very different expectations, and I don't wish that to become a problem."

He slid his hand to her hair. It seemed to have its own energy, curling around his fingers as if to hold them there. "I agreed to get you with child, and once that is accomplished, you will go on your merry way and leave me in peace." He shrugged. "What more is there to say?"

"Well, it will be easier for us if we have the same thoughts about"—she gestured vaguely with one hand—"this."

What more did she want? If she was looking for some emotional promise, she was doomed to disappointment. He had no heart to give, and was glad for it.

"Fiona, I think I've already proven my abilities to provide what I have promised. Haven't I?" He grinned when her cheeks pinkened more. "You may rest assured that I will fulfill my part of the bargain. Then you can fulfill yours. Although," he drawled, "had I known marriage would be so stimulating, I might have rethought my position on never marrying."

Her gaze was riveted on his face. "Really?"

"Oh, yes. I would have done so several times, at least. Perhaps even once a month."

"That is not funny, Jack."

"I think it is."

She stirred restlessly, then sat up. "Goodness, I still have my boots on."

"So you do." He sat up and slid a hand down her leg, pulling her foot into his lap. "Allow me."

"I can untie them."

"You already tried and made knots of them." He deftly tugged on one knot, getting it undone fairly quickly, then tugged her foot from the boot. The warmth of the leather made him remember the feel of her boots upon his ass, an erotic moment he'd never forget.

He dropped the boot over the edge of the bed and turned to the other, which soon joined its mate on the rug. "There." He settled back onto his pillow, pulling her against him.

She sighed, resting her cheek against his chest. "We always did well in bed."

"Yes, we did." Somehow, over the years, he'd forgotten how well they'd matched. He slid his fingers over her cheek and buried his fingers in her hair.

She lifted her face and met his gaze. "It was in other areas that we did not fare so well."

He paused, his fingers still in her curls. She was right. He had two very vivid memories of Fiona from long ago. One of her lying naked upon a blanket under a warm summer sun, her peach-hued skin flushed with passion, her hair curling wildly about her, a satisfied-woman smile on her lips. He'd been young and bursting with pride that he'd been her first and had still managed to give her that glow.

The other memory was not so pleasant. He was standing in the rain, the world scented with lilac, as he read her words on an ink-smeared scrap of paper, thunder roaring in the distance.

Jack refused to remember the pain that day had caused him, the weeks and months of desolation. He'd learned his lesson well, though; he'd never again allowed himself to believe in love or anything else he couldn't see. Since then, life had been much simpler and far less painful.

He regarded her through half-closed eyes, glad his heart was now Fiona-proofed. It was a good thing he hadn't realized how her brothers had interfered in their relationship by letting slip Jack had a mistress. He had, of course. He couldn't remember the woman's name now, for there had been too many, but he'd had a mistress since he was seventeen. It was his right as a man of independence, something his parents would have regarded with disapprobation, which had made him all the more determined to enjoy it.

He'd been mad to think of marrying Fiona, a fact that had dawned on him within days of her jolting rejection. Mad to think that passion alone was enough to carry them across the bridal bridge.

Oh, but what a passion it had been. Every moment

had been consumed with thoughts of her, of her hair, of her scent, of the way her eyes crinkled when she laughed.

Thank God he'd eventually gotten over that madness. He would make certain those old feelings—so strong and out of control—remained naught but the fantasies of the wild youth he'd once been.

Suddenly, he realized that the worst thing he could do was stay where he was, snuggled in bed with Fiona. He could not allow the natural tenderness of the afterglow to soften his heart.

Perhaps that was what she meant by "expectations." It would be awkward if she began to expect more of him than he was prepared to give. It would be a good idea to set her expectations to a believable level right from the beginning, so she wouldn't develop any unreasonable hopes.

Frowning a bit, he sat up, allowing Fiona to move out of his way. "What time is it?"

She glanced past him to the clock on the mantel. "It's almost four."

"Ah. It's still early, then." He flicked back the covers and slid his feet over the side of the bed.

Fiona watched in disbelief as Jack stood and began to gather his clothes. "You . . . you are leaving?"

He didn't look up from pulling on his breeches. "Of course. The gaming hells never close, and I've acquaintances I've yet to greet since my return to town."

Fiona's heart sank. "You are leaving," she repeated, disbelief in her voice.

He sat on a chair to pull on his boots. "As you suggested, perhaps we should discuss our expectations." He rose and crossed to a wardrobe, where he pulled out a fresh shirt. "I normally have my valet attend me, but I thought you might want more privacy. However, to make my comings and goings less disturbing, we can move you into one of the guest rooms and—"

"No." Fiona gathered the sheets and sat upright. "I will not be relegated to a guest room."

He shrugged. "As you wish. I just did not want to awaken you. I come in at varying times. So long as you are a sound sleeper—"

"I sleep just fine," she retorted. "But I cannot believe you are leaving."

"I cannot believe it, either," he said, fastening his shirt. "I usually need a good hour's sleep after a romp like that."

So that's all it was to him. *Of course it is,* she told herself fiercely. *This is not a real marriage. This is a marriage of convenience.*

Still, she could not help but feel slighted. It seemed wrong that he should jump out of bed and head to town. "Jack, I hope . . . I hope people think us a well-suited couple."

He opened the wardrobe again and removed a waistcoat. "Why does it matter what people think?"

"If my brothers were to hear rumors that things between us weren't as they should be, they might come to town." It would take weeks for rumors to filter back to Scotland, but she hoped Jack did not think of that.

He paused, his gaze resting on her for a moment. "I don't wish to see your brothers ever again."

"And I don't wish them to come to town. But if they thought I was unhappy or that you were carousing . . ." She shrugged.

Jack's face darkened. "That sounds like a threat."

"It's not a threat," she said defensively, though a twinge of guilt made her hug the sheets a bit closer. "It's just the truth."

Jack finished buttoning his waistcoat, then came to sit on the edge of the bed. He reached over and threaded his fingers through her hair. "Your brothers will come anyway; you are their only sister, and they care for you."

She sighed. "I suppose they will."

"Once they get here, they will scrutinize our every move and annoy us to death." He trailed his fingers over her cheek to her lips.

She had to admit that his words rang true. She didn't want her brothers to come to London, nor did she want them to become involved in her marriage. It would only complicate things. She also wished Jack would quit touching her; that complicated things as well. It distracted her and made it difficult to think.

He wound a tendril of her hair around his fingers and lifted it to his lips.

Fiona's breath caught in her throat. Perhaps with

time, she'd feel more settled with him. But right now, every nerve screamed for attention.

She pulled back, her hair sliding free from his fingers. "This plan has become more complicated by the minute."

"Simple plans are often like that." He recaptured a long strand of her hair and brushed the tip of it over her lips. Her entire body still quivered from their passion, and the light touch sent an answering flare through her.

He smiled. "But I would expect no less. With you, nothing is as simple as it should be."

Fiona wasn't sure that was a compliment. Her lips tingled; her skin danced with goose bumps; her breasts tightened in anticipation. Every bit of her was aware of the man who faced her.

At least they still *had* passion; she hadn't been sure after so many years apart. It had been the mainstay of their relationship—if you could call three jumbled weeks a relationship.

Yet Fiona knew from bitter experience that passion would not solve their problems. At best, it would give them a respite from the cares of the world and a means to become closer. But that was all.

Her heart ached, and she wished she could talk to Callum. He would know what to do; his innate ability to understand people was far greater than hers. But Callum would never again be able to give her advice. He'd never again be there when she needed him.

"Fiona?" Jack's soft voice cut through her thoughts.

She looked at him, caught on the edge of tears. "You are thinking of Callum."

She swiped at her eyes with the back of one hand. "I'm sorry. I just wish I could talk to him." She swallowed, trying to regain her composure. "I have not been able to discuss his death because my brothers have been so upset themselves."

Jack's warm hand closed about her chin. He tilted her face until her gaze met his.

"You may speak of Callum any time you wish."

Jack's offer soothed her heart in a way she couldn't explain. She grasped his hand between hers. "Thank you." A shy smile touched her mouth. "I would take you up on your offer, but I don't think you have enough shirts."

Jack looked at where she clasped his hand between hers, his expression frozen. Then, ever so carefully, he disengaged himself and stepped from the bed, saying in a rather clipped voice, "It will dry very quickly."

"I feel like a watering pot, tearing up so much."

"A lot has happened."

Hardening his heart, Jack crossed the room to find his coat.

In silence, he dressed, catching a glimpse of Fiona from the corner of his eye. She sat pensively, the sheet pulled up to cover her breasts, her arms wrapped around her knees, her teeth worrying her bottom lip.

The sight of her even white teeth set in the full, soft morsel of her bottom lip stirred him ruthlessly.

He had the right to bed Fiona if he desired, the one woman he'd—

No. She was no different from any other woman he'd bedded. It was just that they'd never been able to draw a satisfying conclusion to their relationship. The other women had stayed long enough that he'd grown tired of them. But his and Fiona's relationship had abruptly ended before it had reached that natural end. *That* was why he still felt this odd stirring of frustrated lust.

He found a new cravat and stood before the mirror. He was careful not to stand where he could see Fiona.

"Jack, where are you going?"

"To a select house party."

She was silent a moment. "What if I wish to go with you?"

"This is not the sort of amusement one takes a wife."

Her eyes flashed.

Jack ignored her, smoothing his waistcoat. "I agreed to this marriage only because I was forced. I did not agree to change my life in any way, shape, or form. This"—he turned to face her—"is who I am."

"I know that," she said stiffly, her chin lifted. "I merely thought you might wait at least one day before you resumed your raucous pursuits."

He shrugged, turning his shoulder to her. "Why should I wait? There are cards to play, bourbon to drink, women to—"

Lightning flashed outside. "There will be no other women."

He lifted his brows, his jaw tight. "I will not be threatened."

She flushed. "I didn't mean to—"

"We shall discuss this another time. Fortunately for you, after our"—he almost said "romp" but caught himself—"exertions, I will not be in the mood for another woman. At least not tonight."

In the distance thunder rumbled, and she gave a decided flounce as she wrapped the sheets more tightly about her.

Good. She was angry. That would keep them both from stupidly thinking this union was something more than it was. Still, he could not help but feel as if he'd just kicked a kitten. Repressing the oddest desire to apologize, he turned back to the miror.

"We don't know yet if this gamble will succeed. We might not be able to produce this heir. Or perhaps our families will simply ignore our noble sacrifices and hurl into one another anyway."

"They will not. I know they won't."

"We'll see," he said, placing a ruby pin in his cravat. His clothes didn't appear too wrinkled, which was a wonder, considering he hadn't used the services of his valet.

Time to go. There was no more reason to stay, and yet . . . he found himself facing Fiona. Her gaze met his, her expression a mixture of disappointment and frustration.

She wanted him to stay. He knew it without her saying a word. He supposed he didn't blame her; she was alone, in a house she didn't know, and still sad about the death of her brother.

Jack steeled himself. None of that mattered. If he stayed, she would begin to expect such things, and he was not about to let her think he was something he was not.

"When will you return?" she asked.

He paused by the fireplace to stir the embers back into flames. "Tomorrow." He replaced the poker in the stand by the fire. "Sleep well." He walked toward the door.

"Jack?"

He paused, his hand on the knob. "Yes?"

"You really do have no heart."

His jaw tightened, but he offered no defense.

"You always seem to hate that name, Black Jack," she said bitterly. "Yet here you are, striving to prove it true."

"I am what I am. I am exactly what I was before you married me, and I'll still be that after."

Her eyes flashed. "I have expectations, too. I do not wish to be left in this house alone all the time. I would like to see London while I am here."

"Of course, sweetheart. I am sure the coachman knows the way to Anstley's Amphitheatre."

Ignoring the angry set of her mouth, he bowed. "Meanwhile, I bid you good night." He slipped from the room and shut the door, quickly making his way to the foyer.

"My lord." Devonsgate stood at the bottom of the stairs.

Jack eyed the coat that was carefully hung over the butler's arm. "You knew I would be going out."

"You always do, my lord."

"Yes. I always do, don't I?"

"Yes, my lord. Once you have, ah—" The butler's gaze strayed up the stairs, then back, a faint touch of color in his high cheekbones. "Once you have awakened from your nap, you inevitably go to one of your clubs, leaving your companion sleeping."

"I didn't realize I was so predictable."

"We are all creatures of habit, my lord." The butler helped Jack into his coat.

"And my habit is to visit gaming hells and buy gifts for unsuitable women," Jack said. "What a wonderful set of habits, to be sure."

The rumble of thunder sounded in the distance, and a sharp wind whistled, so stiff that it rattled the heavy door.

Jack sent a harsh glance up the staircase before buttoning his coat to his neck. "I will need a hat, Devonsgate. I believe a storm is brewing."

"That's impossible, my lord. I was outside earlier, and it was clear—"

A flash of lightning lit the foyer before disappearing into a loud crack of thunder.

"Heavens! That sounds ominous."

It *was* ominous. Devonsgate just didn't know how much.

Jack took a deep breath, the familiar scent of lilac tickling his nose. Damn Fiona. He placed his hat firmly on his head. He would go out and have a good time, no matter what. What was a little rain, anyway?

"What ill luck, that it should rain right now," Devonsgate said, eyeing the front windows with misgiving.

"That is the way things seem to be going for me lately. Ill. *Very* Ill."

"I have heard many times that you live a charmed life, my lord. There are many who envy you."

And why not? He had wealth, properties, and unlimited opportunities to do whatever he wished. He was indeed fortunate. So why did he feel as if he stood on the brink of a great cliff, a strong wind pushing him forward, toward the edge?

Jack's gaze wandered past the butler, back up the stairs to the shadow of his bedroom door. For a long time, he stood there, staring. Then, with a muttered imprecation, he turned on his heel and left for the waiting carriage.

# Chapter Seven

The White Witch was used to seeing fair men, but none
so fair as the MacLean. Och, they are bonny lads and
lassies, those MacLeans.

OLD WOMAN NORA OF LOCH LOMOND
TO HER THREE WEE GRANDDAUGHTERS ONE COLD NIGHT

*P*reston House was situated on the edge of May-
fair. Built of white brick and decorated with
stylish brass sconces and ornate trim work, it was as
understated and quietly elegant as the dinner par-
ties and soirees Lord and Lady Preston hosted. The
location was a favorite of the bon ton and it was not
unusual for Preston events to end with a leisurely
breakfast for some of the more hardy guests.

Tonight, the bright lights of the house were barely
visible from Jack's carriage, dimmed by the rain that
beat mercilessly upon the roof.

The coachman pulled up to the front door, and
Jack jumped out, not waiting for the footman to
appear. The rain slashed at him as he raced up the
steps, head down against the onslaught. He reached

the portico, protected from the rain by a large over-hang.

Damn Fiona for this deluge. He knew it was her; the faint scent of lilacs fanned his ire. How dare she attempt to dissuade him from seeking his amuse-ments? It simply made him more determined to enjoy his freedom, and the sooner she realized that, the bet-ter for everyone.

Still grumbling to himself, Jack took off his coat and shook it.

A footman opened the door immediately. "Ah, Lord Kincaid! Welcome to—" The man caught sight of the rain and blinked, plainly shocked.

Jack glanced back. It wasn't just raining; it was a torrent streaming down in sheets.

"When did it begin raining?" the footman asked in a blank voice. He caught himself and flushed. "I'm sorry, sir! It wasn't raining a moment ago, and—" He broke off, his mouth agape.

Jack followed the man's gaze. His carriage was mov-ing down the drive, and as the horses trotted away, the rain near the house slackened. The storm came from a single thick, black cloud that hung directly over the carriage.

The footman blinked. "I've never seen such a thing!"

Jack looked up at the now-clear sky. The moon gleamed peacefully, stars twinkled all around. Jack gritted his teeth and shoved his coat into the foot-man's arms. "Summer storms are damned unpredictable." He walked past the man and into the gaming hell.

The next time he saw Fiona, he'd—

He frowned. What could he do? She couldn't control the rain—not completely, anyway. He would have to discover exactly how this family curse of hers worked. And if she *could* control it in any way, he'd have something to say about it.

Another footman greeted Jack in the foyer, politely asking if he'd like his usual bourbon and if he'd had his dinner. That was more to Jack's liking, and he replied pleasantly to the man, even as he realized with a faint sense of unease that while he'd been to this house often enough that the staff knew him on sight, he didn't know any of their names. Fiona would have chided him for that.

He scowled. Fiona's expectations were completely unrealistic. Worse, they were getting in the way of his amusements. Ignorance was a good part of comfort. His life had been much happier when he hadn't been thinking about Fiona and what she did or didn't feel.

The sounds of card play and laughter emanated from the main salon, despite the lateness of the hour. Jack headed inside, where he was greeted by the reassuring clink of glasses and the sweet smell of cigar smoke.

He paused, taking a deep breath, catching the eye of a delicate-looking blond beauty on the other side of the room. She immediately made her way to his side.

Twelve years ago, Lucinda Featherington had been the surprise debutante of the season, her fragile blond loveliness winning over her rather plebeian bloodlines and creating an instant fashion in the ton after years of reign by a bevy of dark-haired beauties.

At the tender age of eighteen, Lucinda had caught the eye and eventually the heart of Paul Featherington, one of the wealthiest men in England. After four years of being restricted by the boundaries of marriage, she was delighted when Lord Featherington's political ambitions were realized, and he was appointed ambassador to a remote province in India. Lucinda had cried off going with him, saying the heat would be disastrous for her health. She'd very prettily promised to behave herself and had even brought an old, rather deaf, and somewhat blind cousin into her house as chaperone. Reassured that his wife would be living within the lines of propriety, Lord Featherington left for foreign climes, returning every so often to visit.

Lucinda had always been attracted to men of great wealth, which was why Jack had been rather flattered by her attentions. Wealth he might have, but he also possessed other qualities that made him stand out in her crowd of admirers. Qualities he'd used to good advantage with Fiona that very evening. Jack smiled a bit. His skills had left his bride panting and flushed with pleasure.

The thought instantly stirred him. Never before

had he felt such a blaze of pure passion. With all of his experience, he had never experienced such mindless—

Jack forced himself back to the present. He was there to regain his balance, not to obsess over the very satisfactory flames between himself and Fiona.

"Ah, Jack! There you are." Lucinda almost purred as she came forward, a flutter of pale blue silk and white lace, the cloying scent of rose lifting from her white skin.

She smiled up at him and slipped her arms through one of his, pressing her breasts against him. "I didn't expect to see you so soon."

"My dear Lucinda, I was in your bed but four days ago. Surely you remember. The night your husband returned home and you bade me leave through the window?"

Her smile dimmed a moment, her eyes searching his face to see how displeased he might be. Seeing nothing in his expression to help her, she managed a false laugh and said, "Poor Featherington! He was here only one day before he was called to Dover for a meeting with Lord Burleson." She gave him an arch smile. "Had I known he would be gone so quickly, I would have asked you to stay at the inn in the village, so you could return immediately."

Jack looked down at Lucinda's generous breasts and waited for a flicker of attraction, an answering heat of some sort. But nothing happened.

Had this been Fiona standing beside him, her

breasts barely covered by thin silk and pressed against his arm, he'd have picked her up, tossed her over his shoulder, and taken her back to the carriage so he could slake the growing passion. He shook his head, trying to stop his errant thoughts.

"Jack?" Lucinda's voice sounded uncertain. "What is it? You . . . you are looking at me in the oddest way."

He frowned. "I'm sorry. I was thinking of something else."

Her expression tightened, an unpleasant glitter rising in her eyes. "What are you thinking about? Or should I ask whom?"

The proprietary note in her voice gave him pause. He eyed her a moment, then removed her hand from his arm. "My thoughts are my own. I will share them with whomever I wish."

For a moment, her eyes flashed, and he thought she would retaliate. But something in his expression caused her to swallow a retort. She gave a brittle laugh. "I'm sorry. I didn't mean to imply that you owed me anything."

He bowed, saying nothing.

She flushed a little at the silent rebuke, fixing her large blue eyes on his face, a faint pleading note in her soft voice. "Jack, I was merely funning. It's the heat and the lateness of the hour." She managed a charming smile, peeping up at him through her lashes. "I am famished, you know, and breakfast is not for two more hours."

He smiled a little. "You are spoiled."

"Perhaps." She pressed against him once more, her full breasts rubbing the sleeve of his coat. "Most men *want* me to notice when they are not present."

"I am not most men." Fiona would be the first one to point that out, though not in a complimentary way.

Lucinda ran a hand along Jack's arm, then glanced up at him through her lashes. "Perhaps we should leave. Featherington won't be home for a few more days. We could take your carriage and—"

"No. We cannot take my carriage."

Lucinda blinked at his vehemence.

Jack's jaw tightened. "It's not working correctly. It—it has developed a leak."

"But . . . it's not raining."

"It was storming when I came in."

"How odd. I arrived only an hour ago, and it was beautiful."

Yes, but that was before he'd made Fiona angry. Suddenly, Jack felt an overwhelming need to remove himself from Lucinda's cloying presence. He'd been wrong to come here. There would be no other women for him, not until he'd resolved his issues with Fiona. Besides, Lucinda's charms had palled.

"Jack, is something wrong?"

"No. I am just not in the mood for conversation right now." Once again, he extricated himself from her grasp. "I believe I'll find an open table and play some cards."

Her cheeks flushed unbecomingly, her mouth thinning. "Have a care what you are about, Jack. I shall feel ignored, and I do not like that." Her voice quivered with outrage.

Jack had never seen this side of her, and, frankly, he didn't like it. "My dear, our relationship is far from exclusive. In fact, I believe you are also visiting Sir Melkinridge?" Jack looked pointedly at the diamond necklace that hung at Lucinda's white throat.

The color in her cheeks did not fade. She managed a shrug. "Only now and then. You know that."

"You may have him with my blessing. Just do not pretend that you and I have more of an arrangement than we do. We have been mutually satisfying friends but no more."

Lucinda almost gasped at the coolness of Jack's tone. She'd come there tonight without the expectation of seeing him; he was unpredictable and it was impossible to say when and where he might show up. It was one of the many things she found fascinating about him. One of the reasons she was beginning to think she might be in love.

She had everything a woman could want: her own wealth, the admiration of a multitude of men, a fond but absent husband, several lovely homes. And yet something had been missing. Until she met Jack Kincaid, she hadn't known what that was.

She stole a glance at the strong slash of his jaw, the deep auburn of his hair, the familiar slant of his lips. She shivered. None of her numerous lovers had touched her, shaken her, the way Jack Kincaid had.

There was something about him, an air of inaccessibility, almost of indifference.

All her life, Lucinda had demanded and received the constant attention of those around her. Jack was different, which made life frightening and exciting. Oddly enough, the more he pulled away, the more she felt this demanding tug of attraction.

His attention was even now wandering to the card tables. Coldness seeped through her. Had she done something to lose him forever? He'd seemed upset when she'd asked him to leave through the window. Had she wounded his pride? "Jack, perhaps I should tell Featherington about us so we can—"

"Don't be ridiculous. Would you also tell him about Melkinridge and the others?"

She flushed. "No, of course not. I just think it's horrid you had to leave in such a manner. It pains me to think of it."

His eyes darkened, an unknown thought flickering across his face. "It was a bit painful." A secretive smile touched his lips. "But only at first."

What did he mean by that? She eyed him narrowly. There was something different about him. What was it? "Jack, did you—"

"Ah, Kincaid!" came a deep voice. "I didn't expect to see you here."

Lucinda stiffened as a tall, elegantly dressed man with black hair and blue eyes took her hand in his and pressed a kiss to the back of it. "And the lovely Lady Featherington. How nice to see you."

Jack nodded, wondering why he found every acquaintance so irksome this evening. "Campbell."

"Ah, Black Jack! I haven't seen you in forever."

Lucinda's brows rose. "Ah, yes. Black Jack. I wonder how that name came to be?" Her chilled tone indicated that she thought she knew.

Campbell smiled, his gaze never leaving Jack's. "It's an old childhood name. One given to him by his own mother when he fought his stepfather down the steps of the stately Kincaid manor."

"I don't remember," Jack said tersely.

Campbell shrugged. "That's how I remember it, anyway. And the name has stuck over the years, which I find very telling."

Long ago, Alan Campbell had been a playmate of Jack's. That had changed when Alan had reached his majority. Determined in his ambition to restore his family to greatness, Campbell became a less and less enjoyable companion. He spent his time gathering properties the way some men collected snuffboxes, stepping on quite a few people along the way.

Campbell bowed to Jack, but his gaze lingered on Lucinda. Jack ignored the look; every man present had a fondness for Lucinda. They could have her; he was discovering that he preferred women more spontaneous in nature.

"You look lovely," Campbell was saying to her.

She withdrew her hand and placed it on Jack's sleeve. "How are you this evening, Campbell? I trust you are having a good run of luck."

The man's mouth twisted. "Since when did the Campbells ever have any luck? Of course"—he slid a sly glance to Jack—"our luck is nothing compared to the MacLeans'. Jack, you know the MacLean family, don't you?"

"I know them," Jack said shortly.

"I thought you might." Campbell's gaze dropped to Lucinda's hand on Jack's arm. "By the way, Kincaid, I forgot to congratulate you."

"Congratulate him?" Lucinda looked from Jack to Campbell. "What for?"

"On his marriage, of course."

Lucinda's hand convulsively tightened, her nails digging through his sleeve.

Jack sent a cold look at Campbell.

Shock and disbelief warred in Lucinda's blue eyes. "You've married?"

"Yes," Jack said, seeing her stricken look. *Good God, she cares for me.* Never would he have believed such a thing. "I am sorry."

"So am I," she snapped. She let go of his arm.

"I should have told you sooner, but—"

"Who is she?" Lucinda said in a tight voice.

For some reason, he felt Fiona's name was not for this place, these people. "It doesn't matter."

"What's wrong, Jack, my friend? Shy?" Campbell flashed a smile at Lucinda. "I believe I can answer your question."

Jack sent the man a furious glare. The bastard had done enough as it was. Damn! He should have told Lucinda about his marriage the second he stepped through the door. But perhaps this was best—now she was furious with him, thus ending the relationship quickly. Though Campbell thought he was causing Jack problems, he might, in fact, be doing him a great favor.

"The lady's name is Fiona MacLean," Campbell said.

"I have never heard of her," Lucinda said.

Campbell shrugged. "She has been a recluse of sorts."

Jack eyed Campbell dispassionately. "I didn't realize my marriage was common knowledge already."

"I returned this evening from my holdings in Scotland. Since my valet is the brother of the upstairs maid in the MacLean house..." Campbell smiled. "Needless to say, your name was on everyone's lips. I hear the lady's brothers are not happy with the elopement."

Jack sent a quick glance at Lucinda, who stood as if turned to stone, her eyes glitter-hard. Still, she managed to say with credible composure, "Jack, you really must tell us all about the wedding. I am sure it was quite spectacular."

If she only knew. "It was not fancy."

Campbell chuckled a bit. "Oh, do not hide your light, my friend! I hear it was quite romantic." The man leaned toward Lucinda and said in a low voice, "He literally stole the lovely Fiona from beneath her brothers' noses—quite a feat, indeed." Campbell's smile tightened. "Of course, with a woman as lovely as

Fiona, who can blame him? I might fight a few dragons myself for someone like her."

"She's beautiful, is she?" Lucinda's voice sounded flat.

Jack frowned at Campbell. "How do you know Fiona?"

Campbell shrugged. "I once worshipped at that altar, long ago. Her brothers offered to remove my head from my shoulders for daring to speak to her when they were not present, though they punished me enough. It rained for two weeks at my home after I left."

"Rained?" Lucinda frowned.

"Oh, yes. The MacLean family is cursed. They can cause the weather to storm, rain to fall, lightning to strike. Yet they cannot direct it. I drew their ire, hence the rain."

"I don't believe in such things," Lucinda scoffed.

Campbell eyed Jack with a smirk. "Now that I think on it, you look a bit damp yourself, my friend."

Jaw clenched, Jack met Campbell's gaze evenly. "I bathed before I came."

Campbell pursed his lips. "I cannot help but think there is a fortune to be made, if one could discover how to control the curse."

Jack quirked a brow. "Then it wouldn't be a curse, and the power would cease to exist."

"Do you think so? Of course, they *all* have to perform their deed."

"What deed?" Lucinda asked.

"In order to break the curse, all members of a generation must perform a deed of great good. Personally, I cannot see that happening. The lady's brothers are not the softhearted sort."

"I find them all quite pleasant," Jack said with a smile, though he felt like planting his fist in Campbell's face. "I suppose that's why I am now a member of the family and not you."

Campbell stiffened. "Had I known the lady could have been persuaded to ride to the anvil, I might have been more insistent."

The thought burned through Jack, though he knew better than to show his anger. "I will tell my lovely wife you said so. I am certain it will amuse her no end."

Campbell took a step forward, then caught himself, forcing out a laugh. "I am certain she will. Of course, she has not had time yet to realize what a *prize* she has gained in her husband, has she? She will learn soon enough." Campbell's gaze narrowed. "Has she met the lovely Lucinda? Or are you saving that surprise for a later date?"

"Campbell!" Lucinda said, her color high. "That is quite enough."

Jack was suddenly tired of it. He used to think innuendo and flirtation the spice of life; now it all seemed insipid and tiring.

He turned to Lucinda. "I believe I'll join the faro table. There is an open seat." He bowed to her, then nodded to Campbell. "Good evening."

For the next few hours, he played without cease, tossing back glass after glass of brandy. Lucinda watched him from the other side of the room, but he didn't care. They were finished.

Campbell was a more visible irritant. He joined the table next to Jack's, talking behind his hand to the gentlemen on his right and left, glancing frequently at Jack.

The details of Jack's marriage would be all over town tomorrow, damn it, along with the story of Fiona's "abilities." While no one would believe it, they would unconsciously be on the lookout for signs.

What a bloody mess. If he kept Fiona in seclusion, the rumors would only grow. The only answer was to present her to society quickly, and make her known. Which meant he would have to attend all the boring, bland affairs he studiously avoided.

Damn it all. He was just beginning to realize how much his life *had* changed.


The bright sunlight awakened Fiona, and she opened her eyes to an unfamiliar room. Ah, yes. She was in London. With Jack.

But the bed was empty. She sat up uncertainly and looked at the clock. Nine o'clock. And no Jack.

Blast him. She threw aside the cover and scooted to the edge of the bed. The movement tickled her aching muscles, reminding her of how heavenly making love with him had been.

She swung her feet over the edge of the bed, hugging a pillow to herself. Heavenly.

Now she had to face the other realities of her marriage, namely her absent husband.

"This will not do," Fiona announced. "I did not come to London to sleep by myself."

She slid from the bed, her bare feet sinking into the thick rug. Her clothes lay on the floor, a puddle of muslin and silks topped with her boots. She scrunched her nose; if she put her gown back on, it would be a wrinkled mess. Still, she had little choice. She gathered her clothes and went to the washbasin on a stand in the corner. She washed as well as she could and dressed, then put up her hair.

She crossed to the door and flung it open, then stood, listening, trying to discern where she might find some breakfast.

She could hear the rumble of carriages outside, the shout of a coachman, dogs barking, vendors shouting their wares—all the normal street noises of a city. She also caught the faint murmur of voices inside and came out onto the landing, smoothing her gown as best she could.

She had just taken the first step down when a plump lady dressed in the neat gray and white of a housekeeper came into the foyer below. Fiona recognized her from the night before and said, "Good morning."

The woman stopped dead in her tracks, her face instantly folding into disapproval.

Fiona paused. She had done nothing to merit such a look. It was almost as if the woman—

Realization dawned. Jack hadn't introduced her to the servants when they'd arrived last night; he'd carried her into the house and straight upstairs to his room. They must all think she was a ladybird.

Fiona's hands fisted at her sides. Blast Jack for leaving her alone! Well, she'd just have to deal with it herself.

Head held high, Fiona descended the stairs. She nodded pleasantly to the housekeeper. "I am looking for Lord Kincaid."

The woman's chin lifted. "If he didn't tell you where he was going, then 'tis none of your concern."

Fiona's back stiffened. "I beg your pardon, but it *is* indeed my concern. He is my husband."

The housekeeper gawked. "*What?*"

Fiona didn't think she could have shocked the woman more if she'd announced she had just grown another head. "I am Lady Kincaid."

A door at one side of the foyer opened, and a tall man emerged from a side room, a neat swath of linen folded over his arm. "Mrs. Tarlington, I believe this is—" He stopped when he caught sight of Fiona. "Oh, I am sorry. I did not see—forgive me, Miss—?"

"Lady Kincaid."

The butler blinked, then bowed. "Good morning, my lady. I am Devonsgate, his lordship's butler."

"It is a pleasure to meet you," Fiona said. "I am looking for his lordship. Do you know where he might be?"

Mrs. Tarlington sniffed but didn't say anything more.

Fiona gave the plump housekeeper a stern look before turning back to the butler. "His lordship went out last night shortly after we arrived. I thought he would be home before now, but he is not. Unless he is taking breakfast?"

The butler cleared his throat. "His lordship doesn't take breakfast. At least, not before noon, and only if he arrives home in time, which he didn't."

"I see," Fiona said.

"Yes, my lady. It is not unusual for his lordship to stay out all night."

That would have to change; she could not imagine that such behavior was healthy.

She frowned, catching sight of herself in one of the large mirrors that flanked the hallway. Her gown was hideously wrinkled, her hair barely contained with her few pins, her face flushed. It dawned on her that the gown she wore was the only one she possessed.

She turned her gaze to the butler. "Before he left, did his lordship make any arrangements for me?"

"No, my lady. He just called for his carriage and left." The butler gave her an apologetic look. "Usually when his lordship has a *guest*, he will tell us she is not to be disturbed and to see to it that she arrives home safely. He did not make such a request in your case."

"Mrs. Tarlington, please send a bath to my chambers and have someone come help me with my hair and gown. I was forced to leave my home in a hurry and did not bring anything else with me, so I shall need to have this gown cleaned and pressed."

The housekeeper's lips thinned, but Fiona turned to the butler. "Devonsgate, please send a tray to my room. Just tea and toast will do."

"Yes, madam. Will there be anything else?"

"Yes. I wish to send a note to his lordship. Do you know where he might be?"

The butler's expression froze. "I might be able to locate him," he said cautiously.

"Excellent. Pray send him this message. Tell Lord Kincaid that his *wife* wishes him to come home, and if he does not make an effort to do so soon, she will come and fetch him."

Devonsgate paled, but for the first time, Mrs. Tarlington's wide mouth split in a reluctant grin.

Fiona turned back to the stairs. "I shall expect the bath and the maid immediately. Breakfast can wait until after that." She paused, one foot on the bottom step. "Actually, make that breakfast for two. I am certain his lordship will waste no time in returning home."

*That* should set a precedent of no small order. Feeling better, Fiona walked briskly up the steps.

Mrs. Tarlington said, "Well, I'll be! His lordship has a wife!"

Devonsgate stared up the stairway after Fiona, his mouth agape.

# Chapter Eight

Don't think the MacLean was not affected as well. He was. He took one look at the White Witch, and he tumbled head over heels. MacLeans are like that, ye know. They only love once, but och! What a love that is!

OLD WOMAN NORA OF LOCH LOMOND

TO HER THREE WEE GRANDDAUGHTERS ONE COLD NIGHT

"My lord?"

Jack looked up at a footman who seemed to have appeared out of nowhere. "Yes?"

"My lord, I have a message for you." The footman glanced about the table, then back to Jack. "An *important* message."

Jack blinked blearily around the room, noting with faint surprise that the company had greatly thinned.

"What time is it?" he asked.

"It is almost ten o'clock, sir."

Jack squinted at him again and recognized the livery. "You're one of *my* fellows?"

The footman gave a sigh of relief. "Yes, my lord."

"Well, then, what's the message?"

The footman again glanced at the other gentlemen, then bent near Jack's ear. "It's a *private* message, my lord."

"Ah!" said the duke of Devonshire, filling his and Jack's brandy snifters again. "A *private* message, is it? Then by all means, tell it!"

The footman looked pleadingly at Jack. "Perhaps we could retire to the hall?"

"Hell, no," Jack said. "I'm winning!"

The duke nodded. "He's right. He is winning."

Lord Kennelsworth shook his head. "Aye. He can't leave with all of our money."

"*And* my new jeweled buckle," the duke said.

"Sir, *please,*" the footman said in Jack's ear, his expression growing desperate. "We should leave."

"I can't," Jack said. "I'll get wet."

The footman blinked. "But . . . the sun is shining."

"As if that bloody matters!" Jack snarled. "Just give me the message and be done with it."

The footman bit his lip. "But my lord . . . this is not a message you'd like repeated aloud."

"Oh-ho!" Lord Kennelsworth looked up from his cards. "You'd best be ready, Kincaid—here it comes!"

Jack eyed Kennelsworth blearily. "Here what comes?"

"You have a new wife, don't you?"

Jack nodded.

"And you left her at home," Devonshire interjected. "Now here is your man, telling you he has a private message for you."

"So?"

Lord Kennelsworth shook his head. "You don't see it, do you? Poor bugger! Do we have to spell it out for you?"

Jack knew he was missing some great truth, but his mind would not focus. "Spell it out."

"Good God, Kincaid!" the duke said. "It's obvious your lovely wife wants you home. *Now*. So she's sent this young fellow to fetch you."

Kennelsworth tossed his cards to the table. "I'm done here, anyway."

"Poor Jack." Devonshire shook his head sadly, throwing his own cards down as well.

Jack pushed his cards across the table, then pulled his winnings forward. "You are all mistaken. Fiona would never call me home."

Kennelsworth pocketed the coins on the table. "I think you're wrong, Kincaid. Ask your man for the message."

Jack looked at the footman. "Very well. Tell us your message."

The footman took a deep breath. "The message is from the woman you left at the house. She says she is your wife—"

"Aha!" Kennelsworth said, grinning broadly.

"I knew it." Devonshire chortled.

"And her ladyship requests that you come home as soon as poss—"

"Ha!" Kennelsworth banged his hand on the table, sending brandy sloshing onto the felt cover. "I should have asked you to wager on it, too! Come, Devonshire. Shall we go to White's and have a bit of breakfast?"

The duke nodded, clambering to his feet, and the two men wove their way out the door, arms around each other for support.

"My lord? Should I call for the carriage?"

Jack scowled. His damned damp carriage. "No. I think I'll walk home."

He rose, stuffing wads of notes into his pockets. "You may accompany me if you wish."

"Yes, sir," the footman said, looking none too happy.

Half an hour later, they reached the house. Jack staggered as his boot hit a loose cobblestone at the curb.

The footman immediately rushed forward, but Jack waved him off. "I can walk by myself, thank you."

The footman bowed. "Yes, my lord." He stepped out of the way, but not so far back that he couldn't catch Jack's arm if he stumbled again.

Jack noted that but decided to be magnanimous. It wasn't the footman's fault that he didn't understand Jack's superior ability to drink and remain unaffected.

He took a deep breath, straightened his coat, which had somehow come askew, and made his way to the front steps. He stumbled only once more, catching the railing when he did so. The footman, who'd made a grab toward him, stepped back into place and pretended he hadn't noticed a thing.

"I didn't fall," Jack said, carefully watching the footman.

"No, my lord," the footman said immediately. "You did not."

Jack grinned, absurdly pleased. "You are a good man . . . ah . . . Charles?"

"I am Peter, my lord. Charles was here before me."

"Ah, yes. A shorter fellow with dark hair."

"Yes, my lord."

Fiona thought he was callous and hard-hearted because he did not take the time to know his servants. Well, he'd show her. He'd find out what had happened to Charles and amaze her with his knowledge.

Really, Kennelsworth and Devonshire had it all wrong—this marriage thing wasn't such a difficult proposition. All he had to do was modify his behavior in a few small ways but make a big deal over those changes. That would temper her ladyship's annoying propensity to think the worst of him.

Jack turned to the footman. "So, ah . . . Peter, why did Charles leave my employ?"

The footman blinked. "Because he wished to marry Jane, my lord. She is the upstairs maid to Sir Broughton."

"Ah. And when is the happy day?"

"The . . . the happy day, my lord?"

Jack took a deep breath and enunciated each word with great care. "The marriage. When is it?"

The footman gulped a bit. "M-my lord, Charles left three years ago. He and Jane have a child now. She just turned two years of age."

Jack blinked. "Then . . . you've worked for me since?"

"No, my lord."

Jack relaxed a bit. "How long have you worked for me?"

"Twelve years, my lord."

Jack blinked. "Twelve? You said you'd only recently become a footman!"

"Yes, my lord. Before that, I worked under your head groom, Mr. Lachney."

"There you go!" Jack said, feeling vindicated. "*That* is why I do not recognize you. I daresay I rarely saw you if you worked in the stables."

"Actually, my lord," Peter said, looking miserable, "I saw you every day. I was your outrider since I was twelve."

Jack stared. "How old are you now?"

"Twenty-four, my lord."

Good God. The man had been his outrider for nine years and then his footman for three, and Jack could not remember a bit of it. Maybe—just maybe—Fiona was right, and he did ignore his servants.

God, he needed another drink. He could not think this through now. "Thank you, Peter."

The footman managed a bow.

Jack looked across the portico to the front door. It would be opened by yet another footman, and working with that footman would be others, all of whom had names that he did not know.

"Bloody hell, I'll need a bloody list to remember them all!" He rubbed his forehead and wished he hadn't had that last snifter of brandy; he was rather foxed. Well, it would serve his cheeky wife well—that's what she got for being so damned seductive and for sending a rain storm after him.

He needed something to eat. A man could only take so much witchery on an empty stomach.

Jack paused at the top of the steps, one hand on the banister. He'd have to let go of the banister to reach the door, and he wasn't certain that was a wise idea.

He was contemplating his options when a deep voice rich with a Scottish brogue said, "Och, now, what have we here?"

Another voice, even deeper, answered, " 'Tis none other than black-hearted Jack Kincaid, the drunken scalawag who stole away our sister."

Jack sighed and glanced up at the sky. Was God angry? Was that why he kept sending these tests?

"Aye," replied yet another voice, "that's who 'tis. Now kill him. I'm famished and there are warm pasties at the inn."

"Aye, hurry things along," said another. There was a distinctive sound, as if someone had cracked his knuckles menacingly.

Jack turned, one hand still clutched the railing. Fiona's brothers, all four of them, were standing on his walkway, and here he was, ape-drunk.

He closed his eyes and said a short, fervent prayer. When he opened his eyes, they were still there, all four of them obviously angry.

There was nothing for it but to face them, the jackasses. Jack put his foot back on the steps and made his way down, holding on to the railing and hoping they wouldn't notice the world was slowly slanting to the left.

The morning sun outlined Fiona's brothers with rays of gold, as if they were Gabriel and his archangels come to enact vengeance.

But if there was one thing Jack knew about the MacLeans, it was that the only angel in the family was now residing in *his* bed.

The thought made him grin. They may be furious with him, but it didn't change things. Fiona was his. They'd not do anything to dishonor their sister or cause her embarrassment.

The thought gave him courage. Jack squinted in the light, then cursed and moved to the other side of the stairs so the sun did not shine in his eyes.

*Tall* did not begin to describe Fiona's brothers. They were massively built, with bulging muscles and thick necks. All were dark-haired like Fiona except Dougal, which Jack found amusing, as the name *Dougal* meant "dark stranger." Unlike Fiona, whose green eyes showed her every emotion, her brothers' eyes were so dark they appeared black. And every one of them glared at Jack.

"What a pleasant surprise." Jack leaned against the railing, tipping his hat down to shade his eyes a bit more. "The lost brothers of Fiona MacLean. Oh. Wait. Fiona *Kincaid.*"

"Do not push us, fool," Dougal growled. "We came to be certain our sister is well."

"Aye," agreed Hugh. Older than Dougal by a year, he appeared much older because of the streak of white that touched his brow. He eyed Jack icily. "And if our sister's not well—" He smacked his huge fist into his palm.

Jack decided he didn't particularly care for Fiona's brothers. "There's no need for any of you to be here. Your sister is in *my* care now. Not yours."

His words sent a wave of displeasure through his audience. Alexander, the oldest, glowered, while Gregor, Hugh, and Dougal sent dagger glances.

"She's *our* sister and *our* charge, marriage or no," Dougal said.

"Not according to Father MacCanney," Jack said, his mind clearing by the moment. "Fiona is mine now—mind, soul, and body." Jack let his tongue linger on the last word, fueled by a combination of drink and anger.

Dougal started forward, fists clenched, but Alexander placed his huge hand against Dougal's chest. "No!" Alexander rumbled. "That is not the way."

Dougal grabbed his brother by the wrist, and for a tense moment, Jack thought Dougal might attempt to fight Alexander. It would not have lasted long, for the oldest MacLean was half a head taller than his brother.

Finally, Dougal dropped his hand from his brother's wrist.

Alexander slapped his brother on the back. "Easy, lad. There are other ways."

A distant rumble of thunder met this, and Jack glanced uneasily at the sky. It had been glaringly bright before, but now a thick line of black clouds marred the distant horizon. "Bloody hell, not again."

Alexander sent a glance at Jack from beneath a thick slash of brows. "You are a disgrace to us all."

"From what I've heard, you were planning to disgrace yourselves without any help from me."

Alexander eyed him for a moment. "Fiona told you."

Jack didn't answer.

"Don't push us, Kincaid," Gregor snarled. The thin scar that ran down his face, marring him from brow to chin, gleamed white as he clenched his jaw.

Jack had heard women say that had it not been for that scar, Gregor would have been too beautiful to behold. Jack couldn't see it, but then he didn't have a woman's fanciful eye.

Alexander glowered at his brothers. "We cannot all speak. So hold your tongues, the lot of you."

They nodded, the thunder rumbling closer.

Alexander turned back to Jack. "We want your word that you will not harm our sister."

Jack shrugged. "Of course. You have my word."

Alexander's gaze remained on Jack. "We will accept that. For now."

Jack gritted his teeth to keep from saying something reprehensible. Fiona was waiting for him, yet here he stood, wasting time with these barbarians. "Are we done now? I am anxious to return to bed."

He emphasized the last word a bit, delighted to note how every one of them grew red.

Alexander moved forward now, his gaze hard. "We cannot do anything about this sham of a marriage without embarrassing our sister. But we will be watching. If Fiona even *looks* unhappy, we will blame you."

"Fiona and I are married," Jack said grimly. "That's that. If I could set it aside, I would."

"You bloody bastard!" Gregor burst out. "How can you say that when she's carrying your child?"

Damn—he'd forgotten about that. Jack thought about telling them the truth, but the furious gazes locked on him convinced him of the stupidity of such a move. "I merely meant that I wished to marry under other circumstances."

"We all wish that." Alexander crossed his arms over his massive chest. "I have to say, I have my suspicions about Fiona's condition. She hasn't been near you in fifteen years."

"You don't know that."

"I do. I spoke to Hamish."

"Hamish doesn't know everything," Jack said without hesitation.

"I think 'tis all a sham," Hugh said.

"Then why are you not inside the house, speaking with Fiona?" Jack asked abruptly.

Alexander and Hugh exchanged uneasy glances, and finally, Alexander spoke. "It is our fault this happened, that she was forced to such desperate lengths as to marry a man she did not love."

Dougal nodded grimly. "We were all mad with grief over Callum. Fiona tried to talk to us, but we would not listen, so she made up this wild plan. Now we must find a way for her to get out of it without destroying her honor."

"Her honor will come to no harm at my hands," Jack said.

" 'Tis not her honor but her tender heart that I worry about," Alexander said.

"She's a delicate lass," Hugh added.

"Aye," said Gregor. "A Scottish rose."

"Your tender, delicate rose had me ambushed, knocked unconscious, and forced to wed," Jack ground out. "Facts you all know, if you've spoken to Hamish."

Dougal grinned, his teeth flashing whitely. "She has the devil's own temper, our Fiona does."

Jack was now cold sober. "However she feels about me, she was very angry with the lot of you."

"Aye," Alexander agreed. "She would not have been forced to such lengths had we been willing to listen to her."

Dougal frowned. "Callum must be avenged."

Jack crossed his arms. "The Kincaids are now bound to the MacLeans."

Alexander scowled. "There is no child."

"No?" Jack said. "Your sister and I were married yesterday. If she wasn't with child before, she might be now."

A shocked silence met this pronouncement.

Then, a sudden gust of wind blew, stirring dust and rattling leaves and branches. Thunder rumbled closer than before.

"You—you—" Gregor stomped forward, but Alexander halted him with a sharp "Hold!"

"Bloody hell." Alexander's face was as glum as a thundercloud. "Kincaid is right. There may be a child."

"But Fiona—" Dougal began.

"Is married," Alexander finished firmly. "We would not be doing her a favor if we pretended it was otherwise. It would just cause her and her child embarrassment, if there is one." Alexander shot a black look at Jack, thunder rumbling close. "You have put us in an untenable position, Kincaid."

"Aye," Gregor said. "This does not end here."

Jack pushed himself from the railing, cold fury burning the alcohol from his veins. "It *all* ends here. I am married to your sister. And we *will* have a child. I plan on making certain of it."

"You bastard," Alexander snarled.

"It's what your sister wants—because of *your* behavior," Jack reminded them. "Now, if you'll excuse me—"

Gregor barred him from climbing the steps to the door. "It may be too late to stop this marriage," the Scotsman returned, "but we *can* make certain our sister is happy."

"Aye," Hugh said from directly behind Jack. "One of us will always be watching."

Alexander crossed his arms over his chest. "I have business out of town, and Hugh is needed at home for the next fortnight, but Gregor and Dougal will be here. They will keep a close eye on Fiona."

"That is not necessary," Jack snapped.

"It is to us." Gregor squeezed Jack's shoulder. His eyes gleamed. "She's too precious to leave unprotected with the likes of Black Jack Kincaid."

These men clearly didn't understand Fiona's strength; there was nothing fragile about her.

Gregor's hand tightened on Jack's shoulder. "Every frown that passes her lips, every sad look, will earn you one of these." Gregor's fist slammed into Jack's stomach.

"*Ooof!*" Jack bent over, lights exploding behind his eyes. He couldn't catch his breath, couldn't move, could only struggle to remain conscious.

"Aye," Dougal said. He moved up to stand beside his brother. "We will be watching. And if Fiona ever looks anything but radiant—" He balled his fist, but Jack lunged forward, ramming his head into Dougal's stomach.

The huge Scotsman went backward, hitting the railing and then flying over, feet over head.

Gregor started forward, fists raised, then stopped. "Damn it. She will see it if we mark him."

Hugh rubbed his chin, eyeing Jack thoughtfully. "If we don't hit his face, she'll never know it."

"They're married, fool," Gregor said. "She will see him without his shirt."

Thunder rumbled directly overhead, the entire street cast in a dark light as a huge bank of clouds covered the sun.

Alexander's dark gaze flickered to Jack, who stood leaning against the railing, one hand pressed to his side where Gregor had struck him. "I believe we have made our point." He sighed. "Kincaid, make certain she's happy. She deserves that since Callum—" After a moment's struggle, he turned and walked away. The others followed.

Jack watched them go, his stomach afire from their altercation. Overhead, the trees swayed, an ominous threat in the air. He turned and grabbed the railing, reaching the portico just as the storm broke.

# Chapter Nine

*'Tis a pity about the MacLean temper. They are fierce in both anger and love. They are a close clan, and what affects one affects them all. Together they'll sing in heaven, or together they'll suffer in hell.*

OLD WOMAN NORA OF LOCH LOMOND
TO HER THREE WEE GRANDDAUGHTERS ONE COLD NIGHT

"There you are, my lord!" Devonsgate hurried forward as one footman took Jack's coat while another waited for his hat. "I was beginning to wonder if you had been found."

"I most certainly was!" Jack shook off the attention of the footmen, noting that two more stood beside the library doors. Good God, how many were there?

As he turned, his sore stomach protested the sudden move. He grimaced. Between Fiona and her brothers, he wasn't going to have an unbruised muscle on his body.

Thunder rumbled outside, and with a shattering burst, the sound of rain turned into something more.

Devonsgate blinked. "Is that hail? In *April*?"

Jack glanced up at the darkened windows, where small balls of ice bounced off the windowpanes and danced along the sills. "Damn MacLeans," he muttered.

"I beg your pardon, my lord?"

"Nothing. Where is her ladyship?"

"In your bedchamber." The butler folded his hands and stared straight ahead. "You should be made aware that there was a bit of a situation this morning."

The ominous note in his voice made Jack pause. "What happened?"

The butler sniffed primly. "You failed to inform us that you had *married* the lady you so informally—and, might I add, scandalously—carried into the house last night."

It took Jack a full moment to realize the full implication of Devonsgate's words. So when Fiona woke up . . . No wonder she'd sent the footman for him. "I am in trouble."

"Indeed. I only hope her ladyship will forgive the staff for not reacting as we should have when she arose and requested breakfast." Devonsgate eyed Jack steadily. "Mrs. Tarlington was initially of the opinion that 'the imposter' should be tossed out on her ear."

He'd been such a fool. He'd never thought about the fact that the servants wouldn't know Fiona. Hadn't thought about her waking alone and hungry, looking for breakfast, and meeting hostility and disbelief. "I should have introduced her."

"Yes, my lord."

Jack rubbed his neck. "Is she upset?"

Devonsgate looked at the ceiling.

"Wonderful," Jack muttered. He'd gone out this morning determined to prove that his life hadn't changed merely because he was married, and all he'd succeeded in doing was upsetting everyone. Jack sighed. "I suppose I should go and see her."

"She is waiting, my lord." The butler offered in an undertone, "She also requested a breakfast tray for *two*. Perhaps a heartfelt apology will smooth things over."

That was surprisingly heartening news. "Thank you, Devonsgate. I will indeed attempt that." Jack looked about the foyer, his gaze falling on a vase of fresh flowers. He crossed to them, reached into the bouquet, and grabbed a handful. He pulled them out and shook them over the carpet.

"My lord!"

"Don't worry, Devonsgate. It's only water." Jack held the bouquet at arm's length. It was a bit bedraggled after being yanked from the vase, but it would serve. He would have picked some flowers from his own garden, but with the hail now raining down outside, he doubted there was so much as a blade of grass still left on the entire street.

Devonsgate glanced uneasily out the window before turning his attention back to Jack. "I hope her ladyship was not too offended by my or Mrs. Tarlington's disbelief this morning."

"The blame is mine, not yours." Jack made his way

up the steps. He was beginning to think that perhaps he'd made an ass of himself last night. Damn it; all he'd wanted to do was to establish himself as master of his own life.

Jack's jaw tightened. He would not give that up. Although he'd been wrong to leave Fiona without seeing to her comfort, he still had the right to go where he wanted and when.

He reached the bedchamber door, then looked down at his mussed coat. The least he could do was make himself more presentable for her. He placed the flowers on the floor by the door and straightened his cravat and coat. He used the edge of his sleeve to polish the toes of his boots, then reached for the flowers. His hand had just wrapped around the stems when the door was thrown open.

Jack found himself looking down at the toes of Fiona's boots. The boots that had rested so tantalizingly on his ass just last night.

His body reacted instantly, flaming to awareness. He hurried to stand. *"Oof!"* His forehead bumped into something hard, the flowers flying.

*"Ow!"* Fiona staggered back, one hand over her forehead above her eye.

Jack grabbed her just as her knees buckled. "Fiona! I'm sorry! I just—oh, for the love of—"

He lifted her into his arms and carried her inside, kicking the door closed. He absently noted the large brass tub off to one side while a breakfast tray sat on the small table before a newly stoked fire.

He carried her across the room and gently placed her on the settee, then lifted her chin and examined her forehead. An angry red mark marred her smooth skin. Without thought, he pressed his lips to the spot.

Fiona closed her eyes at his touch. It was a simple gesture, almost chaste, but it flooded her with a warm feeling of comfort. She leaned into his embrace, refusing to think about anything else.

She'd spent the morning fuming at Jack's absence. That had given way to a seething determination to let him know how she felt about his failure to inform the servants of her position. Then she'd spent a considerable amount of time practicing a pithy, well-thought-out speech that would let Mr. Jack Kincaid know in no uncertain terms what was what. She'd even planned which chair he'd sit in while she astonished him with her calm logic: the red chair received direct light, so she could see every expression on his face.

She'd planned to establish herself as the epitome of dignity and grace, of reasonable discourse and womanly pride. And now this! He hadn't even crossed the threshold, and they'd banged heads like a comedy act at Vauxhall.

Life was not fair.

Jack sighed, his gaze meeting hers. He looked tired, deep lines tracing from the corners of his mouth to his chin. Her fingers itched to soothe those lines, to touch his stubbled chin, to press a kiss to the corner of his lips and perhaps more—

Blast it! She was angry with him, and rightly so.

She could not just forget that. Fiona curled her fingers into her palms and jerked her gaze away. What was it about him that had her craving his touch, even when she was fuming mad?

"I am sorry we had an accident," she said now, struggling to remain calm. "I thought perhaps you'd lost something, so I was bending down to see what it was."

"I was polishing my shoe with my sleeve." He looked down at his wrinkled clothing. "I was just trying to look more presentable." He glanced behind him, where a broken flower stuck out from beneath the door. "I even brought you some flowers."

She bit her lip, looking at the flower smashed beneath the door's edge, a quiver of laughter tickling her lips. What a horrid muddle. "Why did you bring me flowers?"

"Because I'm an ass. I am very sorry I did not introduce you to the servants. I should have, but—" His expression hardened. "I was busy proving my life has not changed."

"Both of our lives have changed."

"Some," he said shortly.

She shrugged, turning her face away. There was no mistaking the challenge in his gaze. "I see."

He brushed his fingers over her forehead. "Had this been a bit lower, you would have had a black eye. It's going to make a hell of a bruise as it is."

"Perhaps some ice would keep it from turning colors."

He immediately rose and crossed to the fireplace, reached over the mantel, and tugged twice on a long gold cord tucked beside the picture frame.

"So *that's* where the bellpull was."

Jack looked surprised. "Didn't you use it when you called for the servants?"

"No," she said tightly. "When I wished for the servants to do something, I walked down the stairs and told them."

He looked at the breakfast tray, the bath, and the robe laid upon the bed, a flicker of regret crossing his face. "Fiona, I'm sorry."

"Yes, you are." She bit her lip. *Control. Grace. Composure.* "I think we—"

A soft knock sounded on the door, followed by Devonsgate's entry. "My lord?"

"We need ice," Jack said in a terse tone. "Her ladyship's head came into contact with my own, and you know how hard that is."

"Yes, my lord." The butler turned to go, then hesitated. "My lady?"

Fiona forced herself to look away from Jack. "Yes?"

"I apologize if my previous demeanor lacked the respect due your position as mistress of this establishment. I did not know—"

"Please," Fiona said, throwing up a hand. "The circumstances were awkward for us all. Shall we begin again?"

Devonsgate looked relieved. "Yes, please, my lady. I will fetch some ice for your forehead." With another respectful bow, he disappeared, the door closing softly.

Fiona got up and walked to the window, her hands clasped before her. How did one begin a conversation like this? *Could* she demand that he alter his actions? She'd abducted him and forced him into this marriage. Could she now demand that he be more ... devoted?

But that wasn't what she really wanted. She deserved respect, if nothing else, and—

An odd ticking sound came from the window. Frowning, she pushed open the thick velvet curtains. Hail clacked against the glass, standing in small mounds upon the sill. She sent an amazed gaze toward Jack. "My brothers arrived?"

Jack nodded.

"Where are they? In the sitting room? Why didn't you tell me—"

"They left. But they will return." He gave a humorless smile. "They promised."

"Where did they go?"

"I don't know, though I believe two of them plan an extended stay in town."

"Oh, dear. Which two?"

"Dougal and Hugh." Jack frowned. "Or perhaps it was Hugh and Gregor. I don't remember. You will find out soon enough, as they have promised to be quite visible."

She raised her brows. "What does that mean?"

"You may ask them when they come to visit. I don't

feel qualified to speak for them." Jack quirked a brow. "I don't suppose you know which one of them can cause hail?"

"Gregor. He has a cold temper. The rest of us just make rain."

"Like the cloud that's been hanging over my carriage since last night."

Once again, her blasted temper had gotten her into trouble. Her gaze fell on the breakfast table, and she moved toward it with obvious relief. "We should eat."

He crossed his arms over his chest and rocked back in his chair. "By all means."

She spread jam on two pieces of toast and placed them on plates, along with thin slices of ham and a poached egg.

Another knock sounded on the door, and Devonsgate appeared with a small chunk of ice wrapped in a square of linen. He handed the ice to Fiona, filled Fiona's teacup, and poured some ale into a cup for Jack, then left.

Fiona pressed the ice to her forehead, watching Jack. When he took a deep drink of his ale, his coat pulled tight over his muscled arm. Fiona's stomach tightened at the sight. He was so handsome, so attractive. "Where were you this morning?"

*Blast it! I wasn't going to ask that! What happened to my prepared speech?*

He replaced his ale on the table, his expression shuttered. "If you must know, I was at a gaming hell."

In for a penny, in for a pound. She cleared her

throat. "Jack, I did not like being left alone last night. The next time you go out, I would like to go with you."

That didn't sound unreasonable. It sounded calm, well reasoned, and—

"No."

"What?"

"You heard me. A gaming hell is not a proper place for a gently bred lady."

"Nor for a gently bred man," she returned stiffly.

Jack's mouth hardened. "Are you asking that I give up my amusements?"

"No. I mean, yes. I mean—oh, blast it, I don't know what I mean—except that you should not be carousing."

"I was not 'carousing.' If I had been, I do not see what business it would be of yours."

She clenched her hands into fists. "Everything you do is my business. We are *married.*"

"In name only." He leaned back in his chair, his arms crossed over his chest. "I agreed to get you with a child, but I will not give up my freedom in the process. If I wish to go to a gaming hell, I will do so. You cannot stop me."

A flicker of irritation rose. Fine, then. If he thought she would sit tamely home while he flitted about town, ogling women and doing God knew what else, he had another think coming. "Fine. But anything you can do, I can do also."

"Fiona, this is not a race."

She shrugged. "If you wish your freedom, take it. As I will take mine."

"Damn it, Fiona, you cannot—"

A soft knock sounded on the door, and Devonsgate entered the room, followed by a line of footmen carrying buckets of steaming water. They poured it into the large tub one by one, and then left.

Devonsgate folded a towel neatly over the lip of the tub and poured bathing salts into the steaming water. The room filled with the rich scent of sandalwood.

Devonsgate gathered their dishes, then turned to Fiona. "Will there be anything else, my lady?"

She looked at her wrinkled gown. "This will need cleaning and pressing."

"Fiona's clothing was lost in a storm," Jack drawled. "We will be buying new gowns for her this afternoon."

"Yes, my lord. I shall order the carriage." The butler bowed and left.

Silence reigned. Fiona fidgeted, her gaze flickering to the tub and then back.

"Aren't you going to take your bath?" Jack asked.

She looked at the tub, her color high. "I was hoping for a little privacy."

He gave an unexpected chuckle, the sound warming the room. "Fiona, I have seen you naked and writhing. Why would you mind disrobing before me now?"

Somehow, last night seemed a long time ago. "I was just . . ." What? Going to refuse to be close to him because he hadn't agreed to all of her requests? They had to continue their intimate contact if they were to have a child.

Besides, she had never felt anything as powerful as their lovemaking, and she refused to give it up.

She flicked a glance toward Jack and almost smiled. He lounged in his chair, looking relaxed, except for the hand that clutched one arm of the chair so tightly his knuckles were white.

The truth dawned on her. He had been as affected by last night as she had been! Her heart skipped a beat, triumph washing through her.

Fiona stood and walked to the tub, bending over to trail her fingers through the water. Hot swirls of steam arose, tickling her nose with the fragrance of sandalwood.

Jack's body was suddenly taut with tension. Fiona smiled. There was more than one way to skin a cat. She faced him and slowly undid the neck of her gown.

Both of his hands now clenched the arms of his chair.

Oh, yes. There was indeed more than one way to capture the attention of a very naughty Scottish lord. And oh, how good that attention felt.

She pushed her gown from one shoulder, then stopped. "I'd best remove my boots first."

His eyes darkened with amusement. "Would you like me to undo them?"

"That would be much faster, I'm sure."

He stood and walked toward her, proud and unbowed. She supposed there were benefits to not winning an argument; they were still able to face each other with their heads held high.

They were two of a kind in many ways. She didn't like losing, either. And they both enjoyed the heat of passion.

She shivered as he knelt before her, his hands cupping her calf. He slowly untied the lace and glanced up at her. "Put your hand on my shoulder."

She did so, marveling at the warmth that soaked through his coat.

He held her leg with one hand and pulled her boot free. "There," he said, dropping the boot onto the floor.

Fiona caught her breath as his hand slid a bit farther up her leg.

He flashed a wicked smile and lifted her other foot; in seconds, he dropped her other boot beside the first.

She looked at the tub. "Do you think we might *both* fit in your tub? It seems quite large."

He chuckled, standing up. "It's plenty large if you sit on my lap."

Her body quivered at the thought. "Shall we, then?"

Jack bent to nuzzle her neck, kissing a line from her collar to her ear.

Fiona pulled loose the ribbon that held her gown closed, and it fell to the floor. Pretending she didn't notice Jack watching her, she picked up her gown and tossed it over a chair, then untied the ribbons of her chemise. Shimmying free of that, completely naked, she stepped over the edge of the tub and slid into the water.

"Ahhh!" She closed her eyes, the heat and steam caressing her as the water lapped against her.

"Move forward, sweetheart."

She opened her eyes. Jack stood before her naked, a faint smile in his eyes. She gawked. She couldn't help it; he was so magnificent, his body a ripple of muscles and taut skin from his broad shoulders to his flat stomach to his well-developed thighs.

She slid forward in the tub, pulling her knees up as Jack climbed in behind her. He slid his legs to either side, lifting her and settling her in his lap. It was heavenly, sitting in a bath surrounded by nothing but Jack. His thighs made a perfect seat for her. His muscular arms stretched to either side of her, his shoulder enticingly near her head.

They sat there for a long moment, just soaking in the luxury of the water and each other. Fiona snuggled against him, tilting her head back so that she could see his face.

He kissed her forehead. "I apologize for not introducing you to the servants. I didn't think of it. That was inexcusable."

She shrugged, her skin sliding along his, the wetness holding them together. "I am more interested in discussing your propensity for gaming hells. I know what goes on in those places. I have brothers, you know."

He slid a hand to his side and grimaced. "I am very well aware of that." He reached around her to cup her breasts with both hands, then rubbed her nipples, the warm water lapping at her sensitive skin.

Beneath her bottom, she could feel the distinct stir of his manhood, and her body arched as sparks of desire flashed through her. Fiona lifted her lips to his, sliding her arms around his neck as he slipped his hand between her thighs.

And then she was lost, lost in the heat of his touch, and she gave herself up to Jack's embrace.

# Chapter Ten

Like all women, the White Witch was possessive. Therein lay her mistake. It does not pay to be possessive of a man determined to remain free. All you'll win is an empty bed and an achin' heart.

OLD WOMAN NORA OF LOCH LOMOND
TO HER THREE WEE GRANDDAUGHTERS ONE COLD NIGHT

The sun was sinking below the horizon when the last footman staggered up the front walk, carrying bundles and boxes of countless shoes, boots, gowns, an evening wrap of silvery tulle, three new reticules, and a blue pelisse trimmed with ermine.

Jack followed behind Fiona. "Well, my lady, are you pleased with our many purchases?"

"Yes," she replied breathlessly. "You didn't need to buy so much."

He shrugged. "My grandfather left her entire fortune to me—yet another reason my stepfather cannot abide me."

Fiona titled her head. "Surely you exaggerate."

"No, I don't. Not that it matters; I have long since ceased to need a family."

She halted. "You cannot mean that. Everyone needs a family."

She looked so outraged that he grinned. He touched the end of her nose. "After spending some time with your brothers, I find the thought of needing a family ludicrous."

"Oh, Jack! You just don't know them yet. Gregor has a heart as big as the world, though he'd rather no one knew it. And Hugh writes the most amazing poetry. He carves, too; our house is filled with his work. And Alexander is—"

"A saint, I'm sure." Jack placed his hands on Fiona's shoulders and turned her toward the shrubbery. "*Now* tell me how wonderful your brothers are."

Before them stood a large tree, the leaves shredded, the bark faintly scarred. The ground was covered with torn bits of foliage, leaves, and the ripped edges of the rosebushes surrounding the house.

Fiona winced. "The hail."

Jack nodded, sliding his hands from her shoulders down to her arms. "Your brothers may be wonderful to you, but they have been less kind to me."

She sighed. "My brothers are sometimes overzealous in their endeavors, but they are good people, and—"

Jack kissed her, hard and fast, oblivious to anyone who might be passing by on the street. He wasn't sure why he did it. All he knew was that the urge was overwhelming. Once it was over, his lips lifting from hers, he knew he'd done the right thing.

For the past two days, they'd done nothing but shop, make love, sleep, and talk. Uncharacteristically, he hadn't gone out the last two nights, but that was the nature of freedom: he was free to *choose* to stay home and sleep in his own bed. A soft and passionate woman with ripe curves and a smoky laugh was a very compelling choice.

Jack knew Fiona was using their marital bed as a way to keep him home, and he was all too willing to allow her to do so—for now.

He traced the line of her lip with his thumb, amazed at the sensual response that flashed in her eyes. She *needed* to be kissed, damn it. Every passionate, ardent inch of her, and he was just the man for the job.

Fiona watched the play of emotions across Jack's face. The embrace had left her breathless and wanting. Her cheeks hot, her lips tingling, she smiled. "I thought you'd had enough of that this morning."

He grinned roguishly. "Is there such a thing as enough?"

"I don't know," she answered truthfully, "but I look forward to finding out."

He chuckled and tucked her arm within his. They strolled up the walkway and entered the house.

Inside the foyer, a line of footmen staggered up the stairs with their burdens. Jack shook his head ruefully. "My dear, I fear there is nothing left to purchase in London."

"I think you're right. We shall have to wait a week before our next foray so the shops can restock." Fiona turned to one of the mirrors that lined the foyer and looked twice to be certain it was really her. A bronze pelisse covered her new walking gown and set off her hair and eyes admirably. Her hair was no longer so unruly but had been cut and styled à la Sappho. Lovely ruby ear bobs sparkled on either side of her face, and new half boots adorned her feet. Jack had been insistent about buying her a goodly number of boots, all made of the softest leather.

She relinquished her pelisse to a waiting footman, then reached up to untie the ribbons on her bonnet.

"Allow me," Jack said, his eyes meeting hers as his hands brushed her neck.

A loud snore erupted. Jack glanced over his shoulder. "What the—"

Hamish was propped up on a chair beside the library door, his booted feet planted wide, his chin sunk on his none-too-clean shirt.

Fiona smiled fondly at him. "When did he arrive?"

Devonsgate sighed. "Right after you left, my lady. He refused to leave the foyer, though I suggested he might be more comfortable in the kitchen, near the fire."

"Bloody bastard," Jack said, looking grim. "As big as he is, his snore is larger."

"Shall I wake him, my lord?"

Hamish, stirred by the voices around him, shifted and began to snore even more loudly than before.

Jack gritted his teeth. "Devonsgate, will you at least throw a tablecloth over him? I cannot abide having to look at *that* every time I come and go."

"I shall see what can be done, my lord."

"Thank you," Jack said, wondering how much Fiona's brothers had to do with Hamish's appearance. Probably everything. They probably thought his lack of activity for the last two days was a result of their little "talk."

Jack stiffened. *That was* unacceptable. He glanced at the clock. The day had flown by, and with the encroaching darkness, a faint restlessness overtook him.

"Jack?"

He turned to find Fiona smiling up at him, a question in her eyes.

She'd read his unease. He forced a smile. "I'm tired from our excursion. Are you?"

Fiona shrugged. "A bit. I was hoping you might take me to the British Museum tomorrow."

"I would be delighted." He glanced at her from beneath his lashes, his gaze lingering on her new boots. He liked the way they fitted about her neat ankles, the leather so soft. Perhaps . . .

Jack captured Fiona's hand and pulled her toward the stairs.

"Where are we going?"

"To our bedchamber to unpack."

"But the servants will—"

He glanced over his shoulder, a gleam in his eyes. Her breath caught, color blooming in her cheeks.

"Oh! Yes. I—I suppose we should unpack at least a few of the boxes."

"Just as I thought." They had reached the landing. "No sense making the servants do all the work."

"Exactly." They were almost running down the hall.

"One should always straighten up after oneself."

"I couldn't agree more." He threw open the door and kicked it shut behind them. The key clicked loudly in the quiet.

He picked Fiona up and carried her to the bed, her arms slipping around his neck. This time, when he left for the night, he would make certain she was fully satisfied and deeply asleep. That was why he was there—for that reason and no other.

Jack bent and captured her lips, halting all further discussion, all further thought. For now, he had better things to do.

Much later, Jack quietly pulled on his breeches, then paused by the bed to pick up his boots. Fiona lay sleeping deeply, her chest rising and falling, her lips parted, her hair mussed from their lovemaking.

The bed was warm; the sheets carried her scent. The urge to rejoin her was almost overwhelming. Jack clenched his jaw and turned away.

It was disconcerting, the ease with which he fit into her life, and she into his. But that was only because this was temporary. If they had to face being bound for life, neither of their tempers would have fared so well.

Jack finished dressing and paused by the bed to tuck the sheets around her. She smiled in her sleep and snuggled deeper into the pillows. He had to fight the oddest urge to smooth her hair, though he could not resist placing a light kiss on her forehead.

She murmured his name in a way that made his blood simmer. It was a reflex, he told himself firmly. Nothing more.

He turned and left, closing the door behind him. At the bottom of the stairs, Hamish still slept in his chair, the footmen eyeing him nervously. Gesturing for them to be silent, Jack quietly walked across the thick carpet. He'd just reached the front door when Hamish spoke. "Where are ye going?"

Jack sighed. "You're awake. Finally."

Hamish stretched, the chair creaking beneath him. He scratched under one arm, regarding Jack with an unfavorable glare. "Ye haven't answered me. Where are ye going?"

"That is none of your business."

Hamish crossed his arms and grinned, his teeth white against his beard. "Where ye go is *all* my business."

"Did your mistress request that?"

"No. Master Gregor seems to think ye might do the mistress wrong."

Anger tightened Jack's jaw, and he pulled on his gloves. "I am going out. That is all you need to know."

Hamish lumbered to his feet. "Then go. I'll just meander after ye a bit."

He would inform Fiona's brothers, damn it. Then they would arrive and ruin his evening.

Jack scowled. "The MacLeans can be damned. All of them." Jack put on his hat and left.

Lucinda Featherington paused before the large gilt mirror in the duke of Devonshire's front hall. Though a huge vase of flowers blocked her view, she could see enough to know that she looked perfect. Her honey-blond hair framed her face and her full lips. Her eyes were darkened with a hint of kohl—not enough for anyone to notice in a lamp-lit ballroom but enough to give her an advantage over the women who did not bother with artifice.

Fools, the lot of them. In this world, artifice was the least of sins one had to commit to win what one desired.

Lucinda knew she was beautiful, well off, and in demand as a guest and a lover. Yet as much as she had, she found herself in the unfamiliar position of wanting something that was out of reach.

Her lips tightened. Until recently, she'd been able to boast that no man had yet withstood her. And she'd had more than her fair share, more than any knew.

Men were fools. They all wanted to believe they were different, special, but so few of them really were. "I love you" was too easy to say.

Only once had Lucinda believed the words she'd spoken. Only once had she felt the stirrings of something other than conquest.

It was maddening.

Over the months, her interest twisted and grew until she found herself lying awake at nights, unable to sleep, unable to stop thinking of him.

Then, without a single sign of remorse, he'd cut her from his life. Rejected her. And in front of Alan Campbell, too. That stupid Scotsman had made certain everyone in town knew it. Four different people had made sly remarks about it today alone. She, the beautiful Lucinda Featherington, was the laughing-stock of London.

Her chest burned with the thought, her eyes gleaming in the reflection in the mirror.

She loosened a tendril over one brow, struggling to conceal how her hand shook with fury. She would never give up. Never. She'd seen Jack's wife—a plump little mouse if there ever was one. He couldn't be in love with such a plain dab of a female. No, it had to be something else. There had to be some reason he'd never mentioned this woman before, then had suddenly married her.

Lucinda was determined to discover the secret, whatever it was. And once she knew it, she'd—

"Beautiful."

The deep voice held a hint of a brogue. Lucinda's breath quickened, but it wasn't Jack. It was that damned Alan Campbell. His dark hair fell over his brow, and an intricate cravat was tied at his throat. It was really a pity she didn't have feelings for Campbell. His dark, dashing looks were a perfect foil for her own blond loveliness. Unfortunately, he didn't present a challenge—unlike Jack Kincaid.

"Campbell. I didn't know you would be here."

He smiled, and she had to admit he was indeed fairly handsome. Pity he had no wealth. He might have been an acceptable flirt otherwise.

He leaned a hip against the narrow marble table, standing uncomfortably close. "Surprised to see me?"

She shrugged. "A little."

His smile grew unpleasant. "You didn't think I merited an invitation to such an august gathering."

She smoothed her gown, pleased to see his gaze follow the rise of her creamy breasts over the top of her décolletage. "The duke of Devonshire is plain in his likes and dislikes. You are one of his dislikes."

"Devonshire is upset over a land proposition gone sour. He accused me of making a profit off his loss."

"Did you?"

"Not that he can prove in court."

"Then I am doubly surprised to see you on his guest list. Or are you?"

He laughed, though his gaze flared with an odd mixture of anger and lust. "I am, indeed. The charming duchess and I played cards last week at the Mayfields'. She was moved to invite me."

"Ah, she lost, and you forced her into it. They say her gaming debts are extraordinary."

"Yes, I hear the duke is going to have to do something to avoid embarrassment."

"How perfectly dreadful," Lucinda drawled. She regarded Campbell from under her lashes. Though his manners were impeccable, there was something about him that bothered her.

Yet she couldn't help but picture the two of them reflected in the mirrors she had around her bed. His darker skin would augment the remarkable whiteness of her own, her blond hair and his black hair perfect foils. They made a beautiful couple. A pity they also would make a poor couple.

Lucinda had lived with enough poverty. She wanted money. A life of leisure and wealth. Campbell was good for a momentary distraction; that was all.

Campbell stepped forward, his gaze dropping to her lips, so close his chest almost touched hers. "You should not look at a man like that. It encourages them to think you mean something . . . dangerous." His lips twisted, a cold gleam to his eyes. "But then, you know that."

She lifted her chin. "I don't know what you are talking about."

"Don't you?" He captured her loosened tendril and threaded it through his fingers. The faintest scent of cologne engulfed her. "We are creatures who crave comforts. Who luxuriate in our own sensuality." He was so close she could see his eyes, the centers black and velvety.

She should move away, for he was taking liberties

she allowed few. Yet she still smarted from the slap Jack had given her vanity, and Campbell's admiration poured a balm over her spirit.

But he was still a poor substitute for Jack Kincaid. Very poor.

Lucinda turned away, pulling her hair free from his fingers and repinning the curl. "We are alike in some ways, but there is one big difference."

"What's that?"

"Our birth. I am not of common stock."

Lucinda could feel the icy cold rage that filled him. A flare of power flushed through her, making her nipples peak, her breath quicken. This was the true rush: to control the actions and feelings of another, to incite them to painful passion or the anguish of rejection. She loved it.

His smile was cold. "I beg to differ. I am not of common stock." He threw up a hand before she could reply. "I did not seek you out to engage in a flirtation. I came for another reason."

"Oh?" she said in a disinterested voice. "And what is that?" She took a step toward the ballroom, expecting him to follow.

His hand closed over her wrist, halting her. "What I have to say should not be said in public."

"Then send me a letter. Let me go."

"It's about Kincaid."

Lucinda eyed Campbell for a long moment. "What about Jack?"

"Ah, that caught your interest, didn't it?"

"What do you have to say? I cannot stay here forever, listening to you. I am to dance the waltz with Lord Selwyn during the next set."

"He can wait. This cannot. Not if you wish to know the dirty details of Kincaid's marriage."

She'd known something was amiss! "What about it?"

"Kincaid did not marry Fiona MacLean willingly."

Lucinda's heart pounded an extra beat. "No?"

"Fiona had Kincaid trussed and bound, brought to the altar like a sacrificial lamb."

Her mind roiled with this new information. "I cannot see him allowing such a thing to occur. He has too much pride."

"True, but she has convinced him it is for the best, to avoid a war between their families. Her brother was killed; his brothers were implicated . . ." He waved a hand. "You know a Scotsman's temper. Had war broken out, there would have been more deaths."

It made sense. Jack was not the sort of man to do something heroic, but perhaps, once married, he could see no way out of it without inciting the feud.

What delicious information! How he must hate the entire situation. No wonder he'd broken off with her; he probably couldn't bear to tell anyone what had happened.

She eyed Campbell with suspicion. "Why are you telling me this?"

"Because I've seen how you look at him. I didn't

wish you to lose hope." He smiled and turned toward the ballroom door. "I believe there is still hope for us both."

"What do *you* want, Campbell?"

"I want it all. Jack's money. His position." Campbell's mouth twisted. "And to remind him that he cannot embarrass my family without cost, I also want his wife."

"That plump thing?"

His gaze flashed. "There is much more to her than you might think."

"That stupid curse?" Lucinda smirked. She didn't understand how anyone could be attracted to such a dowd, but it didn't matter.

She smiled at her image in the mirror, imagining how she would turn this information to her benefit. She'd ever so gently let Jack know she was aware of his circumstances. She'd offer her sympathy, her companionship. Jack would see then that she was a much better companion for him than his frumpy wife.

"Don't worry, Campbell. I shall continue to remind Jack of my presence. Is that what you wished?"

"Of course." He grinned back. "Meanwhile, I shall make certain the lovely Fiona knows of her husband's past affiliation."

"I like how you think, Campbell."

"If things play out as I hope, we will both be rewarded." Campbell bowed and gestured to the door. "After you, my dear. Lord Selwyn awaits his dance. But after that, you are all mine."

# Chapter Eleven

*I've oft heard it said that men and women speak different languages, but 'tis not true. They speak the same language, they just hear it with different ears.*

OLD WOMAN NORA OF LOCH LOMOND
TO HER THREE WEE GRANDDAUGHTERS ONE COLD NIGHT

Hours later, Fiona awoke, blinking sleepily in the semidarkness. The silence caught her, and she knew as she reached beside her that the bed was empty. Jack was gone.

Disappointment washed over her. What was her husband doing right now? Was he playing cards? Perchance he'd gone home with a friend? Maybe a *female* friend?

Fiona's jaw tightened, and she threw back the covers. She could not just lie there and wonder; she would find out for herself. She had two feet and two willing legs. Wherever he could go, she could go. She'd warned him, and now she'd show him she meant it.

She marched to her wardrobe and found one of her new gowns, a beautiful green silk with a décolletage far lower than anything she'd ever owned. Jack had been insistent on purchasing it, declaring he'd been delighted to see her wear it. She hoped he'd think so when she walked into one of his precious gaming hells. It was probably tame, compared to what the other women would be wearing, but it was pretty and a little racy.

Racy. Yes, that's what she'd be. Racy and seductive and dangerous. Just like the women who frequented Jack's gaming hells.

"Blast him!" she said aloud.

It felt good, saying that. So she said it again. "Blast him, blast him, blast him!"

She dressed, pulling on stockings and then slippers to complement the gown. Then she crossed to the dresser and quickly put her hair to rights. She would not sit tamely by while Jack made a mockery of their marriage. She was through with waiting.

But how would she find him? She paused a moment. Perhaps there were certain places he frequented. The servants would know; they knew everything.

Yes, that was a good plan. Fiona stood back from the mirror, then tugged her neckline down to a more precarious level. Oh, yes, that would do. That would do very well. She looked stylish and determined, a powerful combination.

"Jack Kincaid, you had best have a care," she announced. "You have raised the ire of a MacLean. Woe betide you now."

Outside, there was a distant rumble of thunder. If

she didn't wish to get wet in her own downpour and ruin her entrance, she had to maintain her calm. She didn't want to get angry; she wanted to get even. That required finesse.

With one last glimpse in the mirror, she turned on her heel and left the room, closing the door firmly behind her.

Devonsgate blinked. "I— I beg your pardon, my lady?"

"I said I am going out." Fiona took her cloak from the hovering footman.

"Yes, my lady. I heard that. I just didn't—I mean, I wasn't certain—I mean, I shall—" The butler paused, then took a deep breath. "What I mean is, where shall I tell his lordship you are going, if he should ask?"

Fiona fastened her cloak about her neck. "Oh, he is not here, so it should not be an issue."

"But—but—he could return, and then what will I tell him?"

She pursed her lips. "I suppose it would be best if he knew."

Devonsgate nodded miserably.

"Very well, then. If his lordship should ask, pray inform him that I have gone out."

The butler blinked. "Just . . . out, madam?"

She smiled. "Actually, inform him that I have gone *carousing.*"

The butler choked. "My lady, did you say . . . carousing?"

"Yes. I am going out just as his lordship does only I shall seek out male companions."

The butler's eyes could not open wider.

"Yes," she continued, warming to her subject as she tugged on her gloves. "I shall seek out the most unsuitable, most lecherous men in London. I will also gamble and drink and—" What else did one do while carousing? She supposed there were wild horse races in the dead of night and such, but she was not dressed for that. "I suppose that's it."

"I should hope so!" Devonsgate burst out.

Fiona raised her brows.

The butler colored. "My lady, *please*. This cannot be safe. Let me send a note to his lordship—"

"You know where he is?"

"No, my lady. There are several places he likes to visit, most of them *quite* unsuitable for a lady of quality."

Excellent. Then that was where she would begin. "Does the coachman know these places?"

Devonsgate nodded miserably. "My lady, surely you do not mean to do this. Perhaps you would prefer a nice cup of tea or a—"

"No, thank you. I'm going to discover the late-night attractions of London, either with his lordship or without him. But feel free to inform him of what I am doing." She smiled. "And tell him that I expect to have an exciting time."

With a wave of her fingers, Fiona swept out of the house, down the steps, and into the waiting carriage.

❧ ❧

"Are you playing, Kincaid, or sleeping?"

Jack looked up from his cards at the man across the table. "Damn you, de Laughsley. I'm playing."

"Then place your wager. You are holding up the game."

Lord Cane looked into his empty glass with an expression of profound disappointment, then sighed. "This place has wretched service. Why do I come here when there are better establishments—"

"Place your wager, Kincaid," Lord Carlyse interrupted. His forehead glistened in the lamplight with the stress of play.

Jack noted the man's pasty demeanor. Carlyse had been losing steadily for the past several hours and seemed more desperate by the moment.

Jack placed a card on the table. "I'm still playing." He met Carlyse's gaze. "Are you?"

The man's swallow was audible, but he nodded jerkily. "Of course."

"Then play!" Cane said, holding his glass aloft and hoping a footman would catch sight of his dilemma.

"Is this chair open?"

Jack looked up to see one of Fiona's brothers standing beside Carlyse's chair. "What are you doing here, Gregor?"

"Dougal and I came to see what mischief you might be in."

"How did you know where to find me?"

Dougal wandered from the crowd behind Gregor, and leaned an arm against the back of Cane's chair. "Hamish told us where you were."

"Do you mean to have me followed wherever I go?"

Gregor nodded. "That's about it."

Dougal caught sight of Cane's empty glass. "Brandy?"

Cane blinked in surprise. "Why, yes."

"I shall find a footman to bring us some. I'd fancy a glass myself."

"Good man!" De Laughsley pushed his empty glass forward as well.

Dougal looked across the room to find a footman. "There's one." He cupped his hands about his mouth. "*Yaw!*"

The room went silent.

Jack winced.

Dougal plucked Cane's empty glass from the older man's hand and waved it toward the footman, who stood, mouth agape, staring at Dougal. "Brandy!"

The footman gulped, bowed, and rushed forward. Talk resumed immediately.

"Well!" Cane said, brightening at his filled glass. "Thank you." He looked at Dougal with raised brows. "Who *are* you?"

Dougal pulled an empty chair from a neighboring table and straddled it, crossing his arms over the chair back. "Kincaid, why don't you introduce us?"

"Aye." Gregor bent down to Carlyse and said in a soft voice, "I believe you are done, my friend."

Carlyse looked astonished. "Here! How can you say that?"

Gregor flicked a careless finger at Carlyse's cards. "You've no face cards at all, and only one eight. I'd say you were done for."

Carlyse choked. "You cannot just read my cards aloud like that!"

Gregor bent down until his face was even with Carlyse's. "Why not?"

The lord blinked, then stood so quickly he knocked a small stack of coins to the floor. "Gentlemen, I fear this gentleman may be right. I am finished. I should have stopped playing hours ago." He bowed. "Good night." He turned on his heel and left the room.

Gregor took Carlyse's empty chair. "Perhaps I should introduce myself and my brother. I am Gregor MacLean and this is Dougal. We are Kincaid's in-laws."

"And greatest pains in the ass," Jack added, throwing his cards to the table.

Lord Cane chuckled. "I know what you mean. My wife's brothers are forever haunting my house, asking for loans, eating me out of house and home."

De Laughsley nodded. "It's the worst part of marriage."

Jack agreed. As Gregor picked up the tossed cards and began to shuffle them, Jack said, "Gentlemen, I believe I have spent long enough at this table."

"Oh?" Gregor's gaze narrowed. "Going home, then?"

"Where you belong?" Dougal added. "With your *wife?*"

Cane and de Laughsley exchanged glances, then Cane cleared his throat. "Perhaps *we* should move to another table?"

One of Jack's footmen came up to the table. "Lord Kincaid? You have a message from Devonsgate. He said to tell you it is urgent, my lord."

Jack took the note:

*My lord, Lady Kincaid announced she would be out this evening. When I asked where, she said she was going "carousing." That is a direct quote. Please advise. Devonsgate.*

Jack stood, his chair hitting the floor.

*How dare she?* he fumed. *God, what if something happens to her? What if—*

"Where are you going?" Gregor said, pushing back his own chair.

"To find my wife."

"*Find* her?" Dougal stood as well. "Where is she?"

"I don't know," Jack said grimly. "But when I find her, I shall turn her over my knee and remind her why *I* am the one who—"

Gregor's brows snapped low. "You are the one who what?"

"None of your business." Jack pushed past his brother-in-law and headed for the door, his stride long and purposeful.

By God, he'd make certain Fiona never went "carousing" again.

# Chapter Twelve

'Tis a horrid thing, to possess a power greater than you are. This is the curse of the MacLeans, to be out of control when their emotions run high and their blood runs hot. 'Tis a wicked curse, yet a smart one, for all that.

OLD WOMAN NORA OF LOCH LOMOND
TO HER THREE WEE GRANDDAUGHTERS ONE COLD NIGHT

Fiona entered the Harringtons' house with anticipation. Odd, she'd thought a gaming hell would be more decadent. Situated in one of the best parts of town, the house was large and well appointed. The windows were large, the glass mullioned. The rugs were beautiful, thick, and of rich designs. Everything sparkled and gleamed.

People glanced her way, but no one seemed to think her out of place. A bit breathless at the taste of freedom, she walked into the main salon and brazenly met the gazes of several men who lounged about the doorway.

Jack would not look away from a beautiful woman, so why should she look away from a handsome man?

If any of them approached her, she'd have someone to talk to, and who knew? She might even make a friend or two. She soon found herself speaking to several rather flirtatious but polite gentlemen, a glass of lovely wine pressed into one of her hands, with music playing softly in the background as she talked and laughed.

Fiona clutched her fan a bit tighter. The rooms were very crowded, but all in all, gaming hells were far less intimidating than she'd imagined.

She noted the tables scattered here and there, the sounds of cards and dice, voices and laughter. She should watch a game or two to learn how to play before joining in. After a half hour, she felt confident enough to play. To her delight, she soon had a small pile of winnings.

Her partners were three very different gentlemen. The first was Mr. Grantham, a pretentious braggart; only the amused contempt of her other partners made his presence bearable. The other two players were obviously gentlemen: Count d'Orsay, quite the handsomest man she'd ever met, and Lord Chessup, the youngest son of the earl of Stanwick.

After a while, Fiona tired of playing. She collected her winnings and made her excuses to her partners, who all begged her to stay that they might recoup their money. But the room had gotten hotter over the last hour, and she wished to stand by a window for some fresh, cool air.

A small orchestra had begun to play somewhere

else in the house, and Fiona tapped her foot unconsciously as the orchestra played a lively Scottish reel.

A warm hand wrapped around her elbow, and
Fiona turned to find a stranger holding her arm. He
was tall, with black hair and vivid blue eyes. They
weren't as bright as Jack's, or as deep in color, but the
contrast with his hair was startling.

Fiona didn't think him precisely handsome, though
he was certainly striking and had presence.

"I'm sorry," she said, removing her elbow from his
grasp. "Do I know you?"

Her companion smiled ruefully, his relaxed manner setting her instantly at ease. "I was going to say
something witty, but I can see you don't even remember me." He bowed. "My name is Alan Campbell. I
know your brothers and your husband."

That was a relief. "How lovely. I am sorry I did not
recognize you."

He shrugged. "We've only met once before, and
it was long ago. I'd heard you were in town and had
married Kincaid. I should have called, but . . . I have
no excuse."

"I have only been in town a few days."

"I know." The man's wry smile grew. "Your husband has been keeping you close."

She wished that were true. "How do you know
Jack?"

"Kincaid and I have known each other a long time."
He glanced around, his gaze finding a nearby alcove
with a thickly cushioned settee. "Would you like to sit?"

"Yes, please," she said gratefully. Soon they were settled on the settee. She peeped at him through her lashes, noting how elegant he appeared in his blue coat and buff breeches. With his dark hair, he reminded Fiona a bit of Gregor.

Campbell's gaze followed the bustle of the crowd. "This is a nice little entertainment, isn't it?"

"Little? It looks as if every person in London is here! I never thought a gaming hell would be so crowded."

He laughed. "A gaming hell? What gave you that idea?"

"Why . . . I thought . . . The coachman said Jack sometimes comes here."

"The Harringtons always have cards, but they are hardly a gaming hell."

"Oh," she said, a bit disappointed.

He chuckled at her expression. "If you'd like, I would be glad to take you to some gaming hells."

"Will they be scandalous?"

"Some are, and some are quite respectable. I think you might find the scandalous ones a bit much. Others are quite unexceptional except for the level of play. They can be steep." His eyes twinkled down at her. "I take it you like to play cards?"

Fiona triumphantly held her reticule aloft so that it swung heavily from her wrist. "I won a good bit tonight already!"

He laughed, moving a little closer, his shoulder against hers. "I shall have to take care that I do not lose my funds to you. It's a good thing we met; I can sponsor you for some of the better hells."

She tilted her head to one side. "Sponsor?"

"Yes, someone must vouch for you. It's the only way to keep the lower classes out. I am certain you'll be admitted." A faintly bitter twist touched Campbell's mouth. "Black Jack is received everywhere. Once people know you are his wife—" He shrugged.

"And you?" she asked, tilting her head to one side. "Are you received everywhere?"

"Everywhere there is not an anxious mama with a marriageable daughter."

Fiona laughed. "I can see you are a dangerous man."

Something flickered behind Campbell's eyes. He did have amazingly blue eyes, all the more vivid for his black hair. They weren't as piercing as Jack's, though. Jack's eyes robbed one of speech, stole one's breath, and made the most intimate thoughts invade one's brain. Campbell's eyes were just . . . a lovely blue.

He regarded her for a long moment. "Has anyone ever told you how beautiful you are?"

She pursed her lips. "Not today, no."

He chuckled. "That is a crime. What *is* that husband of yours thinking?" He leaned forward, his breath brushing her ear. "If you were *my* wife, you'd hear that every day."

"Which would make it ever so tedious. Repeating compliments cheapens them."

Campbell glanced about the room. "Where is Kincaid? I did not see him in the card room."

"He had another engagement this evening," she said with credible nonchalance.

"So you came alone? You and Kincaid must be one of those modern couples who do not forever lock arms when you go out."

"We have our own lives," Fiona said coolly.

"If you were *my* wife, you would not be here alone."

"Then it is a good thing we are not married, Mr. Campbell. I would greatly resent being told what to do."

"A woman of spirit. How amusing."

"A man of improper address. How boring."

His laughter rang out. "Jack clearly has his hands full. You are a lovely, spirited woman, Lady Kincaid." He took her hand. "I enjoy that very much."

She pulled free, noticing that some couples had begun to dance. "I love the Scottish reels. Do you dance, Lord Campbell?"

His smile told her he had noticed her change of topic, but he said, "I do indeed. Would you like to join the next set?" He bent closer and said in a low voice, "I would be honored to partner the loveliest woman here."

She'd thought it would be exciting to be admired, but in all honesty, she was finding it annoying. Rather like listening to one's aunt tell one how pretty one was. Of course, it wasn't merely being admired that was nice; it was being admired by someone *you* admired in return.

She looked at Campbell. "I wonder that Jack has never mentioned you."

Campbell shrugged. "Your husband has no love for me, nor I for him."

"Why is that?"

"A little disagreement over a woman."

"Oh?"

Campbell's gaze flickered past Fiona to the other side of the room.

Fiona followed his gaze. Surrounded by a crowd of men was a tall, blond, striking woman. "That woman?"

"Yes. Lady Lucinda Featherington."

Fiona gripped her reticule tighter. "You had an argument with Jack over that woman?"

"Yes. We both wished to be her . . . friend."

"And?"

"She did not choose me."

Fiona's heart sank. It could not be. Surely Jack would have said something. But how? She'd abducted him and married him so quickly. What if his heart had been already engaged?

The thought struck her with the force of a blow. "Is he . . . Is Jack still—" She could not finish the sentence.

Campbell must have sensed her distress, for he immediately said, "I *believe* he ended it . . ." He paused for a significant amount of time.

Fiona's imagination raced. Oh, God, what had she done? She could not look away from the woman's blond perfection. She was beautiful, cultured, fashionable—everything Fiona was not.

Campbell's hand came to rest over hers. "Lady Kincaid—Fiona. Don't allow Lucinda to worry you. It's obvious Jack cares more for you than he ever did for her."

Hope sputtered to life. "Do you think so?"

"Absolutely. He married you, not her."

Fiona's heart sank to the bottom of her jeweled slippers. Suddenly, she wanted to move, stop thinking, stop imagining Jack with that woman. "They are beginning the new set. Did you wish to dance?"

"Absolutely!" Campbell took her hand. "Come, let's—"

"No." A deep voice came from behind Fiona. "I believe this dance is mine."

A heated shiver raced down her body and pooled in her stomach.

"Kincaid." Campbell gave him a thin smile. "What a surprise."

"I'm sure it is," Jack said, slipping a hand around Fiona's waist and neatly pulling her to him. "If you don't mind, Campbell, I plan on dancing with my wife."

"Well, well, well," Gregor said, arriving next. "If it isn't Alan Campbell, the scourge of Scotland."

Dougal took in the situation at a glance. "Making up to our sister, were you? I suppose you didn't realize we were in town."

Campbell's face turned a mottled red. "No," he said stiffly. "I did not."

"Pity," Dougal said. "You might have saved yourself some trouble."

"And some bruises," Gregor added cheerfully. He leaned forward and said in a confidential tone, "I have to keep an eye on my sister, you know. Scare off the scalawags."

Campbell sent him a dark glare. "I was just leaving." He bowed to Fiona. "I hope we may speak again sometime." He turned on his heel and left.

Jack caught a look of sympathy on Fiona's face. "Damn it, Dougal," he growled. "I didn't need your help to take care of Campbell."

"Oh, it's no problem." Gregor waved a hand. "Besides, we're glad to see our sister." He kissed Fiona soundly on the cheek. "Hello, lass. I hope you're doing well."

"I'm fine, thank you," she said in a decidedly frosty tone. "I am surprised you have not yet visited me."

"We were going to do that tomorrow," Dougal said a bit uneasily.

Fiona met his gaze. "At ten?"

Dougal and Gregor exchanged surprised glances, then nodded. "At ten," Gregor agreed.

She turned to Jack. "I would like that dance now, my lord."

Jack immediately took her hand. "So would I." With that, he swept Fiona into the dance.

Fiona tried not to compare Campbell's rather slack grip to Jack's firm one and failed miserably. There was just something *right* about Jack. Which annoyed her very much. "How did you know I was here?" she asked.

He looked down at her, his glance hot and possessive. "I didn't. I've been to three other places. I was fortunate to find you at this one."

He turned her swiftly, his arm firm about her, his hand warm clasping hers. Her skirt whirled, a faint swirl of air tickling her bare skin, and the colors in the room softened and blurred.

The air flowed from the terrace door, the music flowed around them. And there she was, no longer alone but with Jack. She frowned. *And* with Lucinda Featherington.

"Fiona, we must talk," Jack said in a grim tone. "It is not safe for you to go about town alone."

"I came with the coachman and two footmen, so I hardly think I was in any danger."

"Fiona, you know what I mean."

"Indeed I do. You think that you should be able to do what you want to do, when you want to do it, while I should wait at home and not *want* at all."

He frowned. "No, that is not what I mean."

"Then what *do* you mean? I can make no sense of your complaints at all."

He glowered down at her. "You are being difficult."

"If taking action when I am unhappy is being difficult, then that is what I am."

There was a pointed silence.

"Jack?"

"What?"

"Who is Lady Featherington?"

Jack stopped dancing, ignoring the other dancers who stared. "What about her?"

"Campbell said—he said that you and she—"

Jack led her to one side of the dance floor. "What did that scoundrel tell you?"

"That you and he wanted the same woman. And you won her."

"That bastard. He had no right." Jack took a calming breath. "Very well. Lucinda and I were once friends. Now it's over."

"Over?"

"Yes, before we married. I just hadn't bothered to inform her of that."

God, what a horrid evening. He'd been harassed by Fiona's brothers; then he'd spent a good hour dashing about town, trying to find her; now Campbell was making mischief for him. When he had the chance, he'd make the troublemaker pay dearly.

Slowly, Fiona said, "Very well. I believe you."

"Good. Then shall we dance again?" He placed his hand on her waist and pulled her a bit closer, forcing himself to smile. "I enjoy holding you."

Her cheeks pinkened and she nodded.

They merged back into the swirling crowd. Jack twirled Fiona faster this time, her skirts flaring about her, the silk brushing her legs, tickling her skin. Fiona looked up at him and laughed, her teeth white between her lips, her eyes shimmering with amusement.

Her husky laugh was like soothing, cool water over his seething irritation. He looked down at her and admired the sparkle in her eyes, the joy that shone in her expression.

Jack held her tightly and swirled her so that her skirts fanned out behind her. People were beginning to watch, for they were dancing a good bit faster than the music required. He didn't care. He only cared that his wife was with him, where she should be.

Jack didn't know why he had been so furious to see Fiona being led to the dance floor by Campbell. He only knew that he was. Something about seeing her on Campbell's arm had stirred emotions he couldn't contain or explain.

Jack slowed Fiona into a gentle glide. She laughed again, her eyes sparkling at him. Suddenly, Jack wanted to be away from the crowd; he wanted her all to himself.

He guided Fiona toward the open terrace door, bringing their dancing to a graceful halt as a breeze stirred the sheer curtains flanking the French doors.

Fiona fanned herself energetically. "That was so enjoyable! We must dance more often."

Jack had a sudden image of dancing with her before the fire in the master bedchamber, dancing slower and slower, their bodies pressed against each other, their lips within reach . . . His body raged with the need to feel her, if just for a moment.

Her gaze met his, and the fire in her eyes rose to match his. Jack's body responded immediately. He gripped her hand and leaned toward her, toward her lush mouth, her lush—

"Jack." Her breathless voice reminded him that they were in full view of the room.

Damn it, what did a man have to do to kiss his own wife? He took Fiona's hand. "Come. We need fresh air," he said, moving through the French doors to the flagstone terrace.

Jack led Fiona down the wide steps and out into the garden. His shoes sounded on the stone path, the trees above whispered, and somewhere nearby a fountain gurgled. The scents of jasmine and orchids filled the air.

It was madness, this desire for yet another taste of her. He'd thought that once she was his, he'd tire of her. Instead, his desire seemed to grow with each encounter. He wanted to taste her and explore her, discover every inch of her silky skin, taste the lines of her thighs and hips, smell the lilac of her hair, and lose himself in her heat.

"Jack, where are we going?"

He turned at a low hedgerow, the light from the house no longer illuminating the path. He heard the murmurs of other couples but saw no one on the narrow pathway.

"Jack—"

He pulled her into a private alcove made by two narrow benches. The area was shielded from anyone coming down the pathway by an effusion of shrubberies.

"What are you doing?" Fiona asked, her voice slightly breathless.

He peeled her glove from her hand and tucked it into his pocket. "I am stealing a kiss." He traced his lips to the tip of her finger, brushing the inside of her thumb.

Her breathing was ragged, the pale moon's glow reflected in her eyes.

"This is silly," she said in that breathless tone that told him she was as affected as he. "You don't have to steal a kiss from me. I am quite willing to give you one."

"Just one?"

Her lips curved into an amused half-smile. "Did you want more?"

Something quivered through him. He didn't know what he liked better, the innocently wanton fullness of her lips or the pure line of her cheek and chin. He wanted to trace them all with his lips, taste the freshness of her, the wildness of her passion.

He ran his hands down her back to the curve of her buttocks as their lips met. He swept his tongue along the line of her bottom lip, raking her teeth.

She moaned, her arms coming up to clasp around his neck, her body pressed hard against his. For a mad moment, he did not think. Did not care. He just tasted, took, drank from her.

And she did the same to him, pressing closer, her hips unconsciously rocking against him, her moans deep in her throat.

He paused, his heart thundering in his chest, his

body rigid with desire. "We should leave, my love. While the stone bench behind your knees offers some interesting possibilities, we have a perfectly good bed awaiting us at home."

She shivered against him, her arms tight about his neck, her voice husky and as mysterious as the moon overhead. "Jack, I don't wish to wait."

"That bench is not only hard, but it would scrape your tender skin. I won't allow that to happen."

She reluctantly dropped her arms from him and eyed the bench with distaste. "Someone should put cushions on it."

"I agree. Unfortunately, they do not have our understanding of how things should be in a garden."

One of the benefits of being married, he realized, was that one could take one's leisure. He used to think that the urgency of a clandestine relationship was all the piquancy he needed. Now he saw that much of the excitement had been in the clandestine nature and not the relationship itself, which was why they'd swiftly palled.

Anyone who thought being married to one woman would be boring did not know a woman with Fiona's rich passion. The more he drank of her, the thirstier he became.

Jack bent and pressed a kiss to Fiona's brow. "Fix your hair, and we will say farewell to our host."

She smoothed her gown. "Oh, blast. There's a tear in my flounce. I shall have to stop and pin it, or I might trip."

He nuzzled her cheek. "Just be swift. I cannot wait too long."

Jack escorted Fiona inside. "I shall be right here when you return." He kissed her hand, then released her.

"Thank you. I shall hurry." She had a gratifying last glimpse of him leaning against the wall, arms crossed, his eyes glimmering with unfulfilled passion as he watched her go.

Fiona hurried to the chambers where two maids helped with such emergencies as torn flounces and unpinned hair. One of them quickly set Fiona's hem to rights, and she was soon headed back to the ball-room.

A soft voice came from behind her. "If it isn't the lovely little bride. I've been looking for you."

Fiona turned around.

Standing in the hallway behind her was Lucinda Featherington.

# Chapter Thirteen

*They say the MacLean curse will be broken when every member of a generation performs a deed of great good. Can ye imagine that? All seven of ye and yer brothers, out lookin' fer dragons to fight and maidens to save? What a bonny adventure life would be then!*

OLD WOMAN NORA OF LOCH LOMOND
TO HER THREE WEE GRANDDAUGHTERS ONE COLD NIGHT

Fiona felt the urge to wrap her fingers around Lucinda's neck and squeeze.

She lofted her chin in the air and said as calmly as she could manage, "Lady Featherington. How do you do?"

"Ah, Fiona MacLean," the woman purred the name.

Fiona's jaw tightened. "Actually, it's Lady Kincaid."

She wished the woman were not so breathtakingly beautiful, with her thickly lashed eyes and outrageous figure. This was exactly the type of woman one could imagine with Jack. They must have turned heads every time they were together, the woman so blond and Jack with his auburn hair and dark blue eyes.

"Welllll . . ." The woman walked slowly around

Fiona, looking her up and down. "So you are the lucky woman who managed to snare Black Jack Kincaid. I can't imagine Jack getting married." The woman's gaze narrowed. "And here I thought he would only go to the altar kicking and screaming. Or perhaps . . . unconscious?"

Blast it, why had Jack told this wretch how they'd wed? She imagined Lucinda's shocked expression. Or worse, perhaps she'd laughed. Laughed at Fiona's desperateness. Laughed that Jack had been caught.

"Really, *Lady* Kincaid—" The woman made a mockery of the words, her smile as false as she was. "But somehow, you don't *look* like a Lady Kincaid." As her eyes dropped over Fiona's form, Fiona suddenly felt . . . fat. Fat and dumpy and just plain unattractive.

Which was patently untrue. She might be a bit plumper than she should have been, but that did not make her fat. Furthermore, Jack seemed to like her well enough.

His reaction to her in the garden just ten minutes ago was proof of that. Though she wasn't fool enough to think he wouldn't have the same reaction with another woman, it was reassuring to remember the heat of his hands, the quickness of his breath as he caressed her.

"Poor Jack! He was quite humiliated by the whole ordeal." Lucinda leaned against a marble-topped table that held a flower vase. "Jack is pained that he has to spend so much time with you."

"Oh?" Fiona said sweetly. "He certainly seems enthusiastic in his . . . enjoyment . . . when we are private."

"You don't know how close Jack and I are," Lucinda hissed. "If you had not pulled this trick on him, he would have married *me* by now."

Fiona lifted a polite brow. "What a shock that would have been for *Lord* Featherington."

Lucinda curled her lip. "I cannot believe a little mouse like you thought to capture a man like Jack Kincaid. He needs far more than you have to offer. He needs a real woman, someone who understands his wants and needs. Someone like me."

Fiona's nails bit into her palms and a faint rumble of thunder arose from outside. The broad doors rattled against a sudden onslaught of wind.

"It must be difficult for you to know you won your husband only through force and deception," Lucinda said in a falsely solicitous voice. "That you literally dragged the poor man to the altar. I don't know how I would hold my head up if it were me."

Fiona pasted a fake smile on her face. "How amusing to hear you speak of deception. At least *Jack* has a wife he can trust. That's more than your husband can claim." She turned to leave, her entire body rigid with anger.

Lucinda stepped in front of her, blocking her way.

"Move," Fiona bit out.

"I am not through speaking to you," Lucinda said, her eyes flashing angrily.

"You will move *now*," Fiona said.

"Nobody tells me what to do." Contempt roiled

through Lucinda's voice. "Especially a country bump-
kin like you."

Lightning crackled outside as fury bubbled through
Fiona's veins. She picked up the flower vase and
removed the flowers. Lucinda shrieked as the water
hit her full in the face.

Lucinda gasped, her hair hanging in clumps about
her head, kohl streaking down her face. "You—you—I
can't believe you—"

Fiona leaned forward. "Do not attempt to spread
your poison to me or mine. I am a MacLean, and the
MacLeans protect what is theirs. The next time I ask
you to move out of my way, I suggest you do so."

The door to the hallway opened, and two gentlemen appeared, talking animatedly about the merits
of snuff over cigars.

They stopped dead in their tracks upon seeing
Lucinda standing sopping in a puddle in the middle
of the hall. Their startled gazes fell on Fiona. Smiling
stiffly, she replaced the vase on the marble table and
calmly began arranging the flowers.

"Good God! Lady Featherington! What happened?"
The taller man hurried forward.

He had left the door open, and now several other
people were peering out at them as well.

Fiona dipped a curtsey to Lucinda. "Good evening,
Lady Featherington. If you wish to find the repairing
chamber, it is down the hall to your left."

"Oh! You—you—" Lucinda's voice cracked.

Other people crowded into the hallway. A number

of men looked upset, even angered, but every woman within sight had a smile on her face.

Fiona lifted her skirts and stepped over the puddle. "Excuse me. Jack is waiting."

Lucinda sent Fiona a look of such venom that the gentleman hovering nearby took a hasty step back. "You will regret this."

"Try your best," Fiona said coldly. "I shall be ready and waiting."

She found Jack by the refreshment table. He made his excuses to the gentleman he'd been speaking with, and then escorted her to the main hall. A crowd at the other end obscured Lucinda from view.

"I wonder what that's about?" Jack asked as they gathered their cloaks.

"I believe a cat had a mishap with a vase of water."

They stepped outside to find the wind gusting, lightning flashing overhead, and the telltale scent of lilacs.

Jack looked up at the sky, his expression suspicious. "Fiona?"

"Gregor must be about," she said smoothly.

"I've never smelled lilac during one of his storms."

"Really? How odd." She was glad to see the carriage rumbling up.

Jack didn't look convinced, but soon they were on their way home, rain beginning to spatter before they reached the end of the street.

Jack looked up at the carriage roof. "Are you certain everything is well?"

"Positive. I've never felt more invigorated in all my life."

He frowned. "Invigorated? That's an odd choice of words."

She smiled. "I am glad we're going home." She slid across the seat until her thigh pressed against his.

Though his expression was difficult to see in the flickering light, Fiona could feel the change in the air. Emboldened, she placed her hand on his knee, trailing her fingers up his thigh, then down.

Jack's hand abruptly caught hers, and he pulled it toward him, pressing it between his legs. Her eyes widened at the bulge beneath her fingers. "Oh, my! I can see you're glad we're going home, too."

Jack's eyes darkened, and he swept her into a passionate embrace that lasted until the coach reached Kincaid House. Fiona was hard-pressed to get her gown set to rights before the footman opened the door.

Once they alighted, Jack hurried her inside and up the stairs, his hands moving over her beneath the cover of her cloak in a way that left her breathless and panting.

Hours later, Fiona was snuggled against him as he slept, his broad chest rising and falling, his skin still warm from their exertions.

She sighed contentedly. Let Lucinda Featherington smirk. Let Alan Campbell insinuate all he wished. She would not allow anyone to come between her and

Jack. They might not have love, but they had trust and an undeniable passion that made their lovemaking astonishing and memorable.

Fiona closed her eyes, Jack's warmth and closeness lulling her to sleep. For now, that had to be enough.

# Chapter Fourteen

*The White Witch thought to tame the arrogant MacLeans with her curse, and at first she was right. They nearly destroyed themselves. But she did not count on the MacLean gift fer stubbornness. They never quit, do the MacLeans. Not in love, and never in war.*

OLD WOMAN NORA OF LOCH LOMOND
TO HER THREE WEE GRANDDAUGHTERS ONE COLD NIGHT

*L*ate the next morning, Fiona carried her sewing basket into the sitting room. After a leisurely breakfast, Jack had announced that he was going out, and she'd felt some trepidation. She had no doubt that her confrontation with Lucinda Featherington would be on everyone's lips that day.

She moved a chair near the window to take advantage of the light, then pulled out a small piece of lace and began to work.

Time passed, and when she looked up, the sun was high overhead. Fiona glanced at the clock over the mantel. Heavens, it was growing late. Gregor and Dougal had sent word that they'd like to ride in the park with her, and it would be nice to spend some time with her brothers. Now that Callum was gone, she wished she'd spent more time with him.

At the thought of Callum, she smiled wistfully. He would have loved London. He'd always wanted to visit.

A wave of sadness washed over her, but she resolutely focused on the little muslin and lace bonnet she was working on, regarding it with a critical eye.

"It's beautiful."

She started, turning to find Jack leaning against the doorframe, his arms crossed over his chest. He was dressed in riding clothes, his coat smooth over his broad shoulders, his buff breeches tucked into Hessians that had been polished until they gleamed.

Fiona searched his expression to see if he had heard about her run-in with Lucinda, but his face revealed nothing. "I didn't hear the front door," she said.

He pushed himself from the doorframe and walked into the room. "That's because I came in through the back, from the stables."

"Ah." She put the bonnet back into her sewing basket, feeling a little self-conscious.

He pulled a chair up across from hers, then sat, one leg over the chair arm. "Fiona, I must ask you a question."

She became very busy untangling a knot of thread she found in her basket. "Oh?"

"Yes. I heard a most interesting bit of gossip."

*Blast it.* She kept her head over the tangled threads.

"Fiona, did you forget to tell me something last night?"

"Forget? No, I don't think so." She dipped her head and began digging through her sewing basket. She needed . . . blue. Yes, blue thread. *Now.* "Oh, dear! I have completely run out of blue thread." She jumped to her feet. "I shall send the maid to the market to fetch some."

"Fiona."

She caught Jack's firm gaze, sighed, and sat down again. "I suppose I shall just work on the initials on the hem. I have a good bit of yellow thread—"

"Fiona," Jack said more firmly, "put down that blasted sewing basket."

She sighed, folded her embroidery, and placed it in the basket, then clasped her hands in her lap.

"It was a bit disconcerting to discover your name on everyone's lips, Fiona."

She bit her lip. "I suppose I should have told you."

"Good God, what were you thinking?"

"I wasn't. At least, not then."

"And you couldn't just walk away?"

Fiona stiffened. "I did not plan on making a scene, but she was determined to talk to me."

"So? She can have nothing to say that would interest either of us."

"She had quite a lot to say. She told me about . . . the two of you. She also knew I'd abducted you and forced you to marry me." Fiona sent him a reproachful look. "It was painful to learn that you'd shared that information with *her.*"

"I have never told anyone how we came to be married. I don't know how Lucinda came by that information."

"Well, she knew of it. She was very ugly to me, and I am not in the least sorry I threw water on her. If she'd been outside," Fiona added darkly, "she would have been much wetter."

Jack shook his head. "I thought something had happened. The scent of lilacs was too strong."

Her cheeks heated. "I *am* sorry for causing a scene last night." She hesitated. "Jack, when did you stop seeing her?"

"The same night you and I returned to town."

That was not what Campbell had said. Actually, he hadn't said anything so much as implied that there was more. Much more.

"Did you love her?"

"God, no!" Jack frowned.

"She said you and she planned on getting married."

"With Lord Featherington presiding over the nuptials?" Jack asked sarcastically. "Please."

Thank goodness! "I suppose people are talking about me."

He laughed shortly. "Yes, though not in the way you might think. I received no fewer than eight invitations today, three of them from society's highest sticklers. You appear to have climbed a few notches in the estimation of the ton."

"With the women, I am certain I have. I believe Lucinda is not much liked by them."

Jack chuckled. "You might be interested to know that it has rained nonstop at Lucinda's house since last night. I heard her roof has sprung a leak and her wine cellar flooded."

Fiona unsuccessfully fought a smile.

"Oh Jack, don't tell me that! I feel bad enough that I emptied an entire vse of water over her head!"

"She didn't melt, did she?"

"No, Jack, but I didn't mean to drag your name into this."

"Sweetheart, we are married. Whither thou goest and all that."

Their gazes met. Fiona could not breathe; the words were so rich with meaning, hinting at a future they both knew was not theirs.

He frowned and stood quickly, as if to get away from both his words and her. "Fiona, I didn't mean—"

"I know." She gave him a tight smile. "It's just an expression." At least, that's all it was for them.

The clock chimed the hour, and she stood and gathered her basket. "I must go. I promised my brothers I would meet them for a ride in the park, and I haven't yet dressed."

"Wait." Jack crossed to her, captured her hand, and lifted it to his lips. "It's a pity you are in a hurry."

"Why?"

He bent his head and whispered against her ear, "We could leave your brothers cooling their heels for a few minutes, couldn't we? Just long enough to . . ."

Fiona closed her eyes, her knees weakening, and leaned against him for support.

He removed the basket from her grasp and placed it on the table beside them, then pulled her toward him, sinking into a large chair with her on his lap.

Fiona slipped an arm around his neck and pressed a passionate kiss to his lips as he loosened his breeches. With a quick tug, his manhood was revealed, and Fiona's breath caught in her throat. When she curled her fingers over the thick shaft and squeezed gently, his head fell against the back of the chair as he moaned.

Encouraged, she ran her hand up. With the end of her thumb, she circled the engorged head. A bead of wetness clung to the tip.

"Fiona." Jack gasped, his hands tightening around her. *"Please."*

Her heart pounded in her chest, her breath was short, and her whole body quivered. As desperate as he sounded, she was more so. Every sinew yearned for him.

Jack slipped a hand behind her head and pulled her mouth to his for a consuming kiss that burned through her.

God, how she wanted him. *Now.* She shifted, turning toward him, the chair creaking with their combined weight. His hands urged her on, and soon she was facing him, her skirts ruched up, with her stockinged legs straddling his powerful thighs.

There was something wanton about being on top, something powerful.

Her breasts tightened, and her body tingled in anticipation as his erection pressed against her intimately, her chemise all that separated them from each other. She pressed down and rubbed against him, sliding back and forth.

Jack's breathing grew more ragged, his gaze locked on her as if she were the only woman in existence.

Still moving against him, Fiona unpinned her hair, the thick tresses falling down about her.

Jack's hands tightened on her hips, and suddenly, she wanted more. She needed his lips and hands on her bare skin.

She untied her gown and pushed it down to her waist. Her breasts, covered only by the thin chemise, were level with Jack's mouth. He immediately pulled her forward, his mouth hot upon them, his tongue laving her nipples to hardness, leaving the material wet and clinging. Fiona gasped, her head tossing back as he made her writhe with delight and need.

His hips moved restlessly against her, straining upward, then his hands reached under her skirt. He pushed aside her chemise, his fingers sliding across her wetness, tantalizing and teasing. Fiona clutched his shirt with both hands and gasped. His fingers slid over her harder, then into her.

Each stroke lifted her higher, closer to delicious madness. She rocked her hips against his fingers, until sudden waves of pure pleasure flooded through her, leaving her weak and leaning against his neck, gasping his name.

She felt the insistent press of his turgid manhood, and though still throbbing from her release, she yearned to feel him inside. She rocked back, placed her hands on his shoulders, and pressed down.

Jack gasped as she slid over him, engulfing him in a tight wetness that sent his pulse reeling.

He'd never seen a more beautiful sight than the intense pleasure on her face, and he fought for control. She was so tight, so hot, so *his*. He pressed his mouth to her breasts, his breathing ragged and loud.

Slowly, Fiona shifted forward, then back, rocking against him. Jack was held in place by the exquisite torture. His entire body was focused on that one point where they were joined, on the feel of her tightening over him, of the sensual abrasion of her booted feet along his thigh.

God, he loved her half boots—though not as much as he loved the feel of her, wet and writhing over him.

Jack moaned as he watched her ride him, unable to catch his breath. Never had he seen a more arousing sight than when she threw back her head and called out his name, her body quivering as she came.

Her pleasure ignited his own. He exploded into her, his gasps matching hers as wave after wave of pleasure flooded them both.

With a final shudder, she collapsed against him. His heart pounded in his ears as he held her close. Never had he been with a more erotic, more sensual woman.

Fiona buried her face in Jack's neck. What mind-blinding, knee-shaking, thigh-quivering lovemaking! Her body still shook with the aftershocks of desire.

She drew in a shuddering breath and pushed herself upright.

He leaned back against the chair, a deeply satisfied smile on his face. "I am spent."

"So am I."

She suddenly realized that the episode with Lucinda had proven one thing: if she didn't take care, her emotions could grow until they were as out of control as the storms that attended her. With this man, there was no calling back the thunder. It rolled over her every time he so much as looked at her.

And once she had a child, Jack would be gone.

She pushed herself from his lap.

He tried to hold her in place. "Not yet."

"I would stay if I could, but I must wash and change into my riding habit. And you know my brothers will not wait patiently. If I do not meet them soon, they will come for me. I didn't think you'd want them here."

"No, Hamish is enough angry Scotsman for me."

Fiona smiled. "After I ride with my brothers, I thought I'd visit Bond Street and look for some ribbon for the bonnet I'm making."

He spread his arms wide. "You are as free as a bird, love."

She was. Nothing bound them together. Some devil made her say breezily, "Free indeed. I've not even decided which amusement I shall attend tonight— perhaps a gaming hell. So don't wait up for me."

Jack shot to his feet.

"You will *not* go to a gaming hell."

She merely raised her brows.

"You don't understand how dangerous they can be. They are filled with scoundrels and thieves and—"

"Men like you. If it's good enough for you, then it will be good enough for me. Jack, I know you value your freedom more than anything. When we first arrived in London, you made it clear that you would do what you wanted and expected no complaints from me."

Jack rammed his hands into his pockets to keep Fiona from seeing how upset he was. She was right; he had said that, as idiotic as it sounded now.

"Fiona, I just—"

"There is nothing more to discuss, Jack. You may do as you please, and I will never again complain."

That was good—wasn't it? She would allow him his freedom, his life; that was what he'd wanted all along. He frowned. "But what about you?"

"Naturally, I will go wherever I wish, too. I'm finding this idea of a modern marriage surprisingly appealing." She placed her hand on the door handle. "Now, if you'll excuse me, I must go, or I will be late."

For a long time after the door closed behind her, Jack stood where he was, conflicting emotions crowding his mind. Apparently, he'd just won an argument, yet he didn't feel as if he'd won.

He raked a hand through his hair and stared out the

window with unseeing eyes. Fiona constantly confused and confounded him. Just when he thought he knew her, she surprised him. Like her battle with Lucinda— who was no meek miss. Underneath Lucinda's air of sophisticated helplessness, she was brittle and hard. At first, he'd found her callousness amusing, but that had paled.

Fiona had changed everything, no matter how much he'd tried to stop it. She'd given him his freedom, but he wasn't sure if he'd lost something in the exchange. All he knew was that once she began to expect more of him, he'd come to realize that maybe his perfect life wasn't so perfect after all. There were things he should have done, should be doing, that he'd not bothered with. In a lot of ways, before he'd married Fiona, he'd let life drift by. That was no longer enough.

"My lord?"

Jack turned to find Devonsgate standing in the doorway, a bottle of brandy in one hand. "I came to refill the brandy decanter. Will I disturb you?"

"No, no. Go ahead."

The butler bowed and moved to the small table by the window.

Jack watched as Devonsgate refilled the decanter, then carefully wiped off the glasses and tray. "Devonsgate, do you think I'm a good master?"

The butler's face was almost comical as his brows rose to echo the roundness of his head. "My lord?"

"You heard me. Do you think I'm a good master? And do not mouth platitudes; I want the truth."

Devonsgate opened his mouth. Then closed it. Then he went to the door and closed it firmly. "My lord, that is a difficult question. You are a good master . . . and you aren't."

"What do you mean by that?"

The butler eyed him cautiously. "Well, you are certainly generous with your wages. I've never heard you complain about paying someone more than they are worth."

That was because Jack had no idea how much his servants were paid.

"Furthermore," Devonsgate said, looking thoughtful, "you rarely interfere in the completion of household tasks." The butler caught Jack's grim gaze and hurried to add, "I assure you that servants appreciate that quality in a master."

"I do not interfere with my staff because I do not notice what they do. That is hardly a good quality. Devonsgate, how many footmen do we have?"

"Twelve."

"That many?"

"Yes, my lord."

"I had no idea. They all wear livery and look so much alike that I—" He shook his head. "As for wages, I don't complain because I have no idea what they are. Who takes care of that, anyway?"

"Mr. Troutman used to, my lord."

"My man of business? He used to be here twice a week, pestering me about this and that. I haven't seen him of late."

"That is because you banished him, my lord."

Jack frowned. "When did I do that?"

"Two months ago, my lord. You said you were tired of him always wanting you to sign things. You had one of the footmen throw the man out."

Jack raked a hand through his hair again. Fiona was right to let him go his own way; she would never stay with such an irresponsible man.

He crossed to the window and looked out, his mind whirling. He'd never had to worry about his fortune since the majority of it was tied up in investments; all he had to do was spend the profits. Until now, he'd been perfectly happy with his deliberate lack of knowledge. "Devonsgate, I am beginning to see myself in a new way, and it is not pretty."

"You are being far too harsh on yourself. Most household details would fall to the lady of the house. There hasn't been one until now."

Jack straightened thoughtfully. "That's true. I daresay I run my house in a manner quite acceptable for a bachelor."

Devonsgate did not respond.

Jack turned to look at him.

The butler offered an apologetic smile. "Ah, yes. Quite."

Jack's gaze narrowed. "You worked for the earl of Berkshire before he married. Did he know how many footmen were in his employ?"

Devonsgate hesitated.

Jack's heart sank a bit. "He did, didn't he?"

"Yes, my lord."

"And did Berkshire know how much they were paid?"

"Yes, my lord. He and his man of business kept a close eye on that."

"I never liked Berkshire. I daresay that bastard also knew the names of all of his servants."

"He kept an eye on the entire household. He was quite a generous man, giving gifts on various birthdays and such. He even arranged for the upstairs staff to have an extra day off at Christmas."

"What a bloody paragon." Jack sighed. "Devonsgate, it is time I put my house in order. Please inform Mr. Troutman that I wish to see him tomorrow afternoon, and I promise not to have him tossed from the premises."

"Yes, my lord!" Devonsgate said, brightening.

"Good. When you've done that, bring me the household accounts and a list of every servant with a description of each."

"A description?"

"Yes. Height, hair color, eyes—that sort of thing. If I'm going to learn their blasted names, I will need all the help I can get."

"Yes, my lord. I shall see to that myself." Devonsgate cleared his throat. "My lord, I cannot help but feel it is a good step. Her ladyship will be most pleased."

Jack frowned. "I am not doing this for her." He was doing it because it needed to be done and for no other reason, damn it.

Devonsgate bowed. "Of course. I didn't mean to suggest—"

"On your way out, please have Lady Kincaid's horse brought to the door."

"She will be riding today?"

"Yes, with her brothers. They will arrive shortly."

"I will see to it at once." The butler turned toward the door, then halted. "Oh, yes. Cook asked if you and her ladyship would be having dinner here before you leave for the evening or if you will be dining elsewhere."

Hmm. Fiona had given him his freedom on a platter. All he had to do was order the carriage, and off he'd go, out to any number of places where he would drink to excess, throw away his money, and flirt with women who had more hair than wit.

Yet his victory felt oddly hollow, almost anticlimactic. And after last night's contretemps with Lucinda, it might be a good idea to spend some time away from gossiping tongues. Staying home would also give him time to find a more compelling reason to discourage Fiona from gadding about in the evenings without him.

Jack nodded at his butler. "Tell Cook that Lady Kincaid and I will be dining here tonight."

"Yes, sir. Will there be anything else?"

"No. That should do it for now."

Maybe he should make the evening a bit more special. He could get some flowers from the garden, he supposed. And perhaps a gift of some sort. Fiona might not be his wife of choice, but she was to be the mother of his child. Surely that deserved some recognition.

His gaze fell on the chair they'd just vacated, and he smiled. Perhaps he'd buy her a new chemise—one made of lawn so fine he would be able to see through it.

Of course, such a chemise would be delicate and might rip. The thought of ripping off Fiona's chemise and then burying himself in her made him shiver. Perhaps, if he played his cards well, he could persuade her to wear one of her new chemises *and* a pair of boots.

Jack glanced at the clock. If he wanted to reach the shops and return before Fiona, he would have to leave right away.

Grinning, he reached for the bellpull. It would be a night to remember.

# Chapter Fifteen

Ah, lassies, be sure ye make good decisions, firm and fast. Those who don't know what they want get what they deserve.

OLD WOMAN NORA OF LOCH LOMOND
TO HER THREE WEE GRANDDAUGHTERS ONE COLD NIGHT

Fiona paused before the mirror in the foyer and set her tall-crowned riding hat at a jauntier angle over one eye. A large ostrich feather swirled over the brim.

The matching new green velvet riding habit fit like a glove; and the severity of the style suited her shorter form and rounder curves.

Gregor and Dougal would hate it, she was sure. Grinning, she pulled on her gloves, smiling at John the footman, who opened the door and bid her good day.

Gregor and Dougal stood at the end of the walkway, holding the reins of their horses. They were both dressed in the height of fashion, simple jewels resting in the folds of their cravats, their boots well polished. Their stay in London had been good for them in many ways, but even more amazing was how well London had taken to her handsome brothers. Especially Gregor.

Though Dougal was much admired, with his blond hair and dark eyes, it was Gregor who caused the most sighs with his dark angel looks and brooding gaze. She'd even heard one woman say that, if not for his scar, he would look just like the statue of Apollo in the British Museum, and far too good to be true.

Gregor was leaning against a tree, the reins to his mount draped over his arm. His hat was pulled low, the brim throwing a shadow over the scar that marred his face. Beside him stood Dougal, large and blond, a roguish twinkle lighting his eyes.

"It's about time," Gregor said, pushing away from the tree with a lithe move.

"I apologize for being so late. I was talking to Jack and lost track of the time." Fiona shaded her eyes to see if the groom was bringing her mount.

Gregor quirked a brow. "Is something wrong?"

"No," she said, a mite too quickly.

Dougal frowned. "What's that scoundrel done now?"

He'd smiled and made her heart flutter, had made love to her until she could barely walk, and was the stubbornest of all men. "He hasn't done a thing. Really." She pulled on her gloves. "However, I do need your advice."

"What sort of advice?" Gregor asked cautiously.

"About Jack."

Dougal gestured to his brother. "You can handle this."

"Me? What do I know about relationships? Mine never last more than three weeks."

"That's because you lose interest the moment you tup them."

Gregor glared at Dougal. "Our sister does not need to hear such language."

Dougal flushed. "Sorry. I didn't think."

Fiona broke in. "Gregor, you've had relationships before. You've been close with Venetia Oglivie for years and years."

Gregor sent her a disgusted look. "Venetia and I have known each other since we were five years of age. That's not the sort of relationship that would qualify me to give you advice on your marriage."

Dougal scratched his chin. "I always thought you and Venetia would make a match of it."

"She's not my type of woman," Gregor said, sending his brother a hostile glare.

"I think she's charming," Fiona said. "She's intelligent and funny and cultured and— Oh, you're right. She's not the woman for you."

"Are you finished?" Gregor asked.

"She's plump," Dougal said. "That's the real reason he doesn't lust after her. Gregor has a fascination with breastless women." Dougal ducked as Gregor swung at him. "It's true! That Tratham chit is flat as a board."

"You certainly didn't think so when you were chasing after her."

Dougal shrugged. "That's because I was dazzled by her face. After I tore my gaze from there, it didn't take much time to notice the rest. Or lack of it."

Gregor smirked. "You just haven't seen her naked. She has everything she needs to—"

"Excuse me," Fiona said with some asperity. "We were talking about *me*."

Gregor chuckled. "Sorry, lassie. Of course, we're willing to help you as much as we can."

"Here's your horse," Dougal said as the groom walked up. "Let's walk the mounts to the end of the street and finish this conversation away from the servants."

Fiona looked a little ruefully at her new riding boots. She supposed it wouldn't hurt to walk a bit. She allowed Dougal to take Ophelia's reins, and they walked out of earshot of the servants.

Upper Grosvenor Street was a wide, shaded avenue lined with beautiful houses. Flowers abounded, and the recent rains had given the place a fresh, green look.

She glanced at her brothers as soon as they were away from Kincaid House. "I need a man's opinion. My marriage to Kincaid is a bit more complicated than I thought. There are certain things we don't agree on, and—"

"You wish to change his mind about something," Gregor finished.

"How did you know?"

"I've noticed that women often have a desire to change men, even the ones they love."

"I've noticed that, too." Dougal frowned. "Which is odd, when you think about it. Because if you didn't like the way a man is, why would you attach yourself to him to begin with?"

Gregor glanced at Fiona. "Maybe you know the answer to that?"

"Me? I can't even find a way to keep Jack from wandering out at night to gaming hells. He feels that since he had no choice in being married, he should be allowed to live exactly as he did before we were married."

Dougal shrugged. "That sounds reasonable to me."

Fiona eyed him a moment. "Does it, now? And I suppose you'd have no issue with your wife going out 'til the wee hours of the morning, drinking and gambling and whatnot?"

Dougal scowled. "I'd never allow that! Why, if I thought—" He caught himself and gave Fiona a sheepish look. "I see your point."

"So? What would you do about it?"

Dougal looked at Gregor, who walked silently as if in thought.

"Well?" Fiona asked.

Gregor nodded. "I know what you need to do."

*Thank goodness.* She'd begun to think that asking her brothers for help had been an error.

"I think you should shock him, surprise him, do

what he least expects. Men like an unpredictable woman."

She blinked and glanced at Dougal, who looked as disbelieving as she felt.

He said, "Gregor, I'm not sure—*oof!*" He hopped on one foot. "Damn you, Gregor! That was my toe!"

"Did I step on you?" Gregor asked. "I'm sorry."

Dougal bent to examine his boot. "You're ruining my shine, too."

"Here." Gregor threw his handkerchief at Dougal, who caught it with his free hand. "While you are buffing, Fiona and I will continue our conversation."

Gregor tucked Fiona's hand in his arm and continued down the street. "Fiona, you need to challenge Kincaid, force him to see your way of things."

"But he gets angry."

"Ignore it. In fact, ignore him. No matter how angry he gets, just do what you think is right. He'll come around in time."

Fiona looked up at him, her green eyes wistful. "Do you really think that will work?"

He patted her hand. "Try it. See if I'm right."

She smiled. "Thank you, Gregor. I knew I could count on you."

When Dougal caught up, they mounted and rode to the park, the sun shining gently from the blue sky above.

❧   ❧

A short time later, Dougal and Gregor sat at White's, savoring the best the men's club had to offer. A bottle of brandy sat before them, with a plate of bread and cheese.

Gregor thumped his glass down on the table. "I think I handled that very well. No man likes a woman who bosses him about, and Fiona already tends in that direction."

Dougal nodded. "She's a bossy wench. Kincaid's days of peace are numbered. She'll challenge him every step of the way."

"Which she should be doing, if she had any sense."

"Women," Dougal said, sighing. "No sense at all."

"None of them. Just look at this ridiculous plan of hers to marry Kincaid to begin with. Pure nonsense."

Dougal nodded glumly, toying with his glass. "She did manage to halt the feud."

"Yes, but if Fiona and Kincaid are estranged, we won't have to see him at family dinners for the rest of our lives."

Dougal brightened. "I hadn't thought of that." He took another long drink. "It's a pity Alexander says we cannot lift a finger against the Kincaids."

"Aye. He threatened to strike us with lightning for the rest of our days if we even thought of it." Gregor grunted. "Petty tyrant."

Dougal looked thoughtful. "Perhaps Fiona will call the bairn Callum. That would be better than vengeance."

The idea pleased Gregor until another thought intruded. "What if it's a girl?"

"Callumia."

"That sounds like a stomach ailment."

"Callia?"

"Hm. Maybe."

They were silent a moment, contemplating the addition to their family. Dougal poured more brandy into his glass. "Gregor, do you think Fiona's sacrifice qualifies as her deed?"

Though they didn't speak of it often, the curse was ever in their minds.

Gregor caught Dougal's hopeful gaze and shrugged. "Perhaps. It was a sacrifice, made with a pure heart. That's all the curse requires."

"That's true. The curse doesn't say it has to be successful."

"Aye. We all just have to make the effort."

Dougal frowned. "Gregor, perhaps you shouldn't have given Fiona such bad advice. She's going to do something to thwart Kincaid, and it might be something unsafe."

Gregor scowled and shoved his empty glass across the table. "She's not a fool, Dougal."

"No, but she has a temper, like all the MacLeans. There's no telling what she might do if angered. Ask Lucinda Featherington."

"Bloody hell, Dougal. Must you be the death knell of every good idea I have?"

"At least I know what I am," Dougal retorted. "Unlike you, who thinks you were supposed to be a prince!"

"That's not so, but I wouldn't complain if I were one." Gregor looked into the amber depths of his glass. "Whatever happens, Fiona will find the right path."

"And if she doesn't?"

"Then it's up to us to make certain she does."

# Chapter Sixteen

*I've only met the late laird MacLean once. It was a long time ago, and I was no bigger then ye are now. I don't remember much, of course, except for his eyes. Green they were, but dark, like moss at the bottom of a deep river. I've often thought ye could get lost in eyes like those. Lost and never find yer way back.*

OLD WOMAN NORA OF LOCH LOMMOND

TO HER THREE WEE GRANDDAUGHTERS ONE COLD NIGHT

"*I* trust you had a pleasant ride, my lady." Devonsgate hurried forward to take Fiona's hat.

"It was lovely," she said, pulling off her gloves and handing him those as well. "I shall try to ride every day."

"That is a wonderful idea, my lady, providing it doesn't rain."

"It was beautiful today."

"Excellent, madam, although lately—" The butler looked out the window, so as to make certain the sun was still in view. Satisfied that it was, he nodded. "We've had more than our fair share of unexpected storms. You might want to take an umbrella with you when you ride, just in case. A sudden storm could be a—if you'll pardon the expression—damper on being out-of-doors."

Fiona, already on her way up the stairs, replied without thinking, "I'm sorry."

She slowed in her steps at the silence that followed and looked over her shoulder at the butler.

Devonsgate was frowning. "Madam, I didn't mean to imply fault. The weather is merely unpredictable."

She stopped on the top landing. "I know. I just meant . . ." *Oh dear. How was she going to get out of this one?* "I meant I am sorry you felt you had to warn me about the sudden storms. We have a lot of that in Scotland, so it doesn't seem odd to me."

"Indeed, madam, I have heard that to be true."

"Oh yes. We have lots and lots of weather." She sent the butler a bland smile. "Perhaps it followed me here, to London."

"Then we can only wish it will find its way back home," Devonsgate said. "Shall I send up a bath, madam?"

"No, thank you. Perhaps later." She started to turn, then paused. "Devonsgate, do you have any brothers?"

"Me, madam?" The butler looked surprised at the question. "Why, yes. Three."

"Are they older than you?"

"Yes, madam. Quite a bit."

"Have you ever asked them for advice and received only empty-headed drivel in reply?"

Devonsgate's lips twitched. "Yes, madam. I went to visit my older brother some years ago and had the misfortune of coming down with an earache. My brother informed me that the best way to rid myself of the pain was to place a roasted garlic in my ear."

"Oh, dear! Did you do that?"

"Yes, madam. At the time, I would have tried anything."

"Did it work?"

"Not a bit. The very next day, he told me that remedy only worked on horses. The worst part of it was, even after I removed the garlic, the scent had soaked into my skin, and it was days before I could come near other persons without sending them running. Even the doctor balked at examining me. I was fortunate the earache resolved itself."

"At least your brother was attempting to be of service."

"I am not wholly convinced of that," Devonsgate said with a dark look. "I believe Robert would easily sacrifice my pride just to have a story to tell our other brothers."

Fiona laughed. "My brothers have never done anything that evil to me, though today I asked their opinion of something, and they offered me such ridiculous advice. They hope I'll follow it and make a fool of myself."

"I am glad to see you weren't taken in, madam."

"When you are the only female in a house full of males, you learn quickly." She shook her head, thinking about poor Dougal's toe. He really needed to be more attentive when Gregor was trying to pull the wool over her eyes.

"Devonsgate, where is his lordship?"

"He left while you were out riding, but I don't know where he went." Devonsgate beamed. "He asked for the accounts and said he would not be going out this evening."

"Not at all?"

"No, madam."

Jack had capitulated! Fiona smiled, happy all the way to her toes. "Thank you, Devonsgate. I think I will have a bath."

"Yes, my lady. Would you also like a tea tray?"

"Yes, after my bath."

Fiona thanked him and made her way to her chamber. She should have known better than to ask her brothers for advice, but she had no one else to ask. She'd met several very nice ladies she thought she could befriend, but she'd hadn't yet spent enough time with any of them to become close. Perhaps in a few months.

But no. She placed a hand on her stomach. If she wasn't with child yet, she soon would be.

She undid her coat and slipped it off, placing it on a chair. She was almost certain their child would be a boy. A boy with deep auburn hair and bright blue eyes.

What would life be like after the arrival of their child? She'd probably return to Scotland; it was not unusual for married couples to live apart nowadays, and many seemed to find such an arrangement convenient.

Fiona wasn't so certain she'd feel the same way. She'd miss Kincaid House with its luxurious thick rugs and heavy velvet hangings. More important, she'd miss Jack.

She would miss waking to him in the mornings. She would miss his touch and the passion they shared. She would miss seeing his smile first thing in the morning and the way he spooned against her when he first awoke. All of that suddenly seemed very fragile and precious.

Fiona sighed. If she continued thinking this way, she'd be blue as a megrim. Yet she could not help feeling that in so many ways, her life had changed. For the first time, she wondered if she'd be satisfied going back to her old life. She'd always thought her home in the hills was all she'd ever need. Now she wasn't so sure.

She'd have their child, which was something. Before, whenever she'd thought of being a mother, she'd imagined having three, four, or five children. She'd loved being in a large family and always thought that one day, she'd have a large, noisy, busy one herself.

It was one thing to sacrifice one's future in the desperation of a moment. It was quite another to sit quietly after the desperation was gone and face a string of dismal changes in one's future.

Fiona sighed. She was making herself depressed. Some things were better left unthought. Besides, she had so much to be happy about right now—not the least of which was Jack's admission that their relationship deserved respect. That was what she should be focusing on and enjoying.

A knock on the door announced the entrance of the maid, who assisted Fiona in undressing and brought a robe for her to wear while the bath was being prepared.

An hour later, the tub was filled, and Fiona was more than ready to soak. She sent the maid away and sank into the scented water, steam curling around her. Now her life with Jack would change for the better. Perhaps this new step would bring them closer, and they could— No. Better not to think that way. Still, a trill of hope warmed her, and she smiled softly, her earlier gloom lifting.

That was how Jack found her when, package in hand, he opened the door to his bedchamber. A bright beam of sunlight illuminated the steam curling around her, her skin glistening intriguingly.

She smiled softly, humming as she washed one of her legs, whose curves begged for his touch. Her eyes glowed, and her lips curled in a pleased smile.

Something about it made him smile in return. Then he realized he was standing in the door, staring like an adolescent, his package forgotten in his slack grip.

Excited about the present he'd brought her, he

pushed the door closed, the sound echoing in the silent room.

Startled, Fiona scrambled to sit upright, water sloshing to the floor, her wet hands slipping on the edge of the tub. With a splash, she fell back into the water and slid under the surface with a wild thrashing of arms and legs.

"Fiona!" Jack was at her side in a moment, lifting her back into a sitting position.

She spluttered, her drenched hair falling over her face.

"Good God, you scared me," he said. "It's a good thing I was here; you could have drowned."

She parted her hair and glared up at him, her green eyes sparkling. "I wouldn't have slipped if you hadn't startled me to begin with!"

"I only shut the—" Suddenly, he saw his neatly wrapped package floating in the tub, sinking rapidly. He cursed and fished it out, holding it up while water drained from it in long streams. "Damnation!"

"What's that?"

Jack wrung out the package, the paper ripping and clinging to his hands. "A present," he said grimly. So much for his plan to delight her.

It had been an unusual thought for him. Oh, he'd given presents to his mistresses, because they were expected. This was the first time he'd ever had the impulse to purchase a gift for a woman merely to see her smile.

He hoped the two delicate chemises were not ruined.

"A present? For whom?"

"For you! Who else?"

"You bought me a gift?" She couldn't seem to believe it. "But . . . why?"

Flummoxed was not the reaction he'd wanted. He'd wanted her to be delighted, thrilled, impressed.

She rose a bit, trying to see the package. "What is it?"

As she rose, her breasts crested the water, the peaks taut.

Suddenly unable to breathe, Jack had to force his attention back to the package. "For someone who causes it to rain, you seem very uncomfortable in water."

"Never mind that. I want my present." She scooted to the edge of the tub and reached up for it.

He held it higher, enjoying the way the water was running down her shoulders and over her breasts. "Not yet."

She settled back down and pouted. "It is evil of you to buy me something and then tease me with it."

Jack set the package on the hearth. "I will have to dry them out before I give them to you."

"Them? There's more than one?"

"Yes."

"Hmmm, it can't be something to eat if you can dry it out." She peeked over the edge of the tub at the package as it sat in a puddle by the fire. "I think I recognize that paper. Is it something to wear?"

"I am not saying another word on the subject. You

will just have to wait." He pulled a chair to the edge of the tub and sat, stretching his legs before him.

Fiona colored. "You cannot mean to sit there and watch me bathe."

"No." He let his gaze travel across her. "I mean to sit here and *admire*. That is a totally different matter."

"It *looks* like watching."

"Let me show you my watching stance." He shifted ever so slightly to his left. "See? This is watching. *This*"—he shifted back into place—"is admiring."

Fiona gave a reluctant smile. "Very humorous, my lord." She leaned over and dipped her hair into the water, then smoothed it back, her face in stark relief. "I am almost finished, as it is."

Though Jack had looked at Fiona hundreds of times, held her in his arms, and kissed every inch of her face, he'd never before appreciated the curve of her cheeks, the line of her brow, as he did now.

"How are your brothers?"

She slid the cloth down her shoulder. "Sniping at each other, as usual."

"You didn't enjoy your ride?"

"I always enjoy my ride, even when the company is not the best." She wrung out the cloth and hung it over the side of the tub. "My towel, please."

He sighed his disappointment, then rose and picked up the towel from the table. Instead of handing it to her, though, he held it open and waited for her.

Fiona hid a smile. Her husband was a very physical

man, something she enjoyed very much indeed. She stepped out of the tub into his waiting arms.

"Allow me," Jack murmured, sliding the thick towel down her body.

Fiona luxuriated in his touch. He was being so wonderful. He'd brought her a present, had agreed with her complaints about his behavior and had changed it, and was now touching her in a way destined to make them both very happy.

"There. Everything but your hair."

"I was going to sit by the fire and comb it until it dried."

He wrapped the towel around her and tucked it in place. "I can see through your plan; you are just trying to get closer to that package."

"Me?" She batted her eyes innocently. "Will you at least give me a hint?"

"No." He sat by the fire, waiting until she sat in the chair opposite and began combing out her hair.

As Fiona combed her hair, her heart was full with all his gifts. "Jack, thank you so much."

He waved a hand. "It's just a gift."

"I don't mean the present, though that is very nice."

He looked confused. "Then what do you mean?"

"Devonsgate told me we were staying in."

He still looked confused. "Yes, for tonight."

She stilled. "What?"

"I thought we'd stay in tonight."

"Just this evening?"

He frowned. "I'm sure there will be others, too. Why?"

A cold hand clenched her heart. "You have not changed your mind? You still feel it is appropriate for you to wander from gaming hell to gaming hell and leave me at home?"

He looked blank. "What does that have to do with ... Fiona, I thought you'd be pleased with the present."

She stood and marched to where her robe lay, dropped the towel to the floor, and yanked on the robe. "You cannot buy my approval with a mere present."

"I didn't mean that. I mean, I didn't think a present would hurt anything, though I didn't think you'd— Damn it, Fiona, do not do this!"

She pulled the robe tight. "There's nothing to do, my lord. You've made yourself perfectly clear." She crossed to the bellpull and yanked it forcefully.

"Fiona—"

She pushed the wet present toward Jack with her foot. "You may keep this, too. I would rather have nothing from a man who cares for my concerns than all the gifts in the world from a man who thinks his amusements more important than my feelings."

Anger flew through Jack. He stood. "I am retiring to the library. When you are ready to talk calmly, I will be there."

"I am through talking," Fiona said, fighting the bitter disappointment of her stupid mistake. "You are not willing to give any part of yourself to this relationship, and I am through hoping for more."

For an instant, Jack wanted to tell her that he was willing to give something of himself. The problem was, he wasn't sure how. He'd been alone since he was sixteen, and he didn't know how to open his life to someone else. Not without losing himself in the process.

Maybe he simply couldn't be in a close relationship. Maybe that's the way things were supposed to be. "I don't know what to say, Fiona. I have never misled you."

"No, you haven't," she said, her voice breaking, and for a horrid moment, he thought she would cry. Instead, she straightened her shoulders and said firmly, "I have learned my lesson. I will not ask again. You can have your life back; I want no part of it. As soon as I am with child, I will leave."

Jack's hands clenched into fists, his chest tight with anger and something else. "Very well, madam. If that is what you wish."

She lifted her chin, her eyes bright with unshed tears. "It is."

There was nothing left to say. Gritting his teeth, Jack turned on his heel and left, slamming the door behind him.

# Chapter Seventeen

Some say magic is what ties nature and man together and binds them until ye can't tell one from t'other. I think 'tis love that binds nature to man, and nothing else.

OLD WOMAN NORA FROM LOCH LOMOND
TO HER THREE WEE GRANDDAUGHTERS ONE COLD NIGHT

Jack looked at the paper. Devonsgate had listed all twelve footmen: John, Mark, Luke, Thomas . . . Bloody hell, his butler had hired the entire New Testament.

He threw the list onto his desk and rose, stretching as the clock chimed nine. He had been working steadily in his library since the argument with Fiona. If he was going to be miserable, he might as well do it on a full stomach.

He glanced at the piles of papers on his desk. Mr. Troutman had been so ecstatic over Jack's request to review the investments that he'd sent a portfolio and begged Jack to avail himself of the contents until their scheduled meeting.

After Jack's argument with Fiona, he'd been glad to have something to throw himself into. It was difficult to stay focused on the facts and figures though, and he frequently found himself pacing the room.

Fiona was the most stubborn woman he'd ever met. Once she decided something, she refused to move from it. She wanted Jack to be something he was not: a family man. A man who devoted himself to his wife and children. He was not that sort of man and never would be, and Fiona would just have to accept that.

So why, if he was in the right, did he feel wrong? He shoved his chair from the desk and crossed to the fireplace to stir the flames.

He *wasn't* wrong, damn it. Fiona had forced this marriage on him—on the man he was. Therefore, she had to accept that he had no obligations. This unease merely came from the distastefulness of having an argument—no one liked having his peace cut up. He would wager Fiona felt as bad as he did.

The thought made him look at the door. Perhaps he should speak with her. He remembered the look on her face and sighed, rubbing his tight neck. Maybe he'd give her more time to calm down.

But what if she was upstairs crying? What if she thought him the coldest, most unfeeling man on earth? What if—

Bloody hell, what was wrong with him? Disgusted, he returned the poker to the stand with a clang. A gentle chime from the ormolu clock informed him that it was now a quarter past nine, and he wondered if Fiona had eaten already. He hoped she was not feeling so horrible about their fight that she couldn't eat.

Perhaps by now, she was calm enough to have a rational conversation. She might even apologize for her surprising outburst.

That was a pretty picture, Fiona begging his forgiveness. He paused for a minute to savor the image. Perhaps if he magnanimously invited her to share supper with him, some of their awkwardness would disappear. Jack could then present her with the chemises he'd purchased for her. She would be very sorry then, once she saw the exquisite sheer linen and delicate lace. She would beg his forgiveness, and he would accept. They might even make love.

The thought made him smile. He'd never shared such passion with a woman before. Still, he could not allow that to interfere in his life. After he and Fiona had settled their argument, he would call for the carriage and go about his evening entertainment. After all, a man had to make a stand.

Feeling better already, Jack rang the bellpull. Almost immediately, Devonsgate stood in the doorway. "My lord, I was just coming to speak with you about—"

"Good! I am famished. I had no idea it was so late. Inform Cook that Lady Kincaid and I will have dinner in the dining room. After that, I shall want the carriage." Jack entered the foyer.

"My lord," Devonsgate said, hurrying after Jack. "The carriage is gone."

Jack halted, then turned slowly to the butler. "I beg your pardon?"

The butler flushed. "Her ladyship has the carriage."

Jack didn't know whether to laugh or . . . Hell, he didn't know what to do. "When did she leave?"

"Not thirty minutes ago, my lord."

Bloody hell! "Why was I not informed?"

Devonsgate stiffened. "My lord, you've never asked us to tell you when her ladyship comes and goes."

He hadn't, blast it. But he would have if he'd known his wife was planning— What *was* she planning? Jack had a sudden sinking feeling he knew where she'd be. "Did she mention her destination?"

Devonsgate exchanged a pained glance with one of the footmen. Jack turned to the man. Younger, with wispy blond hair and protruding eyes, he stood at rigid attention, only the shine on his forehead portraying his unease.

What was the man's name? Ah, yes. "Thomas?"

"Yes, my lord?"

"Did you speak with her ladyship this evening?"

"Yes, my lord. She came downstairs dressed to go out."

"Dressed?"

"Yes, my lord. She looked quite elegant."

Bloody hell, she was probably wearing some of the clothes *he* had bought for her, looking charming in a gown *he* had chosen. "Did she tell you where she was going?"

"Yes, my lord." Thomas sent a wild glance at Devonsgate. Jack could not see the butler, but whatever gesture he'd made, Thomas swallowed noisily, stiffened his straight back even more, and said in an expressionless voice, "Her ladyship said she was going to a real, authentic gaming hell."

"Which one?" Jack asked grimly.

"Lady Chester's, sir."

Lady Chester was a fast widow who lived on the fringes of society. She ran one of the most dashing gaming hells in town. Every rakehell, scoundrel, and wastrel would be there. Jack knew, because he was acquainted with them all. "Did she say anything else?"

Thomas swallowed again. "Yes, my lord. She—she said she was going to gamble away your entire fortune."

"She did, did she?"

"Yes, my lord," Thomas said miserably.

"Anything else?"

"Yes, my lord. She also stated that she was going to drink until she was tipsy, and—" Thomas seemed unable to go on.

"Finish it," Jack said in a harsh tone.

"And flirt with every man in sight." Thomas said the words so quickly they blurred.

The absolute nerve of her! To go out on the town and gamble with his funds, drink until tipsy, and flirt with *his* friends—it was untenable.

In a blaze of white anger, he said through gritted teeth, "Was there anything else, Thomas?"

"Yes, my lord. She was talking to herself quite a bit, muttering as if she was angry about something. She said she was finished taking good advice and her life turning out bad, so perhaps it was time to take some bad advice and hope for something better. At least that way, if it didn't work, she wouldn't be surprised."

"What does that mean?"

Devonsgate cleared his throat. "If I may be so bold as to interject, sir. After her ride this morning, her ladyship mentioned that her brothers had given her some bad advice. She wished to know if mine had ever done the same."

"She is taking advice from Gregor and Dougal? I cannot believe they'd suggest she visit a gaming hell. An unescorted lady would be prey to all sorts of unwelcome behaviors."

"She didn't go alone."

Jack stiffened and turned back to Thomas.

"She—she sent word to a Mr. Campbell that she hoped to be out. He replied almost immediately that he would be glad to meet her there."

"Hell and blast! Campbell is the worst of the lot!"

Thomas paled. "I—I—didn't know, my lord!"

"What is she thinking?" Jack snapped. "Have the phaeton brought around."

"But my lord," Devonsgate said, "it has no cover. The weather has been very unpredictable of late."

*Unpredictable* didn't begin to describe it. "Bring it. I will be returning in the carriage, anyway."

"Very good, my lord."

It *wasn't* good. It was infuriating. Muscles tense, Jack ran up the stairs to change, his mind and emotions whirling. *Fiona, what in the hell do you think you're doing?*

But he already knew. She was mimicking him. All the way to hell.

Just as Jack was speeding away from Kincaid House, Fiona arrived at the gaming hell.

Campbell met her outside on the walk, impeccably dressed as ever. He was all smiles and compliments, flatteringly eager to escort her.

Looking up at the brightly lit and noisy house that rose before her, she couldn't help but be glad for the company.

"You look ravishing," Campbell said as they climbed the stairs of the establishment.

She stopped on the top stair. "Campbell, before we begin, I think you should know I am only here because Jack and I had a huge row."

"I know."

She lifted her brows, and he smiled.

"A married woman does not invite her husband's enemy to escort her unless she is making a point."

Fiona flushed. "I do not mean to use you poorly."

"I didn't think you would." He captured her hand

and pressed a light kiss to her fingers, his blue eyes twinkling at her. "Who am I to refuse to escort an intriguing woman to her first taste of sin?"

She removed her hand from his. "I am glad to know I am not inconveniencing you."

"Not at all. I am always willing to discomfort Jack Kincaid."

"Why? What has he done to you?"

"He has more," Campbell said with a shrug of his shoulders.

"More what?"

Campbell's gaze met hers. "Everything."

Suddenly uncomfortable, Fiona turned back to the doorway. "Shall we go in?"

"Of course." He bowed and gestured for her to precede him.

Lady Chester's looked exactly the way a gaming hell should. The foyer left Fiona with a mad impression of a swirl of rich red tapestries and deep wine-colored draperies, gilt-edged mirrors, and pictures depicting Roman debaucheries.

Fiona looked around the crowd, seeing one or two faces she knew but many more she did not. This was the demimonde, those who hung about the fringes of society, mixing only with those who deigned to come down from their lofty perches to visit for such amusements as these.

One of them, Lady Pendleton, who relied on her distant relationship to the duke of Rotheringham to gain her entrance into most houses in London, swooped upon them.

An excessively silly woman given to gossip, Lady Pendleton rushed forward, giggling loudly. "La, there you are, Lady Kincaid! I thought that was you, though I couldn't be certain in this light."

It certainly was dim. Fiona glanced up at the candle sconces and was surprised to see the light blocked by small panels of waxed paper.

"And Alan Campbell!" Lady Pendleton exclaimed, looking between him to Fiona and back with an arch gaze. "I am so surprised to see the two of you here together! That just goes to show that you never know about people, do you?"

Fiona's cheeks burned. Campbell must have sensed her distress, for he quickly bid Lady Pendleton good-bye and bustled Fiona into the front parlor.

"Odious woman!" Fiona said.

"Very much so," Campbell said, smiling down at her. "But please, do not allow her to destroy our pleasure. You wished to see a gaming hell, and this is the best to be had."

Fiona managed to smile back, though she was vastly uncomfortable. The room was filled with cigar smoke and raucous laughter. Tables were crammed into the space with barely any room to walk between them. Everywhere Fiona looked, she witnessed immodest behavior.

The women were all dressed in the height of fashion, though they'd subtly altered their gowns. Fiona tried not to stare, but with so many flashing bosoms in the room, it was difficult not to. "Heavens," she said weakly when a lady with a particularly low décolletage walked by. "I don't know where to look."

Campbell chuckled and pulled her arm through his. "You don't need to look anywhere except at me."

Fiona wished she'd asked Gregor or Dougal to bring her instead of Campbell, but she'd known her brothers would never have allowed her to come, no matter how much she begged. Looking around at the drunken crowd, she thought they might have been right.

Either way, she was here now, and she might as well enjoy herself. At least until Jack arrived. *If* he came. She refused to think what she would do then.

"Lady Kincaid—Fiona," Campbell said. "Let's find a table and try our hand at bucking the tiger."

"Bucking the tiger?"

He smiled, his eyes twinkling down at her. "That's what you call it when you play faro. It's a very simple game but quite swift-moving. I think you'll like it."

She nodded, relieved to have something to occupy her mind. Campbell led her to a nearby faro table and seated her in a plush, gilt-edged chair. "Mr. Chumbly, Lord Penult-Mead, Lady Oppenheim, allow me to introduce a potential partner. This is Lady Kincaid, and she is new here in London."

Lord Penult-Mead brightened immediately. "New, are you? Excellent! Excellent! I am the banker tonight, my dear. If you need a line of credit, just say the word, and I'll open one for you."

She glanced up at Campbell, who stood behind her chair. He bent and whispered, "Shall I frank you, my dear? Would that suit you better?"

She flushed. It wouldn't suit her at all, but she would rather owe Campbell than a stranger. "Would you mind?"

He bent low and pressed a heavy coin into her hand. "It's a pleasure to frank such a beautiful player."

"Thank you," she said. "I will pay you back, of course."

He laughed. "As you wish. Just start low in your bidding. When you feel as if you've lost too much, then quit."

That didn't sound too bad. "Thank you. I am afraid I don't know the rules."

Lady Oppenheim, who looked very much like a large pug dressed in puce silk and ostrich feathers, waved a bejeweled hand. "Oh, it's quite easy, my dear. We are playing against Lord Penult-Mead, as he is the banker. The rest of us are called the punters. You purchase checks from the banker"—she indicated some round, coinlike chips that sat on the table before her—"and use those to place your wagers."

Fiona listened carefully as Lady Oppenheim explained the details of the game. It did seem remarkably easy, though there was a lot to remember.

As if reading her mind, Campbell leaned in and whispered, "Do not worry, my dear. I will be here to assist you."

His breath brushed her ear, and though it felt pleasant, it didn't awaken the response she would have felt with Jack.

It was a dismal thought, and she forced herself to apply her attention to the game, even though part of her was wistfully watching the doorway.

Fiona played only two hands before Jack arrived, and she knew the moment he walked in. Not only did her body tingle as if touched, but the room grew loud with cries of welcome. Even Lady Oppenheim waved her handkerchief.

Jack came directly toward her, looking dangerously handsome in his black evening clothes, his dark auburn hair falling across his brow, his blue eyes steady on her.

She clutched her hand around her markers and tried to calm her racing heart.

Campbell didn't seem to notice Jack's presence until he was almost at the table.

"Fiona," Jack said.

Campbell started, his hands tightening on the back of her chair, yet he said nothing.

"Fiona," Jack said. "It is time we went home."

Fiona grabbed a handful of markers and randomly placed them on the board.

Lady Oppenheim shook her head. "My dear, have a care. That is a risky wager, indeed."

Fiona kept her head up high. "It's what I wish to do."

"Very well," Lady Oppenheim said in a doubtful voice. "Just do not cry to me when you lose."

Lord Penult-Mead dealt the card.

"Excellent!" Campbell said. "You won, my dear!"

Good. Then perhaps she could pay Campbell back before the evening was over. Her Scottish soul detested the thought of owing money.

Jack had crossed his arms over his chest. "Are you through yet?"

Actually, she was. She didn't like the smoke or the hubbub or the quality of people. She'd much rather go home or have a quiet evening with friends, but she was not about to admit that to Jack.

"I am just beginning to enjoy myself."

He reached for her arm. "We are leaving."

She freed herself. "No, we are not. *You* may leave, but I am staying."

He glowered down at her, his powerful hands opening and closing. Her partners at the table watched with interest as he leaned down until his eyes were even with hers. "Fiona, it's time to go home, *now*."

She didn't flinch. "As you said before, we are completely independent of each other. You may do as you wish, and I may do as I wish."

"That is not acceptable."

"It's all you'll get," she said in a heated tone.

Campbell had remained quiet throughout this altercation. Fiona wasn't even certain he was still standing with her.

"Very well," Jack said. "If you wish to stay, then stay. I will do the same. Just don't expect me to change my behavior because you are present."

"I expect *nothing* from you." She waved a hand. "Now, if you'll excuse me, you are interrupting our play."

He glowered, then turned on his heel and left.

Within seconds, he was surrounded by a bevy of attractive women and a group of rather dissolute-looking men.

Campbell's hand came to rest on Fiona's shoulder. "Forgive me for saying this, but your husband is a hothead."

Campbell didn't know the half of it. "He has had a bad day."

"Are we ready to begin?" Lord Penult-Mead asked.

"I hope so!" Lady Oppenheim huffed. "I am quite determined to win back my markers. Lady Kincaid, I believe it's your turn."

Fiona quickly placed her wager.

The next hour was pure hell. Campbell stayed by her side, whispering advice in her ear and paying her overblown compliments. She pretended to be interested in what he was saying, but she was painfully aware of Jack across the room, looking dangerously handsome as he played at another table.

She simply could not help peeking at him, noting the way his breeches clung to his thighs. The way he quite eclipsed everyone else in the room with his broad shoulders. The way his hair fell over his brow, shadowing his eyes until they looked black instead of dark blue. The way every woman in the room was doing exactly what Fiona was doing: watching Jack.

Blast it all, what were they thinking? He was *her* husband!

"Ah, I wondered when she'd arrive," Campbell said softly, looking at the doorway.

Fiona followed his gaze and saw Lucinda Featherington cross the room to Jack's table. She stiffened. "I didn't know that woman came to places like this."

Campbell shrugged. "She goes anywhere she thinks she might find Jack."

Lucinda spoke to Jack. Fiona watched closely, catching a flash of emotion on Jack's face. It came and went so quickly she couldn't tell what it meant, but Lucinda laughed and took the chair next to his.

Fiona fumed. Who did that woman think she was? Hadn't she learned her lesson yet?

Fiona caught Jack's eye. Slowly, their gazes locked, and he reached his arm along the back of Lucinda's chair.

Lucinda needed no more encouragement. She leaned toward Jack, pressing her bosom against his arm, gazing up into his eyes with open invitation.

"Lady Kincaid." Lady Oppenheim's rather strident voice cut through the air. "It's your play again. Please pay attention!"

Flushing, Fiona smacked markers on various cards without paying the slightest heed to what she was doing.

"Careful," Campbell said.

"I am tired of being careful," she said, unable to keep her eyes on her cards.

Campbell looked at her face, then glanced back to Jack's table. Fiona's gaze followed Campbell's. Lucinda was whispering in Jack's ear. He was listening with an absent smile, his gaze locked on his cards. As Fiona watched, Lucinda looked across the room, directly at her. A cool, triumphant smile flickered over Lucinda's lips.

Fiona rose from her chair, but Campbell's hand pressed her back into her seat. Thunder rumbled outside.

"Easy, my sweet. You don't want to give her the satisfaction of making a scene." He glanced at the window as lighting flashed, a thoughtful look on his face.

" 'Making a scene' doesn't even begin to describe what I wish to do."

"Do as you wish, of course. I just thought you'd rather have your dignity than revenge," Campbell said.

It was a pity she couldn't have her dignity *and* slap Lucinda Featherington silly.

"It would hardly be wise," Campbell said coolly. "People will forgive a dousing but not an out-and-out attack."

Her face flushed. "I didn't realize I'd spoken out loud."

"You didn't. I guessed at your thoughts."

"Was my expression so revealing?"

His blue eyes twinkled at her. "You do have a tendency to wear your thoughts on your sleeve." He looked pointedly at the window, where the panes were rattling from the sudden wind. "Much like your brothers."

Fiona didn't know what to say. Many people in Scotland knew of the curse, but few actually believed it.

"Perhaps there is a way we can turn the tables on your husband." Campbell caught her gloved hand and lifted it to his lips, his breath warm through the cotton.

It was a proper gesture, but the insinuation in the length of time he held her hand, the way he let his fingers slide from hers when she pulled free, the manner in which he stared into her eyes—all of it smacked of seduction.

Fiona glanced to where Lucinda leaned against Jack, the two of them deep in conversation. Lucinda's breasts were pressing against his arm, their fullness quivering with each breath.

Fiona's jaw tightened, and, instead of setting Campbell in his place, she leaned toward him and smiled. "Thank you."

His eyes widened, an odd flush entering his cheeks. He pressed her hand meaningfully.

From the corner of her eye, she saw Jack's hand fist on the table, and she knew she'd won a point. Without removing her hand from Campbell's, she tossed her new wager onto the table.

Jack scowled. Then, with a narrow look, he picked up Lucinda's hand and kissed it exactly the way Campbell had kissed Fiona's.

Wind rattled the front window, and the first smattering of rain slashed across the glass.

Jack smirked.

Fiona looked around. Damn him! She had to find
something else to irk him.

She watched as he took a drink from a glass on the
table, smiling absently when Lucinda spoke.

A drink! All of the footmen were on the other side
of the room, so she grasped Campbell's arm. "I need
a drink."

He blinked. "Of course. Someone will be by soon,
and—"

"No, I need one *now,*" she said breathlessly. "Should
we go to one of the footmen and fetch one?"

"They will bring it here. Wait a moment." He lifted
a finger, catching the attention of a footman, who
obediently rushed to their side.

Campbell took two shimmering glasses of champagne from the tray and handed one to her. "Here you
are, my lady. To what shall we drink?"

Sparkling bubbles rolled up the side of her glass,
gathering on the surface. The candlelight reflected
through the glass. "It's almost too pretty to sip."

Campbell's gaze darkened. "All the more reason to
do it quickly."

Fiona glanced past him to Jack.

He paused, his own glass halfway to his mouth,
and frowned when he saw the champagne in Fiona's
hand.

Never breaking his gaze, she lifted the glass. And drank it all.

At first nothing happened, but then a slow, lazy flush moved up her breasts to her neck. "Oh, my!"

Jack's brows lowered. Lucinda, realizing she'd lost his attention, glowered at Fiona.

Campbell laughed. "I see you enjoy champagne."

"I love it." She tossed her head. "In fact, I will have another glass."

Jack's frown grew as Campbell ordered another glass.

Fiona took the second glass and looked directly at him. His expression hardened; he lifted his glass and tossed back his drink, every move a challenge.

Fiona steeled herself, then lifted her glass to Campbell. "Here's to the end."

"The end of what?"

"Of everything." She lifted the glass and quaffed it as she'd done before, but this time, the champagne refused to go the way it was intended. She sputtered a moment, then sneezed so violently two pins dropped from her hair, a thick tress falling to one shoulder.

Campbell laughed. "My dear, I hope you don't take this wrong, but champagne does not seem to be your drink."

"I am not going to drink ratafia. Old women drink that." The two glasses of champagne so close together were taking their toll; she felt frothy and light and completely free.

Which she was, thanks to Jack Kincaid. She was unfettered, free, and damned happy. She lifted her empty glass. "Another toast!"

Campbell laughed and gestured to a footman, saying something to him in a low voice. "There," he said when the footman had nodded and scurried off. "I believe I have solved your problem."

"I don't have a problem," Fiona said, tossing more markers onto the table without caring where they landed.

Campbell took her hand and brought it to his lips. "I never argue with a beautiful woman."

Fiona peeked past him to Jack. His face was like a thundercloud. Good. It was time someone besides her made a little rain. She turned back to Campbell and smiled at him sweetly. "I appreciate your help, but please do not think this means I will allow you any liberties."

He turned her hand over and peeled the glove from her wrist, then placed a kiss on her pulse. "I wouldn't dream of it, my dear. If you want me to stop, just say the word."

The footman returned, a single glass on his tray. Campbell handed it to Fiona, who sniffed it gingerly.

The glass was warm; the scent of cloves and cinnamon and a dozen other delicious spices curled through the steam that rose over the cup.

Fiona took a sip, smiling as the taste caressed her tongue. "This is delicious!"

Campbell smiled. "Drink it up. Then we will dance."

She did as he said, setting the cup down with a *thunk*. "I am ready."

"Good. I promise to hold you much too tightly and make it seem as if I'm whispering sweet naughties in your ear."

"Just do not whisper real ones, for I would laugh, and that would not help matters." She was almost giggling now, and she had no reason to. "What was in that drink?"

"A little of this. A little of that." His eyes darkened. "Did you like it?"

"Oh, yes. Wayyyyy too much." She pushed her markers to Lord Penult-Mead. "I think I am through." She turned to Campbell and started to stand but fell back into her chair.

He swiftly caught her elbow and pulled her hard against his chest. "Easy, my sweet! You don't want to fall."

Fiona realized her chest was pressed against his, his hands holding her intimately. She pushed away from him and smoothed her gown, aware that though many watched, no one seemed shocked. All behavior was accepted and expected here.

Of course, that would not keep anyone from gossiping about what they saw.

Fiona put a hand on a nearby chair and forced a smile at Campbell. "Shall we dance?"

"Of course."

"Good. Just try not to step on my new shoes."

With that unromantic rejoinder, Fiona allowed Campbell to escort her to the dance floor.

They never made it.

One moment, they were walking out of the card room. The next, Jack was standing before them, his face furious.

"Ah," Campbell said smoothly. "I wondered how long it would take you to reclaim your wife."

"She is going home now."

Fiona snorted inelegantly. "*She* is doing no such thing."

Jack's gaze burned into hers. "You don't know what you are doing; you've had too much to drink."

"Nonsense! I only had two glasses of champagne"— she held up three fingers—"and one glass of . . . what was that?"

"Rum punch," Campbell said succinctly.

Jack's face darkened. He grasped her arm and pulled her forward.

She stumbled against his chest, and he caught her firmly.

"No," she said, pushing away from him. "I am going to dance with Campbell, and he is going to whisper to me and not step on my new shoes."

"Like hell," Jack said. He pulled back his fist and smashed it into Campbell's face. Campbell dropped to the floor like a lead weight.

"Jack!" Lucinda rushed forward. "What are you—"

Jack ignored her. He stooped and flung Fiona over his shoulder, and turned for the door.

"Jack!" Fiona's hair fell completely out of its pins, dropping over her like a curtain. "You're hell on a woman's hair, Kincaid! I hope you know that!"

Jack just walked out the front door and into the rain to the carriage, ignoring the faces that stared out the windows at them.

# Chapter Eighteen

*I've often thought it unfair that women are expected to stay at home when there's a fight to be won. If a woman has the strength to bear a child, she can swing a sword as well as any man.*

OLD WOMAN NORA OF LOCH LOMOND
TO HER THREE WEE GRANDDAUGHTERS ONE COLD NIGHT

"May I take your hat, my lord?"

Gregor tossed it to Devonsgate. "Is my sister ready yet? We are to ride this morning."

The butler handed the hat to a waiting footman. "I believe her ladyship will be down in a minute."

Somewhere upstairs, a door slammed and someone stomped across a floor.

Devonsgate looked stoically ahead.

Silence reigned for a moment, then the sound of raised voices—one female, one male—lifted in the distance.

The front door rattled, wind buffeting the heavy panel until it shook.

Devonsgate frowned. "My, but the weather has been abrupt lately."

Gregor smelled the scent of lilacs, faint but unmistakable. He sent a hard glance at Devonsgate. "What's that jackass done now?"

The butler returned his look blandly. "I am sure I don't take your meaning, sir."

The sound of voices raised in discord once again floated downstairs.

"It seems as if the storm may be inside this time," Gregor said.

Devonsgate sighed and nodded in agreement, then caught himself. "I do not know what you're speaking about," he said stiffly.

Upstairs, the door slammed again, voices were raised, and then came the stomp of booted feet on the stairs.

Jack stopped when he saw Gregor in the foyer.

Gregor rocked back on his heels. "Sounds as if you're having a rather windy morning."

Jack eyed Gregor a long moment and then continued down the stairs, past Gregor, and went into his library, slamming the door behind him.

Gregor strode across to open it, his large form filling the entryway. "What's going on, Kincaid?"

Jack dropped into the chair behind his desk and pulled his papers forward. "Ask your sister."

"I plan to. I thought you might want your side of the story to be heard, too."

"I don't need anyone to hear my side, least of all you and your brother. In fact"—Jack's eyes flashed—"if you and Dougal *ever* give Fiona another piece of advice like yesterday's, I will rip your tongues out and feed them to my hunting dogs."

Gregor's irritation faded. "Fiona didn't do anything foolish, did she?"

"You might want to ask your sister what she was doing at Lady Chester's last night."

Gregor stiffened. "She went *where*?"

"With Alan Campbell, who took great delight in giving her champagne and rum punch."

"That bast—"

"I took care of him," Jack said shortly.

"And Fiona?"

"I had to toss her over my shoulder, but I managed to get her home."

Good God. Gregor didn't know what to say.

A sharp clip on the staircase told him his sister was approaching. He looked at Kincaid, whose face was grim, the deep lines beside his mouth and eyes telling their own tale.

A flash of guilt went through Gregor. Since the beginning of this debacle, he'd been angry. Angry with the Kincaids for Callum's death. Then angry with Fiona for sacrificing herself as if she alone could solve their problems. Angry with Jack for not treating Fiona as he should have. But mainly, Gregor had been angry with himself. He should have been with Callum that night. Should have seen Fiona's plan and stopped it. Should have found a way to set her marriage with Kincaid aside.

And he hadn't done any of it. He'd been a selfish

bastard, unable to put the needs of others ahead of his own impulsive emotions. And now, because of that and his misdirected sense of humor, his sister had ended up in a gaming hell where God knew what could have happened to her.

"Thank you for watching over my sister, Jack."

Jack's gaze swung up to meet his. "She's my wife, Gregor. I may not be happy about that, but I *will* take care of her."

"I shouldn't have suggested she cross you. I never thought she'd do something unsafe and—"

Jack threw up a hand. "Just don't be so flippant the next time Fiona asks for advice. She's worth more than that."

Fiona's footsteps could be heard on the steps behind Gregor, and he asked Jack, "Would you care to ride with us this afternoon?"

Jack raised his brows. He'd never thought he'd receive an invitation from one of Fiona's brothers. It was a pity to have to reject it. "I'm sorry, but I have a meeting with my man of business. Perhaps tomorrow?"

Gregor nodded, his expression harried. "Very well. I'll see what's to be done with the lass. Perhaps I can talk some sense into her."

"Don't bother. I've already tried, and—"

But Gregor had already left. Even now, his deep voice could be heard booming through the foyer as he welcomed Fiona.

Jack strained to hear her soft reply, but her voice

was lost when the front door opened and a strong wind whistled in. In a moment, the wind and the voices disappeared as Fiona left for her morning ride.

It had been a long night, and he'd thought he wanted nothing more than the peace of his own library. But now the silence was screamingly loud.

Jack rose to stir the fire, his gaze drawn to the window. The wind whipped wildly, large clouds rolled by, trees bent and swayed. He found himself standing at the window, looking down as Fiona and Gregor joined Dougal.

She was dressed in the green riding habit that hugged every curve, her hair pinned up beneath her hat, tendrils whipping with the wind. Her face was tilted up as she listened to something Gregor said, her eyes intent on his face, her lips slightly parted.

Jack rubbed a dull ache in his chest. Last night had been horrid. Fiona had refused to speak to him after he'd carried her out of the gaming hell, refused to sleep with him when they'd arrived at the house, and, this morning, refused to listen to his attempts to explain his behavior.

She was wrong, damn it! She should not have been at a gaming hell. Period.

Before long, the two of them had engaged in a witless battle that had culminated in a slammed door and terse good-byes.

Jack leaned against the window frame and watched as Gregor helped Fiona onto her mount, a neatish bay named Ophelia. She was the perfect lady's horse. She was a mite restive if left too long in the stables, but after a brief ride, she calmed and offered a sweet gait.

The horse was full of spunk today, prancing so that the groom had to hold the bridle for Fiona to mount safely.

Jack frowned at the man. What was that grooms-man's name? He didn't look familiar; Jack would have to ask Devonsgate about that.

Fiona placed her boot in the stirrup, slid into the saddle, then hooked her knee over the pommel. After she was seated, Gregor turned to his own horse. The groom handed Fiona the reins and stepped back to adjust a strap.

Whether it was the large cart rumbling by or Fiona's skirts blowing in the wind, something startled Ophelia. The horse shied nervously, tossed its head violently, then suddenly reared. Jack watched in horror as Fiona clung to the horse's neck, her hat and whip falling to the ground as she scrambled to hang on. The horse pawed the air, then came down hard.

Jack gripped the window frame, his breath frozen, as Ophelia wheeled and ran madly down the road, Fiona clinging to the horse's mane.

Jack rushed through the foyer and outside. Gregor spurred his horse after Fiona. Jack grabbed Dougal's leg and yanked him to the ground. Jack swung up onto the huge black horse, slammed his boots into the stirrups, and galloped off, leaning low on the horse.

He *had* to catch her, had to save her. Life without

Fiona would have no meaning, no flavor. He couldn't accept it. Not now. Not ever.

Leaning close to the horse's neck, Jack began to pray.

Fiona hung on to the horse's mane for dear life as the mare ran madly through the streets of London, dodging carriages and sending other horses bucking in its path.

Fiona was jolted savagely back and forth. If she loosened her grip the slightest bit, she'd go flying and land on her head. If she continued to hang on, her neck would break from the violent jolting. Every time she went up, she came crashing back down. Her bottom was already bruised and sore, and her neck already pained her.

Suddenly, something snapped, and the saddle slid a bit to one side.

With a pop, the saddle let go and Fiona flew into the air.

The moment slowed, stretched, almost stopped. She was flying up and up. Any moment now, she would begin to fall, and there would be pain. She closed her eyes, reaching out to grab something, anything. But there was nothing to hold on to.

Miraculously, strong hands grabbed her and pulled her against a broad chest, catching her as simply and easily as if she were an apple falling from a tree. Gasping for breath, she clutched the rocklike man who had saved her.

A low, deep voice growled, "Hold on."

*Jack.* She clutched at him in relief, and he pulled her close, settling her in his lap. Trembling head to foot, she turned her face into his chest, inhaling deeply. She was beginning to love his scent almost as much as she loved chocolate.

"Are you injured?"

His deep voice rumbled through his chest beneath her ear.

She shook her head, though her entire body ached, and tears filled her eyes.

Jack felt her quake in his arms, saw her tears. His own heart thundering in his ears, he cursed and tightened his grip. "I have you now, Fiona. You are safe."

"She had bloody well better be," Gregor said from where he'd come up beside them.

Jack halted his horse, Gregor doing the same, at the entrance to Hyde Park. Carts and carriages, horses and passengers milled about, all eyes on them.

Jack couldn't bear to think of what had almost happened—the horse bucking wildly out of control, Fiona hanging on for dear life. If she'd landed on her head—

He held her tighter, trying to block the images in his mind.

Dougal rode up on one of Jack's horses, his face white. "Is she all right?"

"I think so," Jack said, feeling her breathing grow steadier.

Gregor stood in his stirrups. "Fiona? Can you hear me?"

"She's shaken, but fine otherwise."

"Are you certain?" Dougal reached for Fiona as if to take her from Jack.

Jack bared his teeth and backed his horse away. She was *his,* and he would die fighting to keep her.

The power of his reaction startled him. Was it because she was his wife? Because he was the only man who'd ever known her intimately? Or just his misguided, possessive Kincaid blood? Whatever it was, Jack only knew that right now, if anyone tried to remove Fiona from his arms, he would kill him without thought.

Dougal stayed back, but looked at him suspiciously. "You put my sister on an unsafe mount."

"I did not. Ophelia is never difficult. Look at her now."

The horse stood beside the entryway to the park, its saddle hanging off one side as it peacefully grazed.

"Then you did something to make the horse act that way," Dougal said hotly.

"Pshaw!" Gregor said. "Fiona has been riding lively mounts since she was four. She's no tender flower."

"I still think something was wrong," Dougal said.

"Then you'll have something to mull while you collect the mare and her saddle," Jack snapped. "I'm taking Fiona home."

With a dark glance, Dougal swung down from his

horse and tossed the reins to Gregor. He walked carefully up to Ophelia and took the reins without a problem. He started to lift the saddle, then stopped, and bent to stare at something.

"What is it?" Jack asked.

Dougal's brow lowered. "There is a burr under the saddle."

"Damnation!" Gregor swung down, tied the horses to a low branch, and joined his brother. They spoke in low tones, occasionally glancing back at Jack.

"I want to see it," Jack said sharply.

Gregor stepped back. "Let him see."

"It isn't really a burr." Dougal held up the cause of the accident. "It's a thistle. And there's more: someone cut the girth."

Jack looked down at Fiona, still pale. "I will kill whoever did this."

Dougal met Jack's gaze. "Was it you? You've said many times that you did not wish to be married."

"No, damn it! I've never wished Fiona harm."

Gregor said, "Dougal, why would Kincaid put a burr beneath her saddle and then save her as well? That makes no sense."

Fiona stirred. "Please, no more. I—I just want to go home."

Jack led the way, his mind whirling. Who would wish Fiona harm?

He could not see Lucinda going to such lengths. She would get her vengeance on Fiona, but in a more public manner. Maybe Campbell? There was something about him that Jack did not trust. He seemed far too interested in Fiona. What did he want? What would he gain by Fiona's death?

He rested his cheek against her forehead, then looked at her brothers. "If someone wants her harmed, we must go where she'll be safe."

"Jack, I cannot stay behind locked doors," Fiona protested. "I am sure there is an explanation, and—"

"No, Fiona," Gregor said. "Do as Kincaid says."

Identical shocked expressions crossed Jack's and Dougal's faces.

Fiona scowled. "I am not going to be locked away like a porcelain teacup."

"We must find a safe place for you to stay until we find out what's going on."

When they reached Kincaid House, Jack told the groom, "Find Mrs. Tarlington. Tell her to attend her ladyship in our bedchamber." Jack handed Fiona down to John the footman, swung down himself, and reclaimed Fiona. "John, see that her ladyship's saddle is put in my library. I want to examine it in better light."

Then he carried her up to their room. He tucked her into bed, frowning when she caught her breath as he slid her between the sheets.

Within the half hour, the doctor arrived and pre-scribed a daily hot soak in a tub with special lini-ment.

Fiona hated the liniment, which smelled like rotten potatoes, but Jack insisted she use it. He also allowed her to sit in the library afterward and drink her tea, which was a blessing.

Jack watched her every move with dark eyes. Twice she asked him what he was thinking, and twice he didn't answer, pacing the room silently.

Finally, she set down her teacup with a clink and said, "Jack, will you *please* sit down?"

He turned a surprised face to her. "I didn't mean to annoy you. I'm just a bit out of sorts."

"We both are." She gave him a wry smile and pressed a hand to her stomach. "You are making me seasick with all that pacing."

"I'm sorry," he said ruefully. He opened his mouth, stopped, then burst out, "Fiona, I hated our argument last night. I don't want you to think that I wish you harm. I would gladly have taken that fall myself rather than see you suffer."

Her heart leapt. "Why . . . why do you feel that way?"

His gaze raked across her, hot and possessive. "You are my wife."

The words were a branding. She found herself looking at him, too. Her husband. At the broad expanse of his shoulders. At the muscled length of his thighs and—

She looked away, her cheeks hot. That cursed liniment made her thoughts run smoky and hot. She slid her hands into the pockets of her day gown, wishing she had something to keep her mind off her husband's far too attractive thighs.

"Fiona, while the doctor was with you, I looked at the saddle. The strap was cut in two and then bound to look as if it was intact. I think we should leave London."

"What?"

"Aye. We've been invited to a wedding in Scotland, so we could go there for a sennight. It's near your home, so you could see your brothers, too."

She made a face. "I have seen more than enough of Dougal and Gregor."

Jack smiled grimly. "So have I."

"Jack, they don't blame you, do they?"

"They might. Dougal mentioned several times that I gave you that horse."

"You've also given me clothes. I suppose if I am found strangled with one of my own stockings, he will think that a clue, too."

Jack didn't laugh.

She sighed.

"Fiona, I don't relish the thought of going to this wedding, but it's a valid reason to leave town."

She rubbed her shoulder, where a dull ache burned. "I cannot think who might want me gone. Do you think it was Lucinda? Because I embarrassed her?"

"No, but it might be Campbell." Jack raked a hand through his hair. "There is something about him that I don't trust."

"Why would he do such a thing?"

"I don't know. Yet." Jack came to a halt in front of her. "Fiona, Scotland will be safer for us."

"I know. It's just . . ." She threaded her fingers together, fighting to hide a wince. She was getting more stiff and sore by the minute.

There was no disguising the concern in Jack's eyes. Just a short hour ago, they had been arguing fiercely. Now, they were shoulder to shoulder as they dealt with this new danger.

Fiona forced a smile. "So. We are to go to a wedding? Who is getting married?"

Jack flashed her a relieved smile. "A gentleman I went to Eton with. He and I have kept in touch."

"It will be nice to get out of town." She began to shrug, then gasped with pain.

Jack went to the sideboard and poured a glass of brandy, then brought it to her. "This will help. Just sip it."

She took it and sniffed it gingerly. "I don't think—"

He exploded. "For the love of God, don't you *ever* do what you are asked?"

Fiona closed her eyes, her throat suddenly tight. She was so tired, so afraid, and every muscle in her body was bruised and swollen.

The settee cushions sank as Jack sat beside her. "I know things seem dark, Fiona," he whispered, pulling her against him, "but they will get better. I promise they will."

Fiona sipped the brandy to please Jack. After the third sip, a pleasant numbness seeped through her. It warmed her bruised body and soaked into her sore muscles. Her eyes grew heavy, and she closed them for a moment just to rest them . . .

Jack knew the second she fell asleep. The glass slipped from her hand, but he caught it just in time and set it on the table. Then he rested his cheek against Fiona's hair, careful not to disturb her.

In London, they were obvious targets, their habits too well known, Kincaid House too large to protect. In Scotland, they'd have the advantage. There they would have the time to work their way through this mystery.

Jack looked down at where Fiona slept against his shoulder, her eyes closed, her lashes fanned over her cheeks.

He had to get Fiona to safety. Immediately.

# Chapter Nineteen

*We Scots love a good weddin' and a bad funeral. Sometimes 'tis difficult to tell which is which.*

OLD WOMAN NORA OF LOCH LOMOND

TO HER THREE WEE GRANDDAUGHTERS ONE COLD NIGHT

"Oh, Lord Kincaid! Lord Kincaid!" A woman waved wildly from the portico of the country house. "It's me, Miss Hatfield! Oh, *do* say you remember me!"

Jack helped Fiona as she climbed from the carriage, murmuring in her ear, "Don't look now, but it's the bride."

The short, red-haired woman, dressed in pink silk that clashed sadly with her bobbing red curls, rushed toward them. "I told Paul you'd sent word you'd be arriving today, but he wouldn't believe me. La, how he will hate to be wrong!"

Fiona smiled as she murmured under her breath to Jack, "I thought you only knew the groom."

"I met Miss Hatfield only once, just enough to know that she's a bit emotional. You'll want to be careful not to—"

Miss Hatfield stood before them, almost hopping up and down. "It's just *lovely* of you to come, especially when it's still the Season in London and you're in such demand. Oh, is this your wife? Lady Kincaid, how nice to meet you!" Miss Hatfield grabbed Fiona's hand and pumped it heartily, then stepped back and looked her up and down. "Aren't you pretty as a picture! Why, I do think you're the most modish guest we've had yet. And just *look* at the two of you, standing together, the sun on your hair. Oh!" Miss Hatfield pressed her fingers to her mouth, her eyes filling with tears. "You look so *dear*! We really must get your portraits done!"

Hamish, who'd just removed the trunks from the carriage, regarded Miss Hatfield with the same expression he might bestow upon a dead cat in the road.

As the woman paused for breath, Jack took the opportunity to interject a greeting. Fiona did the same but then made the error of asking about the wedding. Miss Hatfield beamed and launched into a litany of all the troubles she'd had planning her wedding, guffawed quite inelegantly at the caterer who told her they couldn't have ices delivered all the way from Edinburgh when she knew for a fact that Lucy Marshall had ices at her eighteenth birthday party only two months ago, and shared a great deal of personal information about her soon-to-be husband that neither Jack nor Fiona cared to know.

Jack tried to interrupt several times, but Miss Hatfield could not be stayed. His irritation was just beginning to melt into distemper when he felt Fiona chuckle.

She met his glance with a barely suppressed smile, her eyes sparkling.

"Oh, yes," Miss Hatfield continued, unaware that she was causing amusement. "*Both* the butcher and the baker died within two weeks of each other! I don't know how we'll have decent food on our table, and here we are, with so many guests! You cannot simply *grow* those types of people overnight."

Fiona had to press a hand over her mouth to keep from laughing aloud, which made Jack grin, too. Thus, it was with an amazingly calm voice that he was finally able to break into Miss Hatfield's monologue the moment she paused for breath. "Miss Hatfield, I am sorry the butcher and the baker have caused you such distress with their untimely demises, but Lady Kincaid and I are a bit weary from our journey. Do you think—"

"Oh, dear me! Here I am prattling away, and you two are probably exhausted! I will have your trunks taken up to the Rose Room." She leaned toward Fiona and said in a confidential tone, "It's the biggest guest chamber we have. Poor Paul's parents thought they were to get it, but I told them that until they grow a fortune or win a title, I'm saving the room for someone *really* important."

"Thank you," Fiona said, casting a laughing look at Jack.

Miss Hatfield, oblivious to everything, gestured

toward the house. "Lord Kincaid, Paul is in the garden with the gentlemen if you'd care to say hello." She tucked Fiona's arm into hers and headed toward the portico. "Come, my dear! I shall take you to your chamber and have my maid wait upon you with some Grecian water. I bought it in Italy, and though I don't particularly care for its odor, I must say I sleep more soundly after I rub a bit on my temples."

"I am really not tired, just a bit stiff from the ride."

Jack sent a concerned glance toward Fiona. She was moving better now, with barely a limp. They'd traveled in easy stages, stopping frequently so she could get out and walk.

She'd done well, though she still appeared paler than usual.

"La, Lord Kincaid! Porterfield here will take you to the garden so that you may watch Paul smoke his silly cigars."

A portly butler bowed in Jack's direction.

"Meanwhile, I shall take good care of your lady." She patted Fiona's hand. "My dear, I hope you don't mind, but my eldest sister knows your brothers well, and she tells me you are in a delicate condition."

Fiona stumbled, and Miss Hatfield tightened her hold. "You must tell me all about it, for I'm sure I don't know the first thing, and like I told my fiancé, I'm certain we'll have a large family, and I just know I'll be in the same interesting condition before you can say 'Sneeze!' "

Jack grinned as Fiona was led away, prisoner to

a chatterbox. It had certainly been a bit off-color of Miss Hatfield to mention Fiona's "condition," but Fiona had taken it well enough.

Jack halted. Was it possible that Fiona *was* in an "interesting condition"? He watched her climb the stairs, noting that her hand frequently rested on her stomach. Had she always done that?

She'd been ill several times on the carriage ride, and they'd had to stop and let her regain her composure once or twice. She'd also cringed at a steak and kidney pie at a posting inn, which had surprised him, as she usually had a healthy appetite.

Good God, she *could* very well be carrying his child. Jack rubbed his forehead, his mind swirling. Bloody hell. He was protecting not only his wife but his child as well.

He slipped a hand beneath his coat to the reassuring weight of his pistol tucked securely into his waistband, then turned on his heel. Hamish stood at attention at the carriage, his face grim with menace. Jack gave his two footmen a warning glance, and Dobson and Peter nodded. They would keep a careful watch over the equipment, taking turns through the night. They'd also report anything suspicious they might see. Tomorrow, after the wedding, Fiona's two brothers would arrive, as would Devonsgate, who was following with the rest of their luggage. All were keeping their eyes peeled as they traveled the Great North Road.

Back in London, someone would have realized by

now that the Kincaids were no longer in residence. Jack felt as if the cares of the world weighed on his shoulders.

The wedding was an elaborate affair. The bride wore a lovely blue gown and flowers in her hair. The groom wore a kilt and a formal coat bearing the family crest on the pocket. There were masses of flowers, numerous bridal attendants, and so many guests that the pews in the beautifully decorated chapel overflowed.

Fiona sat beside Jack. He'd seemed unusually somber since they'd arrived. Miss Hatfield—now Mrs. Cargreaves—spent the entire morning in a mist of tears. She grew dewy-eyed at the sight of her groom waiting for her at the altar, wept as she exchanged her vows, shed a tear at the end of mass, and fell in a sobbing mess upon the shoulder of her husband as they made their way to the receiving line.

Still, Fiona thought the ceremony lovely. The couple had been genuine in their professions of love, and the excitement with which they embarked on their new life was evident in their faces and the way they kept holding hands when they thought no one was looking.

Fiona watched them wistfully. She and Jack hadn't had the luxury of such a blissful sendoff; their wedding hadn't been what either of them had wished for. She slid a glance at Jack and found him staring out a window, his brows drawn. Was he thinking the same thing? The thought tightened her throat.

After going through the receiving line, they joined the other guests for dinner at the main house. The floor of the great hall was flagstone—well worn, uneven, and cold. It wasn't long before Fiona's back began to ache and her feet hurt.

She pressed a hand to the small of her back to relieve some of the pain and caught Jack's eyes on her. His gaze roamed over her, lingering on her breasts, her hips.

A familiar tingle traveled up her spine. Last night, he'd surprised her by the gentleness with which he'd made love to her. He'd seemed fascinated by her body, running his hands over her, cupping her breasts, kissing her stomach, and touching her with a near-reverence that had awed and excited her.

Perhaps tonight she'd seduce him in return. She would slip into bed without her night rail, slide her legs down him, run her hands over his shoulders and chest, touching and tasting as she went—

She shivered, her nipples peaking at the thought. He was so handsome, this husband of hers, and so passionate.

Jack took her arm and bent close. "Fiona, come and let's find a seat."

"Did you wish to dance?"

He looked down at her and hesitated. "No," he finally said. "Did you?"

She would have loved to, but her aching feet decreed otherwise. "I fear I'm still a bit sore."

"Of course." Jack led her away, finding a small group of empty chairs at a long table. "Here." He pressed her into a chair. "I will return."

He did, too. With his hands full—two cups of orgeat and two plates filled with slices of cake, hot tarts, and other delicacies.

He grinned. "I managed to get the last of the apple tarts. The fat man in the blue broadcoat will never speak to me again, but it will be worth it."

Fiona gurgled a laugh. "Your name will be spoken in harsh tones for weeks to come."

"I have no doubt." He handed her a plate with a slice of cake, and they ate and watched as several young couples came together to dance. The bride and groom held hands, looking sweetly shy as she chattered breathlessly and he looked upon her in silent adoration.

A faint ache tightened Fiona's heart. She didn't really long for the missed bridal veil and flowers but for the excitement of beginning life as a couple. They'd missed that and would never have it.

Jack followed Fiona's wistful gaze to where the bride and groom were leading a set in dancing. Was that saddening her? She'd never had a real wedding.

Though he'd disliked the thought of being married at first and had clung to his freedom for as long as possible, now he couldn't imagine life without her. He couldn't remember sleeping alone, eating breakfast alone, or wandering through life instead of living it, which is what he had done before Fiona. With her, he *lived*. Without her . . .

He refused to consider that. He'd always lived in the present; perhaps that was what he needed to do now. He couldn't give Fiona a wedding like this—what was done was done. But he *could* do something to bring a smile to her face.

A few moments later, he sat back in his chair and grinned. He knew what he'd do. All he needed was a little help from Devonsgate.

The morning sun splintered through the crack in the curtains. Fiona opened her eyes, searching the unfamiliar room.

Jack was gone.

She sat up and scooted out of bed. Where was he? She started to tug the bellpull to call the maid but then decided that with the number of guests in the house, it would be quicker if she dressed herself. She washed using the pitcher of fresh water by the bed, then hurriedly dressed.

Jack's riding boots were gone. Maybe he'd just gone for a ride or—

The door opened, and Jack walked in, her cloak folded over his arm. He smiled upon seeing her, and until then, she hadn't realized she was holding her breath.

"I am glad you are up."

She looked at her cloak. "Are we going somewhere?"

"Yes, we are. Devonsgate arrived earlier and he is with the carriage."

"Where are we going?"

"It's a surprise." He looked at her shoes. "You'll need half boots; the ground may be uneven." He went to the wardrobe for a pair of boots.

She sat down to remove her slippers, but he shook his head. "Change them in the carriage. I want to leave before anyone else awakens."

Fiona stood. "Very well, though I have to warn you, I'm starving."

"Excellent. I want you *and* your appetite for this little jaunt." He placed her cloak around her shoulders and fastened the hook beneath her chin.

The gesture was sweet, simple, and completely unexpected. There was something tender about Jack this morning. Was he realizing that perhaps the time would come soon when they would part? Once she was with child . . .

Beneath the voluminous cloak, she rested her hand on her stomach. It was possible she was already with child. She frowned, trying to remember the date of her last courses.

"Ready, my love?" He held the door open.

She went through it, wondering at the gleam in his eyes. He appeared excited, almost playful.

At the carriage, Devonsgate greeted them with a bow and a smile. "Ah, madam! How are you this fine morning?"

"I'm cold!" She rubbed her arms beneath the cloak. "I hope you will not freeze on the carriage."

"I have a toasty topcoat. I find this weather rather invigorating, after the heat of town."

Hamish snorted. "The air is fresher, too."

Fiona agreed; the gentle morning wind carried the scents of fresh hay and roses.

One of the footmen opened the carriage door, and they were soon on their way. It was a lovely ride, over the hills and through a thick forest. Along the way, Jack made her laugh with tales of his brothers and parents.

The carriage pulled up to a wide, grassy spot near a small stream. Fiona alighted, one of the footmen assisting her. "Where are we?"

"Strathmore Forest. I used to come here when I was a child. There is a small clearing down that path. I thought we might set up the food there."

As Devonsgate disappeared down the path with a heavy basket, Fiona drew a deep breath. The scents of damp grass and clean water soothed her. The grass was a deep, rich green that begged for bare feet. A babbling brook rushed past them, the water tumbling clear and clean over mossy rocks. Large trees overhung them, the vivid blue sky dappling through.

Hamish dismounted and tied his horse to the back of the carriage, then pulled his pistol from his belt and stood at a tree not far away, scanning the woods.

Fiona frowned, realizing that not only was Hamish armed, but the footmen were as well. "Jack, do you really think that is necessary?"

"I doubt whoever caused your accident has yet realized we've left, but I feel safer being prepared." He clasped her elbow as he directed her to a little path. "I used to hide here when I was a boy."

"From whom?"

"From my chores, actually."

She laughed.

He grinned back, his gaze sliding down to where her hand rested on her stomach.

Fiona quickly removed her hand and flushed; she hadn't realized she'd been standing so.

A deep look of possessiveness flashed over his face, but he merely gestured to the path. "After you, my lady."

She walked down the winding path, her half boots rustling through the grass, her toes cooling as the leather chilled on contact with the damp ground. She was supremely conscious of the freshness of the air, of the breeze that tugged at her hair and brushed her cheeks, of the warmth of Jack's hand cupping her elbow as he led her around various dips in the path.

"I hope you brought plenty to eat," Fiona said. "My stomach is demanding attention."

They rounded a corner, and she halted. A large blanket was set with grapes and cheeses, tarts and crumpets and sweet breads, accompanied by jellies, jams, and marmalade. Devonsgate stood to one side, a napkin hung over one arm.

"Devonsgate! This is lovely!"

"Thank his lordship. It was his idea."

Fiona turned. "Jack, thank you."

The faintest hint of a smile curved his mouth. "It's nothing. Now, come and eat. You've gotten a bit pale these last few days."

He settled on the blanket next to her. "We've had a wild time of it, haven't we? First our marriage, which was not the usual fare. Then we had to adjust to each other. Your brothers did not make things easier, either. Plus the problems with Lucinda and the runaway horse . . . And now, here we are, attending a wedding." He picked up a knife and began peeling a pear. "I don't like weddings."

"Really? Why not?"

He cut the pear into slices and placed them on a plate. "Devonsgate, please give her ladyship some juice."

Devonsgate poured some juice into a wineglass and handed it to Fiona. "And you, my lord? I daresay you'll wish for some ale or—"

"No. I will have juice, too."

Devonsgate and Fiona looked at each other in amazement, then Fiona looked at Jack. "Juice?"

He shrugged. "What's good enough for my son is good enough for me."

Son? He thought she was— She blinked. She kept wondering, yet her mind skittered around the thought as if it were too hot to touch.

Silently, she began to add up the weeks. It was possible. Yes, it was possible. Her eyes watered. *Was* she carrying Jack's child?

"Fiona, drink your juice," Jack said gently.

She took a convulsive gulp, the liquid tart on her tongue.

"Devonsgate," Jack said, his gaze never leaving Fiona, "I believe we have all we need. You may retire to the coach."

"Thank you, my lord. If you need me I am but a step away." He bowed deeply, gave the blanket one last critical look, then disappeared up the walk.

Jack sipped his juice, grimaced, but quickly hid it. He set down his glass, picked up a small plate, and placed an apricot tart on it, along with a wedge of cheese. "Try these."

She picked up the tart and nibbled on the edge. She'd donned a white muslin morning gown trimmed with pink rosettes that peeked from between the gap in her cloak. In her hurry to dress, she'd used far too few pins, and her hair was in imminent danger of falling down.

She looked fresh and young, the smattering of freckles dusting her nose so appealing that he was tempted to trace their progress with a kiss.

Fiona bit into a tart. "Jack, why do you dislike weddings?"

"I find all the trappings and the flowers and such ridiculous."

"I suppose," she said slowly. "But still . . ." She blushed. "You may think me silly, but the ceremony itself was beautiful. They really love each other. Jack, sometimes . . . sometimes, don't you wish things were different between us? That our wedding had been more normal?" She flushed deeply. "Of course, we wouldn't be together then. But if we had . . . do you miss that?" She sighed. "I am making things difficult, aren't I? I am sorry."

"No, please go on. What did you like about the wedding?"

She looked surprised but pleased. "The whole thing was lovely—the ceremony, the reception. We didn't have that."

He grinned. "No, our wedding was quite different. The groom was drunk and unconscious."

She put down the tart, her cheeks hot and pink. "I wish you wouldn't remember that."

Jack laughed. "I will do my best to forget, though it will be difficult."

She sighed, and silence filled the space between them. Jack's flippant remark died on his lips. She was serious. This meant a lot to her.

"What do you wish our wedding had been like?"

She gave him a quick smile. "It is silly even to wonder. We had no choice in our marriage, especially you."

"I am not sorry we married." The words surprised him, but he knew instantly they were true. Now there was a purpose to his life, a reason for everything.

Her gaze flew to his face. "*No?*"

"Not at all. Considering everything, I think we've done well."

She pulled up her knees and wrapped her arms around them. "I think we've done well, too."

He took her hand, noting how small it was in his. "Fiona, I—"

A shot rang out.

Jack was on his feet, his pistol in his hand before the echo died.

But the thick woods revealed nothing—no movement, no sound. Nothing but an eerie, unnatural silence.

"Damn them!" His chest pounded with shock. "Someone must be hunting."

Fiona didn't answer.

He turned. A stunned expression on her face, she opened her mouth as if to speak, but no sound came out.

He knelt. "Do not be frightened. When I find—"

Blood, rich and red, soaked her pristine white gown.

"No!" he gasped.

Her lips quivered. "I—" Her eyes fluttered, and then, slowly, she fell forward into his arms.

Jack caught her, dropping his pistol to the blanket. *"Devonsgate! Hamish!"* Jack's mind thundered with fear. He had to do something to save her! The blood was spreading so fast.

*"Damn it, Devonsgate!"* he yelled frantically. "Fiona! Please, God, no!" Tears blurred his eyes as he scooped her into his arms.

A whisper of sound brushed across his ears, then—

*CRACK!*

Something exploded across his head. He fell, pushing himself to one side, cushioning Fiona against him.

He fought with all his will to stay conscious, to reach for her again, but thick, black, cold silence swallowed him whole.

Gregor peered through the thicket.

"Can you see anything?" Dougal asked.

"Aye. I can see both of them. It looks as if they're having a picnic." He glared at Dougal. "So much for your thought that Kincaid was bringing her here to murder her."

"I didn't suggest any such thing."

Gregor lifted a brow.

Dougal flushed. "I don't trust him, that's all."

"Sometimes I think he truly cares for her. Right now, he's looking at her as if she's the only woman in the world. I wonder if he knows he does that."

Dougal scowled. "He needs a good thumping to wake him up. She's the best woman on the earth, and he's a fool not to realize it."

"Aye."

"And we should be over there, protecting her. I don't trust him, and neither did you until recently."

"Has it ever dawned on you that he's had many a chance to harm her if he wished? A push down the stairs, a bit of poison in her daily tea. It wouldn't be so difficult," Gregor pointed out.

Dougal scratched his chin, then peered through the leaves. "Oh, God. He's going to kiss her. I hate seeing that."

The brothers turned away, resting against the tree trunk. Silence reigned, except for the bubbling of the brook.

Finally, Dougal looked at Gregor. "I hate to admit it, but perhaps you are right. We don't need to be here."

Gregor nodded, and they headed back for their horses.

Dougal turned to duck under a low branch, then pausing, peering back into the woods.

"What is it?" Gregor asked.

Dougal stared a moment longer, his blond head cocked to one side. Finally, he shrugged. "I thought I saw something, but whatever it was, it's gone. Probably nothing."

They crossed the small stream, and suddenly, a shot rang out.

Dougal turned a white face to his brother, and both of them yelled, *"Fiona!"*

Then they were running, through the trees, over fallen logs, their booted feet thudding, their breath harsh.

They turned the corner in the overgrown path and burst into the clearing.

"Fiona!" Gregor charged across the clearing to where she lay on the blanket, a red stain spreading across her gown, her face alarmingly pale. On the blanket beside her was Jack's pistol. Fury flooded him as he scooped up his sister, and lightning cracked overhead.

"To the village," Dougal said grimly, tucking the gun into his waistband. "Old Nora knows more about medicine than any doctor."

Gregor nodded, striding toward their horses with Fiona alarmingly still in his arms. How had he let this happen? As clouds gathered with amazing swiftness, he handed Fiona to Dougal, who was already astride his mount.

Dougal immediately set off at a gallop.

As Gregor swiftly followed, he silently swore vengeance. And not just on Jack Kincaid, but on the entire family who'd brought that son of a bitch into this world.

Hell was now roused.

# Chapter Twenty

*Aye, they brought her to me, they did. Two more desper-*
*ate men I've never seen. And all the while I was tendin'*
*her, the lightning and wind roared overhead, shakin' the*
*ground and rippin' the trees from the earth 'til even the*
*bravest fell to their knees and prayed.*

OLD WOMAN NORA OF LOCH LOMOND
TO HER THREE WEE GRANDDAUGHTERS ONE COLD NIGHT

Jack awoke slowly, as if layers of gauze were slowly drawn from his mind. He was lying on a plank floor with his hands tied behind him. His head ached powerfully. Overhead, thunder rumbled and roared, so loud it shook the ground.

He shivered at the sound, a part of his mind searching for something—a lost thought or a memory or—

*Fiona.*

Horror trembled through him.

"Here, now. Ye be awake already, eh?"

Lightning split the air, lighting the face of the man who stood in the darkness. He was broad, his arms powerful, his face heavily lined and dirty. Lank hair fell over his eyes; his nose was bulbous.

A crash of thunder made the man glance at the window. He frowned. " 'Tis a horrible storm. I've never seen the like."

Jack knew that storm meant Fiona's brothers were somewhere, their hearts as torn as his own. He tried not to think of the blood on her gown. She *couldn't* be dead. He could not accept it. He'd thought they'd be protected, with Hamish and Devonsgate and the two footmen. What had gone wrong? Who had done this, and why?

He had to escape, reach Fiona. Save her. His heart burned at the thought, and he looked around to see what he had to overcome. He was in a shed of some sort, tackle hanging from the walls, the smell of hay and horses strong.

The man pushed Jack with his boot, the hard leather digging between his ribs. "Awake, are ye?"

The man was too happy by far. "Where am I?"

"Where I was tol' to keep ye until 'tis time."

"Time for what?"

Another flash of lightning cracked, eerily lighting the man's face. "Time to let ye go, o' course."

That made no sense. "You're not going to kill me?"

The man's grin didn't waver. "I could. I've done it afore. But this time, I gets me money fer doin' nothin' more than holdin' ye fer a bit. Ye see, everyone thinks the constable will be wishing to speak to ye. Ye'll tell them ye were captured by a mysterious man, but I'll be long gone by then. No one will believe ye."

The man leaned closer, his foul breath in Jack's face. "They'll think ye're making excuses fer killing yer woman."

Despair gripped Jack, numbing his brain.

"Here, now, perhaps I should stand ye up a bit so I can sees ye better." The man roughly grabbed Jack by the arms and hauled him to his feet.

Pain lanced through him. "The ties. They are too tight."

"What do I care fer that?"

Jack thought quickly. "If they leave marks, they will verify my story."

The man swore. "Damn, they might at that. Very well. I'll loosen them, but just a bit." He reached behind Jack and fumbled with the ropes.

Jack felt the knot loosen, then slip free.

The man grabbed the ends to retie them, but Jack was faster. He flung up his arm, his elbow catching his captor on the chin.

As the man stumbled back, Jack grabbed the lantern and swung it with all his might into the man's face.

"*Argh!*"

Jack bolted for the door, out into the yard of an inn that looked vaguely familiar. Where in the hell was he?

A noise came from the shed, and Jack scrambled behind a barrel. Crouched there, he rubbed his wrists and forced his sluggish mind to work. By God, he would find out who had done this and make them pay.

Blinding lightning flashed, and the shed exploded before Jack's bemused eyes, splintered wood flying through the air. Thunder crashed and rolled, the very ground shaking.

Inside what remained of the shed, fire flickered as the straw began to catch, then smoke poured from the windows. Jack's captor staggered out into the yard, collapsing in a gasping heap.

A shout went up, and people began to pour from the inn. As Jack watched, a man came to one of the windows and stared out into the yard, then disappeared.

Jack trembled with the desire to leap through the glass and take the bastard by the throat, whoever he was. But he was too weak from the attack, his head still swimming, his chest aching.

He slipped from his hiding place and darted through the inn yard between the running groomsmen and stable hands. As the mayhem grew, he disappeared into the darkness beyond, pausing at the edge of the yard to look back at the window.

His enemy was there, but he could not do this alone; he had to have help. And there was only one place he could go for it.

He only hoped they would let him live long enough to explain.


"Good God! Lightning struck the shed!" Campbell turned from the inn's window, his face pale. "It is the MacLean curse."

"Oh, don't be silly. Fires happen all the time, as does lightning." His companion stretched luxuriously before the fire of their private room. "It's a summer storm, that's all."

As if in answer, a deep boom rattled the window. "You don't understand, Lucinda. The MacLeans have power. More than you know."

She held her slippers toward the embers. "Superstitions are for the lower classes."

He glared at her, pulling a handkerchief from his pocket to wipe his brow. "I cannot believe you. How can you sit there so calmly—" He whirled away from her and madly paced across the room. "You never said you'd kill her! You said your men were crack shots, that they could graze her arm from such a short distance. That was all we needed to set the MacLeans against the Kincaids!"

She shrugged. "My men could have grazed her arm or anything else, *if* I'd requested it." Lucinda's face hardened. "I wanted her dead. She stole Kincaid and humiliated me before everyone. *No one* embarrasses me."

He turned on his heel with a jerk. "Oh, God—I can't believe this. Lucinda, the MacLeans will figure it out and come after us." He stopped at the window, staring out at the burning shed, horror on his pale face. "Nothing will stop them."

"Nonsense. They think Kincaid shot their sister. You will get your desired outcome; the families will be at each other's throats."

He sank onto a chair. "So many deaths. I never thought it would come to this, especially a woman—" He closed his eyes and shuddered.

Her gaze sharpened. "Deaths? There have been more than one?"

He slowly opened his eyes. "Yes. Her brother Callum."

Lucinda sat upright. "You revived the feud."

"Yes. It was so easy. Callum had fought with one of Jack's brothers—they were forever tufting, so no one paid it much heed. Callum had been left at the inn, unconscious and lying on the floor. It was late at night and few were about. I came into the room just as some man, ill-dressed and desperate looking, finished rifling through MacLean's pockets. He had smashed MacLean's head against the hearth, probably to keep him from awakening." Campbell shuddered. "It was horrible. I saw the man there and all the blood and I . . . I ran."

"You ran?" Lucinda's lip curled. "How valorous of you."

He glared at her. "I came back, of course. By then, though, the damage was done—Callum was dead. I was horrified. But then I began to think of the advantages to be had if the MacLeans and Kincaids revived their little feud. *Really* revived it."

"They would fight."

"Of course. Then it would escalate, and they'd have to hire men to increase their forces. Eventually they'd begin to sell off property, jewels, whatever they had."

"And you'd be there, ready to 'assist.'"

"Yes." Campbell ran a hand over his face. "I cannot believe it has come to this. I spoke with Fiona, danced with her. It's almost as if I've lost something precious."

"Don't be silly," Lucinda snapped. "She wasn't worth the time of day."

The storm raged overhead, unchecked and wild. Campbell glanced out the window. "Not to you, perhaps, but I suspect she was worth a great deal to some."

Lucinda made a face, watching him from beneath her lashes. "Why did *you* wish that marriage to end?"

He crossed his arms over his chest, his shoulders hunched. "A long time ago, my family owned all of the land along this valley. We were powerful and feared. But my family was never good at holding on to things of value. Over time, the land fell into disrepair. We lost everything. The MacLeans bought that land."

"Why not just offer to buy it back from them?"

"I have. Many times. They will not part with it. I thought if they were drawn into the feud, they'd need ready funds and would reconsider."

"How complicated. My needs are simpler. Now Kincaid is free to marry once again."

"And *your* husband?"

Lucinda met Campbell's gaze.

He flushed but said in a firm voice, "Kincaid will never marry again. He loved her."

"He did *not*!" Lucinda's eyes flashed. "He would not

have married her at all except she had him tied and bound at the altar. Once he has observed the proper mourning period, he will come back to *me*."

Campbell scowled. "You are mad. You cannot think—"

The door burst open. A large, burly man stood in the doorway, his face cut and blackened. He staggered forward. "Lady Featherington! He got away. He—" The man collapsed at Lucinda's feet. Outside, a harsh rattle clacked against the window.

Campbell sank onto a chair, his gaze on the window. "Hail. Gregor MacLean has been roused." The noise rose, ice pounding from the sky, obliterating the thunder, obscuring the lightning.

Lucinda wrinkled her nose at the fallen man and said over the roar, "Call someone, and have him moved."

"But he said Kincaid has escaped!"

"We will send word to the constable that we've seen him. He cannot be too far away. Once he's in custody, I will arrange to have him exonerated, but not in a way that gives peace to the MacLeans."

The window shook under the onslaught, a faint crack appearing in one corner. Campbell looked at the crack as it traced across the glass. "Dear God," he said under his breath. "What have we done?"


Jack slowly opened his eyes to find himself surrounded by boots. Four pairs, all well made and huge.

He groaned. At least he'd made it to the MacLean stronghold.

The last hour had been a blur. He'd found a horse in a field and had ridden it to MacLean House. If the storm had been bad at the inn, it cracked and exploded here. Like a living, breathing thing, it roared with fury, the wind swirling madly, lightning and thunder crashing.

Just as he'd pulled the horse into the yard, the hail had begun to fall. Jack had thrown his arms over his head, trying to protect himself from the icy furor, urging his horse to the portico. Desperate for cover, the horse had obliged.

Jack had not been there a second before the front door had opened, and Gregor—or Alexander?—had yanked him from his horse and thrown him head-first onto the stone steps. That was the last thing he remembered.

Dougal planted a boot on Jack's shoulder and shoved him so hard Jack's head smacked on the stone floor. "That's for our sister, you mangy dog."

"Let him up," growled Alexander, hands fisted at his sides. "So we can kill him properly."

Jack struggled to his feet. "You can kill me if you like, but not until we capture the person who killed Fiona."

Alexander exchanged looks with his brothers, then hauled Jack into a chair. "*You* shot our sister."

"I would never harm her. *Never.*"

A pistol was tossed onto the floor at his feet. "Then where did this come from?"

"It's mine, but it hasn't been shot." Jack pushed it with his foot. "You will not smell powder."

Gregor retrieved the pistol and sniffed it.

"Well?" Alexander said.

"He's right," Gregor said. "There's no powder smell."

"That doesn't mean anything," Dougal said tersely. "It has been hours."

"It's still loaded," Jack said wearily. "Look at it and see." He swallowed hard. "The bastards who shot Fiona left my gun there to implicate me. They tied me up and took me to the stable at the Strathmore Inn, but I escaped."

"And came here?" Gregor said, disbelief in his tone.

"I need help. I cannot do this on my own, and I'll be damned if I let these murderers escape justice."

Alexander continued to stare at him. Finally, he nodded.

"You cannot believe this bastard," Hugh protested. "He tried to kill our sister!"

Jack's head lifted, hope blooming in his chest. "*Tried?*"

"Jack?"

The soft voice came from behind him, its sweetness drawing every iota of breath from his chest. Jack could not move. Could not think. He could only sit and watch as the woman he loved more than life itself came back into his world.

Gregor stepped forward. "Fiona! Nora said you should not even speak, much less rise from bed."

Fiona reached for Jack and he opened his arms, enveloping her in his embrace. He buried his face in her hair, his eyes full of tears. "Fiona. Oh, God, Fiona." He held her tighter.

"Ouch!"

He loosened his hold. "Oh, no! I'm sorry. Is it . . . is it bad?"

"No, though it bled copiously."

"And . . . our baby?"

"He is fine, I think."

Joy rushed through Jack, hot and flashing.

Fiona placed a hand on his cheek, her eyes filled with tears. "I thought I'd never see you again. I couldn't—"

He captured her hand and pressed a kiss to the palm, emotion shaking him from head to toe. Then he gathered her to him, holding her ever so gently.

They stood like that, his face pressed to her chest, his arms about her waist, her cheek resting against his hair, soaking up the feel of each other.

Oh, God, he'd thought he'd lost her. Thought he'd never again touch her, never again feel or taste her. He could hardly believe she was there, before him.

She raised her face and brought her mouth to his. His emotions exploded into passion, and he gave himself to the kiss, pouring his heart into every second.

A hand closed over his shoulder and jerked him back. "Leave off!" Hugh snapped.

"She is my wife," Jack growled. "I have the right to embrace her." He shoved Hugh away and looked directly at Fiona. "I love you, Fiona, with all my heart. I never wish our marriage to end. Not now. Not ever."

Her eyes filled with tears.

Jack sank to one knee before her and pressed her fingers to his lips. "If I had my life to do over, I would marry you yet again. I love you, Fiona."

"Oh, Jack," she whispered, and placed her hands on either side of his face. "I love you, too."

"I hate to break this up," Gregor said, "but if you want our help, we need to know what you require."

Jack pressed a final kiss to each of Fiona's palms, then rose and turned to her brothers. "Gentlemen, it is time to unleash the full MacLean powers. Every bloody one of them."

# Chapter Twenty-one

*When the sun shines o'er the loch and sparkles on the water like diamond drops, ye know one thing: somewhere there's a MacLean who is smilin'.*

OLD WOMAN NORA OF LOCH LOMOND
TO HER THREE WEE GRANDDAUGHTERS ONE COLD NIGHT

"This is an outrage!" Lucinda snapped, upside down over Gregor's shoulder.

"Hsst, you." Gregor tightened his hold on her. "Kincaid? Where in the hell are you?"

"In the great hall." Jack stood with Alexander and Hugh by the fireplace. Fiona sat on the settee nearby. He'd tried to talk her out of coming, but she'd refused.

Gregor entered and dumped his captive into a chair as if she were a sack of potatoes.

"You *lout*!" Lucinda attempted to straighten herself, shooting dagger glances at everyone.

"Where's the other?" Alexander asked.

Gregor jerked his head toward the door. Moments later, Dougal entered, shoving a beaten and battered Alan Campbell before him.

Jack's jaw hardened. "You bloody bastard."

"Yes," Lucinda said, smoothing her hair. "He *is* a bastard. I heard what happened, but I am not a part of it."

"Lucinda!" Campbell's face was red.

She ignored him. "I was just passing through. Campbell had reserved a private room, and he invited me to share it with him."

"Ha!" Fiona scoffed.

Jack had to suppress a grin. She had spirit, his lovely wife. He gestured to the chair beside Lucinda. "Campbell, take a seat."

"I wish to sta—"

Gregor shoved Campbell into the chair with an audible thud.

Jack walked forward. "Which of you ordered Fiona shot, and why?"

Lucinda fluttered her hands, smiling appealingly. "Jack, I don't know what you're talking about."

Campbell said nothing, his jaw set.

"One of you shot my wife, or had her shot. I *will* know who."

"Ask Campbell," Lucinda said with a shrug. "He is at fault here, not me."

Campbell whirled on Lucinda. "Don't you dare lie!"

Fiona stood. "Lucinda, you know exactly what happened to me. Hamish saw your footman in the woods. He also found this." She held out her hand. In it lay a golden hairpin.

Lucinda's hand flew to her hair. "How did—" She

caught herself, then shook her head. "That proves nothing. Obviously, someone put that there to implicate me."

"Perhaps you would prefer to hear the words from your own man's lips." Fiona turned to the door. "Hamish!"

The door swung wide, and the huge Scotsman entered. A deep purple wound marked him from forehead to ear. He carried a large sack to the center of the room and dropped it with a thud and an audible *"Oof!"*

Lucinda had risen when Hamish entered. Now she backed away, her gaze wide. "What's in there?"

"A rat." Hamish lifted his huge foot and kicked the sack. A spate of cursing met this. Hamish reddened. "Here, now, ye bloody fewl! Do not be talkin' such in front of the lady!"

The bag froze in place. "Lady?"

"Aye." Hamish turned his shaggy red head toward Fiona. "What's to do now, mistress?"

"Open the bag, but do not let him escape. We must speak with him."

"Yes, question him," Lucinda said, breathless but composed, an odd gleam in her eyes. "Ask him whatever you want."

Jack frowned. What was she up to now?

Fiona gestured to Hamish, who untied the heavy cord that held the sack. Seconds later, a head popped out of the opening. The man tried to lift his arms through the narrow mouth of the bag, but Hamish quickly tightened the ties, creating a noose around the man's neck.

"*Eck!*" The man's face reddened, his eyes bulged.

"Easy 'ere, ye maggot," Hamish said calmly. "Ye can speak when ye're spoken to and not before."

Fiona swayed a bit, and Jack swooped her into his arms and carried her back to the settee.

"Jack, there is no need. I was just a little light-headed, and—"

"You've done too much already. You should be in bed."

"No! I must see this through."

He saw the determination in her eyes, and he nodded. "Very well. *We* will see this through." He ran the back of his hand over her cheek. "Just as we will see to the birth of our baby."

Lucinda's laugh tinkled like shards of glass. "Oh, stop it, Jack. Everyone knows you were forced into your marriage. That she abducted you and poured whiskey down your throat and made the priest accept your vows by pretending to be with child."

Alexander's hands fisted. "Watch what you say about our sister, witch!"

Fiona reached for Jack's hand and held it to her cheek. "She is right. We pretended I was already with child, so no one would demand an annulment. But now it is the truth."

"Good God," Campbell said, his face even more pale. "I didn't know."

Lucinda stood stiffly by, her jaw set, her eyes blazing.

"Aye," Jack said, his gaze fixed on the two with dark intent. "My wife is soon to be a mother. And whichever of you intended her harm should thank the lord above you didn't kill her."

Lucinda drew herself together. "I would never harm anyone, especially not a woman with a child. Ask my man who gave him his orders. I am certain he has the information you seek."

Jack said, "Hamish, make the coachman sing for us."

Hamish obligingly tugged on the noose he'd made. The man in the bag choked, then blurted out, "What th' 'ell do ye want of me?"

"Did you shoot the lady?"

The man's gaze flickered to Fiona, then away. "I—I—I—"

Hamish gave the rope a sharp tug.

"Gawd!" wailed the man, choking. "I'll tell ye! I'll tell ye! I only did what I was tol' to do!"

"By whom?"

"By Campbell!"

Fiona's brothers boiled over toward Campbell as one.

Campbell stood, his chair toppling over. "I never told him to do anything! I swear it! Lucinda is the one who gave the orders!"

"Halt!" Jack said, throwing up a hand, his gaze still on the coachman. "There is more to this. What *exactly* did Campbell tell you?" he asked the coachman.

"H-he said to follow the carriage and shoot the lady from the brush when I could."

"And kill her?"

The man's weasely eyes flickered to Lucinda for a second, then away. "I do as I'm tol'."

"You lousy excuse for a human!" Gregor snapped. "I should—"

"Leave him," Jack said quietly. He walked up to the man and stooped so that his eyes were level with his. "You know that I could have you hung with the information you have already given me."

The man gaped. "Yes, but—I was tol' to do it! I was tol' to—"

"Aye. And see how the person who sent you to do this deed is now protecting you."

The man's gaze flickered behind Jack and then back. "I don't know what ye're talkin' about."

"You just admitted to shooting my wife. There is not a magistrate in the world who would not hang you. Especially with such august witnesses." He stood. "Alexander, Hugh, Gregor, Dougal, would you testify against this blackguard?"

"If we did not kill him first," Alexander snapped.

Outside, thunder rumbled.

The coachman glanced at the stormy sky and paled.

Jack looked at Campbell. "And you? Would you testify against him?"

"Aye, though he lies about my giving him orders!"

"And you, Lucinda?" Jack asked, his voice softening. "Would you testify against this miserable excuse of a man?"

Her gaze dropped to the floor. "I do not know why you would need my testimony when so many others are available."

"Answer the question. Will you testify to what you just heard? That this man shot my wife?"

Lucinda looked at her coachman, whose gaze was locked upon her face, his expression intent.

She swallowed.

"Well?" Jack asked, moving to stand between the two of them. "Will you?"

Her lips thinned. She tossed her hair, anger blazing out. "Yes, damn you. You know I will."

"*Argh!*" The coachman lunged forward, straining against the rope around his neck, his face twisted with fury. "You tol' me to shoot her! You tol' me to kill her!"

Hamish restrained the man with difficulty, grabbing him by the shoulders. "Easy, muttonhead! Ye about cut yer own throat!"

Jack asked, "Perhaps you have more to say now?"

"Aye! 'Twas Lady Featherington as gived me the orders," the man spat. "She even came to watch. She said if we were caught, we were t' blame it all on Campbell. 'Tis the only reason she brought him with her!"

Every eye turned to Lucinda.

"You bitch," Jack said with quiet fury. "I suppose you also planted the thistle under Fiona's saddle. Why did you do this?"

She paled but said nothing.

"A woman scorned," Alexander said, his fingers flexed around his sword.

Lucinda flicked a look of utter disdain toward the lot of them. "I am not such a fool."

Campbell said, "I don't understand any of this. We had an agreement. We were just going to break up the marriage, cause problems to refuel the feud. She would get her revenge for being humiliated. I would gain the land that rightfully belongs to my family."

"All of this for some property?" Jack asked.

Campbell's cheeks heated. "Aye. I was trying to restore to my family what they had lost. I—I never thought Fiona would be harmed or—"

"Oh, for the love of God." Lucinda's bored voice cut through Campbell's plea. "Be a man, for once in your life."

He colored hotly. "You are poison. I wish I'd never met you." He turned to Jack. "I owe you and Lady Kincaid an apology."

"You owe them more than that," Lucinda said significantly.

Campbell froze.

"You owe them Callum's life."

Alexander's hands balled into fists. His gaze locked with Campbell's. "You . . . *you* killed Callum?"

Slowly, Campbell sank back into his chair. "No. But I saw—"

Gregor started forward, but Alexander caught his arm. "No. This we'll leave for the constable. There has been enough bloodshed."

"Please, Gregor," Fiona added quietly. "Not for us but for Callum. He would not have wished you to dirty your hands."

Gregor turned and walked away, staring out the window with unseeing eyes. Thunder cracked overhead.

Hamish tugged on the coachman's noose. "Shall I take this weasel away now?"

"Aye," Jack said. "And keep him tied well."

Hamish unceremoniously shoved the man back into the bag, then tightened the noose once more, giving the bag a good kick when it began to thrash about.

The bag went still, and Hamish hefted it over one shoulder. "I'll hang 'im in the stables and watch over 'im with a pitchfork. If 'e so much as sneezes, I'll poke 'im."

Alexander grunted his approval.

"I'm off to the stables, then. Lord Alexander, keep yer eye on this one." Hamish looked at Lucinda with disgust. "She's the worst 'un in the bunch." He lumbered from the room.

Jack looked at Lucinda, burning to give her the same pain she'd caused Fiona.

"Well?" Lucinda's mouth curled in a sneer. "What now? Will you turn me over to the court? If you do, there will be a huge scandal, and your precious wife will pay the price."

Jack's hands flexed into fists. God, what he'd give to—

Fiona's hand slipped into his, her fingers warm and trusting. He looked down at her, some of his anger cooling, then turned back to Lucinda. "We are going to turn you over to the magistrate and let justice have its way."

Lucinda's smile slipped a notch. "There will be talk."

Jack shrugged. "There always is when the MacLeans are involved. Besides, my wife and I will not be in London to hear any rumors. We are moving to Scotland, so that we may share our child with Fiona's family."

Fiona's eyes widened. "But you love London."

"You belong here, my love. And I belong where you are. Now and forever." Smiling, he gathered her into his arms. "In fact, we should discuss our new home."

She placed her arms around his neck. "*New* home?"

"You don't think we'll live with your brothers, do you?" Jack glanced at them. "No offense intended."

"None taken," Alexander said bluffly. "We've barely room for ourselves as 'tis."

"Aye," Gregor said, grinning reluctantly. " 'Tis too small even for us."

"I'd rather not have my nephews and nieces running about under my feet," Hugh said. "It would interfere with my fun with the upstairs maid."

"Aye," Dougal said, a smile in his eyes. "I'd rather not have to watch the two of you kissing on each other. Makes it hard for a man to keep his appetite."

"There you have it, my love," Jack said. "We would make your brothers ill if we lived in their house."

Fiona smiled shyly at him. "I suppose you are right; we must build our own."

Jack pressed a kiss to her forehead and smiled. Finally, he'd discovered the secret of having a home. It wasn't the place, or the time, or the people who lived in this city or that. It was the person you shared your life with.

And with Fiona, he knew that their house would be all the home he'd ever need.

Pocket Books proudly presents

*Karen Hawkins's*

*next delectable romance*

*featuring the MacLean family*

## TO SCOTLAND, WITH LOVE

Turn the page for a sneak preview
of *To Scotland, With Love.* . . .

# Chapter Three

*Och, me lassies, I wish't I could tell ye that the path to love is as smooth as a wee bairn's bottom. That 'tis festooned with flowers and gentle breezes and pretty phrases. Sometimes 'tis. But sometimes the path to love takes a different turn, through barren lands o' harsh rock and icy winds where nothin' grows but pain. If ye and yer love make it through that then ye'll find the flowers and gentle breezes and yer hearts will speak the pretty phrases and more, lassies. Ever so much more!*

OLD WOMAN NORA OF LOCH LOMOND
TO HER THREE WEE GRANDDAUGHTERS ONE COLD NIGHT

"Why—that's MacLean!" Lord Ravenscroft said in a bright voice.

Venetia Oglivie stood and smoothed her skirts nervously, aware that her breath was short, her skin tingling oddly. Goodness! Why was she reacting like this? It must be relief that *someone* had come to help. *It's just Gregor*, she reminded herself severely. *It's nobody special, just—*

She heard the front door open, a pause, and then

heavy footsteps on the wood floor and Mrs. Treadwell's startled voice and approach. A deep voice murmured queries to the innkeeper's wife's increasingly breathless replies and then . . . the door flew open.

Gregor stood in the doorway, Mrs. Treadwell hovering behind him. He immediately turned to her and said in a voice tinged with caustic wit, "Thank you for showing me the way to my errant charges. I shall make certain that Mr. and Miss West are kept well in hand."

"Indeed, my lord," Mrs. Treadwell said, sketching a bright curtsey. "They've been no problem at all! In fact, I was just making a bit of tea for the two of them."

"They don't deserve tea."

With something remarkably like a simper, Mrs. Treadwell curtseyed once more and tromped back down the hallway. Gregor closed the door behind him and entered the common room.

Venetia clasped her hands before her. Gregor's coat and boots were covered with quickly melting snow, his face flushed with the cold, and his lips almost white, though from the cold or his temper, she could not say.

Except for the blazing heat of his eyes, one would think him a statue, a tall, cold, lifeless statue. But those deep green eyes, framed in thick dark lashes, burned with an inner fury that only those who knew him well would see. And if there was one thing Venetia knew, it was the man standing before her now.

The gaze he threw at Ravenscroft should have sent that young lord into a flurry of misapprehension, so full of cold outrage was it. But Ravenscroft, ever the eager puppy, did not see the censure in the blazing gaze now turned his way. Nor did he notice the thin-lipped regard he was being subjected to. All he saw, in his eagerness, was a well-connected companion come to save them all.

Thus, when he stepped forward with a quick and sure step, hand outstretched in greeting, it took more than a glance from Gregor to chill the younger man's excitement. It took a cold flicker from those fathomless eyes and a sneered "Ravenscroft, you bloody fool."

Venetia's excitement on seeing Gregor completely evaporated, replaced with a flare of irritation that she welcomed.

Ravenscroft's step faltered, and he dropped his outstretched hand. "Lord MacLean! I don't know—that is, what do you mean by—how can you—"

"Sit down, whelp."

The younger man stiffened and said in an awful voice, "I beg your pardon?"

Gregor didn't spare him a glance. "You heard me. Sit down and let me think. I came to see what could be done to get the two of you out of this mess, though I had no idea you'd already run your carriage aground."

Ravenscroft's face burned redder. "That was an accident."

"It was foolish of you to continue in this weather. And to be pressing the horses—" Gregor shook his head, his gaze suddenly swinging to Venetia. "I would have thought that you, at least, would have known better."

Venetia stiffened, forgetting that for a few seconds she'd actually been glad to see Gregor MacLean. The annoyingly superior glint in his green eyes always set up her hackles as easily as stroking a cat backward. "I did not endorse traveling at such a dangerous speed. Nor was I a proponent of pressing on, though the weather was worsening."

"That's true," Ravenscroft interjected. "She was against it all."

Gregor lifted a brow. "Then I must suppose that you not only abducted Miss Oglivie, but that you put her life in danger by not heeding her advice."

Ravenscroft's hands were balled into fists held stiffly at his side.

Why, oh, why had she thought Gregor's presence would help? The toll of the carriage accident, combined with the shock of discovering Ravenscroft's perfidy in lying to her about her mother's health, had obviously upset her more than she'd realized and caused her to imagine things that could never be.

Ravenscroft sputtered, "There was no need for that! Miss Oglivie and I aren't in a mess of any kind. In fact," he stuck out his chin, "we are doing perfectly well on our own!"

He cast an uneasy glance at Venetia, who immediately nodded and added in as calm a voice as she could, "Really, Gregor, I don't know what you think you're doing, riding to our rescue, but Ravenscroft and I are fine. Just before you entered, we were saying how lovely it was to have found this snug inn during such a horrendous snowstorm." Her gaze narrowed a bit on Gregor. "It's so *unusual* to see a snowstorm in April ... don't you think?"

Ravenscroft didn't seem to catch the accusation in her tone, for he nodded vehemently. "Exactly! It's unusual to see a snowstorm or I'd have planned things differently." He paused, then added stiffly, "Not that we need any help, now. Miss Oglivie and I had our plans all sewn up long before you arrived on the scene. Didn't we, Miss Oglivie?"

Gregor sent Venetia a long, hard look, his gaze taking in her disheveled appearance, a look of obvious disbelief on his face.

She wished she'd taken the time to smooth her hair before he had arrived. "As Ravenscroft says, we have the situation well in hand. There is no need for you to be here."

A mocking light warmed his eyes. "Oh?"

It wasn't a normal 'oh,' but rather a 'that's-a-falsehood-and-you-know-it' sort of 'oh,' which did not sit well with Venetia at all. "Yes," she said in firm tone, wishing Gregor to the devil. She could not stand the way he was standing there, looking at her and Ravenscroft as if they were the silliest creatures on earth. *She* had done nothing wrong.

Venetia sniffed at Gregor. "You wasted your time

coming here. I'm not certain why you bothered."

Gregor unbuttoned his coat and pulled it off, tossing it into a chair in the corner of the room. "Your father sent me here, and begged me to return with you forthwith."

"But it is *his* fault this happened to begin with!"

Gregor paused in removing his gloves. "Is that what Ravenscroft told you?"

Ravenscroft stepped forward eagerly. "Venetia's father has been very supportive!"

"He might have been supportive, but he definitely didn't expect you to abduct his only daughter!" Gregor said.

"It doesn't matter," Venetia snapped, her hands now curled into fists at her sides. "Father can be very vague when he speaks. It has caused many problems."

"But—" Ravenscroft began.

"Venetia," Gregor said, ignoring Ravenscroft completely, "no matter what your father did, *you* were the one who acted so foolhardy."

"*Oh!*" she fumed. "I did nothing wrong!"

"No, she di—" Ravenscroft began again.

"Oh?" Gregor said without taking his gaze from Venetia. "Did you or did you not willingly climb into a carriage with an unknown man?"

"I know Ravenscroft!"

Ravenscroft opened his mouth, but Gregor spoke over him, "You *barely* know Ravenscroft."

"I know him well enough," Venetia huffed.

Ravenscroft dropped his head into his hands.

"Then tell me about him," Gregor said. "Explain his circumstances. How he came to the conclusion he should elope with you."

Venetia glanced at Ravenscroft, who didn't look up. She took a deep breath. "Ravenscroft is a—a fine young man who ah—is quite well spoken," she said, trying not to remember that less than ten minutes ago, she'd wished that poor young man at the bottom of a very deep snow drift. "He has been nothing but gentlemanly since we left London." *More or less.*

Gregor's brows lifted. "Except for the fact he abducted you—"

"I was going to marry her!" Ravenscroft said, though no one looked his way.

"—lied to you—" Gregor continued.

"I also told her the truth, once we were here!"

"—and has kept you imprisoned ever since—"

"I did not!" Ravenscroft said, his face now as red as his waistcoat. "Had it not been for the snow, we would have been married and on our way to the continent by now!"

Venetia's mouth opened, then closed. "The continent?" There was a decided squeak to her voice.

Gregor smiled. "That surprised you, hm? I thought you knew Ravenscroft, that er, 'gentleman'?"

Venetia ignored him. "Ravenscroft, what is this about the continent?"

Ravenscroft sent a resentful glare at Gregor before answering, "I—I—I was going to tell you, but I wasn't sure when to say something and if, perhaps, it wouldn't be better to just wait until—"

"Oh for the love of Zeus," Gregor said impatiently, "just spit it out. Explain why you wished to travel to the continent right on the heels of your surprise nuptials."

Ravenscroft stiffened. "There are many reasons."

"We just want the real one."

"Perhaps I just *like* Italy."

Gregor crossed his arms, his broad chest framed by his powerful arms. Beside him, Ravenscroft appeared even younger and more narrow-shouldered than usual.

"Ravenscroft," Venetia said, "why the continent? You aren't fleeing because of debt, are you?"

"No! Of course not!"

"No," Gregor said. "It's something worse than mere debt."

Ravenscroft glowered. "Look, MacLean," he blustered. "Why I wished Venetia and myself—"

"*Miss* Oglivie," Venetia snapped.

Ravenscroft sent her a harried glance, "*Miss* Oglivie," he said before turning back to Gregor. "My lord, I know you don't mean to insult me, but—"

"Of course I mean to insult you, cub."

Ravenscroft's mouth opened. Then closed. "You *mean* to insult me? On *purpose*?"

"Yes. I find your company unbearably tedious and your actions in regard to Miss Oglivie selfish. So I do not bother to speak in a polite tone, or even in a polite manner."

The younger lord drooped as if his bones would no longer bear his frame. "Oh. I see."

Venetia stamped her foot. "Ravenscroft! Do not let Gregor beat you down in such a way!"

The young lord's cheeks reddened. "I am not allowing him anything! I was merely attempting to understand, that is all."

"He is insulting you. If I were you, I would be furious."

Gregor's low voice drawled with an amused undertone. "I believe she would have you challenge me to a duel."

Venetia whirled to face him. "I do not believe in such fustian, and you know it! I was merely suggesting that he stand up for himself."

"It's no matter. If Ravenscroft challenged me to a duel, I fear I would have to stand in line and await my turn."

Venetia frowned. "What?"

Ravenscroft suddenly came to life, gulping as he spoke. "Lord MacLean! Perhaps we should discuss this elsewhere—"

"No," Venetia said, her gaze narrowing on Ravenscroft. "Is there something you have not told me?"

"Yes—no—a very *minor* thing, to be sure—"

"What is it?"

Ravenscroft winced. "Venetia, don't—"

"*Miss* Oglivie."

Ravenscroft ground his teeth. "*Miss* Oglivie, then!"

Gregor grinned. "I believe I will take a seat for this one." He pulled a chair into the center of the room, where he could plainly see both Venetia and Ravenscroft, then made himself comfortable, crossing one booted foot over his knee. Once there, he gestured. "Continue!"

Venetia placed her hands on her hips. "Would it kill you to be of assistance?"

"I put my neck at risk traveling here in this weather in an attempt to do just that, but you informed me that I was not needed." He shrugged. "So I might as well enjoy myself."

"That is no excuse to do what you can to make things worse."

"I beg your pardon," Gregor said with that devastating half grin that made her stomach warm in the most annoying way. "How could I possibly make things worse?"

Venetia hated it when Gregor was right. She forced herself to turn to Ravenscroft. "You might as well get this over with. Lord MacLean is not going anywhere until you've aired everything."

Ravenscroft sent a resentful glare at Gregor, who threw up his hands and said with a laugh, "Don't look at me like that! I am not the one challenging every male within earshot to a duel!"

Venetia ignored Gregor, which was not easy to do as he was leaning back negligently in his chair, his wet boots now thrust forward across the rug, making it difficult for anyone to walk anywhere. In his wet clothes, his black hair curly from the dampness, his green eyes sparkling with amusement, he was devastatingly handsome. Even the scar on his left cheek seemed a part of him, secretive and hinting at potential danger.

"Well, Ravenscroft?" Gregor said, quirking a brow at the younger man. "Will you tell Miss Venetia your plight? Or will I?"

"Oh, I will tell her," Ravenscroft said in a voice so sulky that it quite put Venetia out of patience with him. "First of all, Miss Oglivie, you must realize that no matter what—*no matter what*—I am here because I love you madly."

"And?" Gregor prompted.

Venetia scowled at Gregor. He grinned, then gestured for her to proceed.

She turned back to Ravenscroft. "And?"

"And I had to get out of the country because of a duel I was to fight."

Venetia blinked. "I beg your pardon?"

He sighed, his shoulders sagging beneath the ridiculous buckram wadding that padded them. "Veneti— I mean, *Miss Oglivie,* I can explain everything." He ran a hand through his hair, sending his fashionable coif into even more disarray. "What happened was— It wasn't my fault either, but— Last week, Lord Ulster and I were playing cards at White's. He accused me of cheating and I—"

"Were you?" Gregor asked.

"No," Ravenscroft said sharply. "I dropped a card on the floor. I bent to retrieve it without thinking and Ulster had the—the—*gall* to suggest I was not playing a fair hand!"

Gregor's brows rose. "In the middle of a game, you picked up a card from the *floor*?"

"Well, yes! I'd dropped it and hadn't noticed it and— I know I shouldn't have, but it was a queen and I particularly needed— That's not to say that if I had it to do over again, I might—"

"Bloody hell." Gregor looked at Venetia, his eyes shimmering with humor. "You really wish to wed this fool?"

Ravenscroft's hands fisted, his face flushing a dark red.

Venetia ignored him. "I never said I wished to marry anyone, MacLean. I only said Ravenscroft had been a gentleman. Or so I'd thought."

"He *is* rather amusing," Gregor said thoughtfully, looking at Ravenscroft. "Quite fun to watch, too. Much like having a pet monkey."

"My lord!" Ravenscroft stepped forward, his eyes blazing in anger.

"Sit down," Gregor said in a bored tone.

"My lord, I cannot allow you to—"

"*Sit down!*" This time Gregor's voice thundered, his eyes the bitter green of an angry sea. Outside, a crashing echo lashed through the air.

Ravenscroft's butt hit the chair, a stunned look on his face.

Venetia's own heart was pounding against her throat. Gregor rarely became angry. Oh, he was perpetually irritated, but never truly angry. In the many years they'd been friends, she could count on one hand the number of times he'd lost his temper.

She clasped her hands together. "Ravenscroft, pray continue with your story. Ulster accused you of cheating, and?"

"I had no choice. I challenged him to a duel."

"Who won?" Venetia asked.

The young lord bit his lip, and said in a very quiet voice, "No one."

Venetia leaned forward. "I beg your pardon?"

He cleared his throat. "I said, 'No one.' We—we have not yet met."

Venetia considered this. "When did this incident occur?"

"Three days ago."

Three days ago. Just before he'd come to steal her away and—She fixed her gaze on him. "*That* is why you wished to go to the continent?"

Gregor's soft chuckle punctuated Ravenscroft's wince.

"You see, my love?" Gregor asked calmly, though something tight snapped beneath the surface. "I not only saved you from an unwelcome elopement, but from a life on the continent, the wife of a banished man."

Venetia tried to stop a flame of resentment, but could not. "Let me get this straight, Ravenscroft. You not only tricked me into accompanying you by claiming that my mother was ill, but you planned on taking me with you into a life of hiding on the continent?"

"Well . . . yes. I thought you'd like it."

She was going to explode. "You really thought I'd *welcome* such a thing? Living from country to country, never returning to England—"

"We would be able to return!"

"When?"

"Once Ulster could be persuaded to drop the charges."

"And how would you get that accomplished?"

"I—I thought perhaps your father—"

"You thought *my* father would undertake to beg for *your* return to England?"

"Your father likes me!"

"And so does my mother. But *they* would not be the ones living with you on the continent, would they?"

"No," Ravenscroft said in a sulky tone. "I didn't think they would mind assisting their son-in-law, though."

"I'm sure *they* wouldn't have minded being banished, either. Indeed, I am certain *they* would have thought it a grand adventure, hiding from the constable, registering at low inns under assumed names. As much as I love my parents, no one would ever think *they* possess the smallest bit of common sense. *I*, however, would have been greatly put out by the entire mess."

Ravenscroft leapt from his chair. "Ven—I mean, *Miss* Oglivie! Truly, I did not think you'd object! I hear it is beautiful in Italy! There are villas and shops and all sorts of amusements—"

"How, pray tell, would we afford these villas and shops and amusements?"

Ravenscroft looked desperately around the room, finding nothing but Gregor's amused gaze and Venetia's indignant one. "V—Miss Oglivie, please, listen to me. Perhaps I should have told you about fleeing from the country—"

"Perhaps?"

"Yes, yes! I should have told you. But I did not think you would mind once we were there."

"Oh? And how were you going to make the experience of losing my own country so painless? What sort of lovely plans did you have laid? Have you purchased a house, perchance?"

"Ah. No. I didn't really have the funds—" He caught sight of Venetia's expression and hurried to add, "I am certain something would have presented itself!"

"I am certain something would have," Venetia said, her voice low and smooth. "I don't know why I thought you were going into this unprepared."

Ravenscroft looked relieved.

Gregor, however, knew Venetia better. He knew the strength of her sarcasm.

She was a wrathful goddess, her gown mussed and crumpled, her hair a tangled mess upon her head, but her gray eyes were flashing silver, her smooth skin flushed with passion. She was a sight to behold. Grinning to himself, Gregor leaned back and waited.

Ravenscroft, ever eager to think things were in his favor, was nodding eagerly. He took Venetia's hands in his. "I am not the sort of man to rush into things without thinking them through. Of course I have a plan, one that has taken into account every exigency."

Venetia's gaze flickered to the window where snow swirled outside. "Really?"

Gregor bit his lip to keep from laughing.

Ravenscroft clasped her hand tighter. "Indeed, my dear! After marrying, we were to go to Italy via France."

"How? That will cost a bit."

"Oh. Yes. Well, no need to worry your pretty head over that! I have quite a sum put away to pay for the trip."

"We were to travel in the first of style, I presume?"

He looked a little uneasy, but his smile remained firmly in place. "Not the first, of course. But well enough."

Gregor cleared his throat. "I know something of crossing the Channel. How much money did you bring?"

Ravenscroft colored. "Enough."

"More than a hundred pounds?" Gregor asked gently.

There was a frozen moment, and then Ravenscroft nodded. "Of course."

The whelp didn't have fifty if he had a pence, Gregor decided. Still, he would show the lad some mercy. "Providing you have a hundred, you will find crossing the Channel quite comfortable. You can have a private cabin, meals, your luggage loaded and unloaded."

There was a pregnant pause, then Ravenscroft said, "And if I have less?"

"If you have fifty, you might get a private cabin but

will have to provide your own meals and load your own luggage. Of course, since you did not inform Miss Oglivie of your flight, I daresay she has very little luggage anyway."

"*Very* little," she said in a resentful tone.

Ravenscroft appeared somewhat put out by the mention of funds.

Venetia's gaze narrowed. "Ravenscroft, I can see from your expression that crossing is much higher than you thought." She drew back a bit. "Did you make any inquiries at all before you began this mad bolt to Italy?"

Ravenscroft glared. "Yes! I made all sorts! People say it is remarkably inexpensive to live over there—"

"It had better be, since you don't even have enough for passage over. How were we going to live once we arrived? If you were planning on my parents assisting, you do not know them well enough, for they are forever living at the edge of their means."

"No, no! I would never ask such a thing! I thought, once we arrived, we would find a pretty little cottage in a vineyard. And once there—" Ravenscroft straightened up, his expression beaming. "Once there, I am going to write a book!"

The clock on the mantel ticked loudly. The snow outside silently swirled, the only movement to be seen.

Gregor struggled mightily not to laugh.

Venetia sent him a fulminating glare, letting him know he was fooling no one. He managed a faint, helpless shrug before she turned back to Ravenscroft. "I have to ask you one thing."

He leaned forward eagerly. "Anything!"

"What was I supposed to be doing while you were working on this . . . this roman á clef?"

"Doing? I don't know. I thought you would be keeping the cottage nice and clean, perhaps washing our clothes in a pail and hanging them on a line in the sun—" He smiled a dreamy smile. "Your hair has the faintest hint of red. It shows every time you are in the sunlight."

Gregor almost choked. Red? He tried to decide where Ravenscroft had gotten that from . . . although the firelight did indeed show some reddish glints in her brown hair. Odd, he'd never noticed that before.

Venetia leaned forward, her face level with Ravenscroft's. "You thought I would *enjoy* washing my clothes by hand, hanging them on a clothesline?"

His smile slid a bit. "I thought you would not mind helping while I wrote my book."

"By hanging up your laundry?"

"And yours."

"*And* mine?"

"And our children's."

She closed her eyes.

"I know just how you feel!" he said eagerly. "You are overwhelmed. I was the same way myself when it dawned on me what we were to do. We'll go to Italy, leave civilization behind, and live a simpler life. A more pure one. There, I will work on my writing, and you will clean and cook and play with our children and perhaps," he added naively, "when you've time, take in a few local children as students and teach music and English."

"Students?" Venetia repeated blankly. "You thought I would do all of that *and* become a governess?"

"Just a *few* students," he said hurriedly, his expression uncertain. "I wouldn't wish you to be overworked."

Gregor almost felt sorry for the man. "Venetia, you always said you enjoyed helping your fellow—"

"MacLean, not another word." She didn't look at him, but her frigid voice said it all.

Gregor settled deeper into his chair, placing his hands behind his head and leaning back. "Ravenscroft, I can see that I underestimated you. I am surprised at the amount of thought you put into this concept, and I apologize for assuming you were impetuously running into things."

The younger man brightened. "Oh, don't think it! I'm certain it sounded like a hare-brained idea to begin with. It did to me! But after a short reflection—"

"No doubt over a few glasses of port," Gregor guessed.

"Why yes! Four, to be exact—"

Venetia pressed her fingers to her forehead.

"I realized that Italy was the place for us. Once there, I know the muse would visit me and my idea for a novel will come to fruition."

"Do you have any of this novel written?" Gregor asked, curiosity strong in his tone.

Venetia yearned to take off one of her boots and hurl it at Gregor. The ass was begging for a set down, and poor Ravenscroft was too dim-witted to do more than cheerfully answer.

"No, I haven't written any of it yet," he said now. "But I have some notes."

Gregor's brows rose. "Oh?"

Ravenscroft reached into his jacket pocket and pulled out a crumpled piece of paper. He smoothed it out and said, "I've named two of my characters, and I've decided to use my travels in Italy as the basis."

"An educational book, then. One about the history of the country. Very good."

"What? Oh no! It's to be a mystery. A murder of some sort has occurred—I haven't decided who or how—and a young man is accused of the crime. Of course, he is innocent, but he must prove it or else he will end up in jail for all time."

Gregor quirked a brow. "Let me guess . . . this young man, he is your age?"

"Why, yes."

"And about your height? And hair color?"

"Yes! How did you know?"

"A fortunate guess," Gregor said, smiling broadly.

"Indeed! I've been thinking of writing this novel for three years now. I am certain I could do it, if I but had the time."

"Which the lovely Miss Venetia will give you, once she begins her life as a cleaning maid."

Ravenscroft looked horrified. "I would *never* think of Miss Oglivie as a cleaning maid!"

"I am glad to hear it," Venetia said dryly. "My rough laundress hands will thank you."

Ravenscroft captured one of those hands and lifted it to his cheek, his gaze fixed on Venetia's face. "Miss Oglivie, you are the most beautiful woman in the world, inside and out. I hope you know I would never do anything to disrespect you."

Up until now, Gregor had been enjoying every utterance that slipped from the pup's lips. But the unconcealed admiration that shone in Ravenscroft's eyes as he held Venetia's hand to his cheek sent an unfamiliar—and devilishly sharp—pang through Gregor.

It was the oddest feeling and it wiped away his amusement in a flash. Venetia should have been offended by such familiarity; she should have been outraged by the callow fool's suggestions.

Instead, she sighed, her lips curling into a reluctant smile as she turned her hand and patted the insolent pup's cheek. "Oh, Ravenscroft! You are so young. I keep forgetting that, don't I?"

It was hardly a compliment, but it only encouraged the fool. Ravenscroft's eyes brightened and he had the temerity—the *audacity*, b'god!—to cup her fingers to his lips and press a kiss to her bare palm.

Something inside of Gregor snapped in half. "*Venetia*." He was on his feet in an instant, both Venetia and Ravenscroft looking at him.

Venetia blinked at Gregor's black expression. Dark as a thundercloud, he stared down at her, his gaze flickering between her and her hand.

She followed his gaze to her hand where Ravenscroft clasped it, holding it almost reverently. It was improper, although there was so much about this entire situation that was improper that holding hands with Ravenscroft seemed minor indeed.

Ravenscroft smiled up at Gregor, unaware of the danger he was in. "Isn't she an *angel*?"

Venetia's cheeks heated, and she freed her hand from Ravenscroft's rather tight grasp. "Yes, well, now that everything has been said that needs to be said, we must find a way out of this mess."

Ravenscroft stepped forward. "I will marry you. That will solve one problem at least."

"No," she said firmly. "That is not an option."

"But Miss Oglivie, I love you. With all my heart!"

"Ravenscroft." Gregor's voice chilled the air.

The young lord sent a harried glance at Gregor.

What happened next, Venetia would never be able to explain. One moment, Ravenscroft was standing there, imploring and earnest. The next, the young lord was backing up, edging toward the door, stumbling a bit in his haste.

"I—I—I just remembered— Important meeting!" He tugged on his neckcloth.

"Here? At this inn?" Venetia didn't know when she'd heard a more ridiculous assertion. Well, other than the thought that she might support the poor youth in his quest for notoriety as a novelist. "How on earth could you possibly have a meeting here?"

But Ravenscroft was gone. Within moments, she heard the thud of his well-shod feet as he hurried out the inn's front door, closing it behind him. Seconds later, he could be seen buttoning his coat as he made his way through the wind to the stables.

Venetia crossed to the window and watched him. "That is most odd!"

Gregor shrugged, coming to stand beside her. "He is a fool."

"Something happened." Venetia glanced up at him. "What did you do?"

Gregor shrugged again. "He was getting out of hand. I merely stopped it."

She frowned at him, suspicion clear in her gaze.

The light from the snowy haze softened the line of her brow and cheek, and he regarded her closely, trying to see her as Ravenscroft evidently did.

Venetia was not an ordinarily beautiful woman. Her figure was a bit heavier than was fashionable.

Still, he noticed that her arms were lovely and round, her breasts were full and lush, as were her hips. She was not a small woman, was Venetia. Which was a good thing. A frailer body could not have contained such a passionate soul. He had to admit that there was something taking about her. If he had just met her he might have overlooked her, but not if she'd met his gaze as she was meeting it now. Her face held an amazing mixture of intelligence, humor, and liveliness.

"What's wrong?" she asked now, frowning. "Why are you looking at me like that?"

"I am just wondering what Ravenscroft is so enamored of."

Her cheeks heated. "Don't strain your eyes."

"Oh, stop being missish. I see plenty to admire."

She regarded him suspiciously, and he laughed. Her eyes were by far her best feature, a light silvery gray, framed by thick black lashes. Her skin was fresh and creamy, though not particularly fair. She tanned easily and even now he could detect the hint of a few freckles on her rather ordinary nose. Her lips were full and remarkably pert, her teeth white and even. Her dark brown hair was unremarkable except for its tendency to wave and curl at the faintest hint of moisture.

He smiled a bit, remembering how many times he'd heard her complain about that trait—one he found rather attractive, truth be told. Now that he thought about it, Venetia was indeed an attractive female. He supposed his prolonged exposure to her had inured him to that fact, which was probably a good thing for them both. He treasured their friendship and had no wish to give it up, especially for a fleeting attraction, as all such affairs were. Still, there was something damnably taking about her. Something that drew him to her plump lips. Her rounded shoulders. Her full breasts. Heat flooded him, and he found himself walking toward her.